I Saw What He Did

Kemi Estephane

Clink
Street

Published by Clink Street Publishing 2022

Copyright © 2022

First edition.

The author asserts the moral right under the Copyright, Designs and
Patents Act 1988 to be identified as the author of this work.

All rights reserved. No part of this publication may be reproduced, stored
in a retrieval system or transmitted, in any form or by any means without the prior consent of the author, nor be otherwise circulated in any
form of binding or cover other than that with which it is published and
without a similar condition being imposed on the subsequent purchaser.

ISBNs:
978-1-915229-14-4 – paperback
978-1-915229-15-1 – ebook

Dedication
If not for friendship, love and support.
Francis, Lara, Lena, Sarah, Suzie, Vanessa - thank you.
We share the victories. x

How it ends

I adjusted my eyes to the darkness beneath. The musty smell of long-forgotten furniture that had dampened and dried many times rose to meet me, causing my nose to twitch. A furtive glance behind me: no one. I could still hear the muffled, exasperated voices. I had seconds, a minute maximum, before they came looking for me where they'd left me.

I leaned forward, pushing the door further open, relying on the dim light from the hallway. Now I could make out the distorted heap blending in with the darkness below. It had to be him. Was he alive? I had to help him. But which battle should I tackle first?

Thoughts scrambled and with a rising panic setting in, I knew my best option was to get out and call for help. I have to move. Now! *The front door. About fifteen metres ahead of me. With one final glance below and whispered words, 'hang in there', I took a step towards my only escape route. That was when I heard it: a sharp, uneven inhalation of breath. I turned round. On his face: hatred. Irritation. The hint of an apology?*

His move was swift: there was nothing I could have done to deflect it or protect myself. I felt myself being yanked towards him. Acute pain, as something heavy and cumbersome was smashed against my head. A shove sent me somersaulting backwards. A broken head, a broken body, falling and flailing into the abyss, saying goodbye forever to the life I had not yet fully lived.

Chapter 1

Seven weeks before the end

Today is a good day. The rare kind of day when everything feels perfect; promising. On days like this I am super-efficient, organised and prompt. So, in my excitement at the rendezvous with my besties, I arrive at Reno's twenty minutes early. Having already secured an outdoor table with a bottle of Rosé chilling on ice, my life feels as free as the diamond droplets that slither down the bottle.

Reno's sits on the eastern side of Brockwell Park, a relatively unpretentious brasserie made popular by the eponymous range of pasta dishes. Not that I'm a huge pasta lover, but I'm definitely a fan of al fresco dining, a friendly and bustling atmosphere and a smorgasbord of sweet desserts, which Reno's has aplenty – not to mention anywhere that puts me in sight of trees and grass. This part of south London is rich with green. On this sunny May afternoon, it's easy to look beyond the graffitied railway bridge behind me and imagine being somewhere less built up and more redolent of country living.

I don't have to wait long before the glam duo, arms linked, totter towards me, bringing with them an aura of joie de vivre. Lex and Kizzy – the sincerest friends a girl could wish for. We met during our tenure at Brunel University: totally different pathways but, having been thrown together through a flat-sharing scheme in our final year, we became firm friends and have remained so ever since.

Lex, stunning in her pixie haircut and Gok Wan-style glasses, this girl can rock any attire and accessories. Tall, and as slim as the first day I met her, she has an elegance that commands authority, despite the frequent unsavoury language that rolls off her tongue once she's had a few. Kizzy, gorgeous too, is five feet and not much more with an athletic physique. She gave birth to her first child just nine months ago. Back in the day, she gave the lads a run for their money on the football field and to this day, she still has a penchant for competitive team sport. Their animated chat and loud cackling turn a few heads as they see me and speed walk towards our table.

'If there's so much as a mouthful missing from that bottle, you're in big trouble, Shephard!' Lex, always with the wacky greeting. I rise from my seat, feeling the ridges of metal unstick from the back of my legs. I look at my watch.

'Two more minutes and I'd have started necking straight from the bottle.' I joke. We hug, swaying dramatically, high-pitched greetings. Our time together, always banter-filled and (more often than not) boozy. The pledge we made to meet once a month had been honoured in the early days, but with each of us journeying along different paths, it's become less frequent and sometimes random. But we make up for it in our WhatsApp group, which is constantly pinging with messages, memes and video calls.

As if he's been awaiting the noisy arrival of my friends, the waiter sidles over and places three plastic-covered menus on our table. We make ourselves comfortable and I open the bottle of wine, pouring a glass for each of us.

'Cheers!' Voices merged, we clink glasses and take the first of many sips.

'So, what are we drinking to today?' I ask, knowing, as is

customary, we will take it in turns to raise a glass to salute something of importance

Lex raises an eyebrow haughtily. 'Well, there's only one thing I want to drink to right now.' Her silver bangles jingle a merry tune. 'Good riddance to bad rubbish!' she says, enunciating each word.

Kizzy winks at me, unsmiling. We know where this is going. Eighteen months into her marriage to Phil, and when most couples are still ensconced in an extended honeymoon period, she found out he was having an affair with someone he'd met at the local gym. So unoriginal. The fallout has been messy. Cheating is one thing – but to get your mistress pregnant when your wife is struggling to conceive is quite something else. Lex was adamant, from the moment she found out, that the death knell had been firmly sounded on their relationship. With the divorce in its very final stages, Lex is desperate to move on and extract the last traces of Phil from her life.

'Let's drink to putting the trash out then,' I say, raising my glass and taking a generous gulp. Lex and Kizzy follow suit.

Thankfully, not all relationship breakdowns end in heartbreak and hatred. It's been three months since my amicable parting from Denny, who was (and probably still is) my soulmate. Super ambitious, unlike me, and already settled into a promising career as a solicitor, his devotion to a relationship gradually became insubstantial. Coupledom lagged behind his commitment to work. It may well be that my capricious and fickle parents have had an impact on my ability to brush things off; I was sad about our break-up, but not devastated. What would be the point? One thing we both agreed on: we would rather part with our respect for each other intact than for bitterness to seep into the crevices of the relationship and present us, damaged and resentful, to whoever we get together with in future.

Lex turns her attention to Kizzy. 'Raise this one high, Kiz. What are you drinking to? Apart from this being your first drink in yonks!'

Without pause, Kizzy says, merrily: 'Farewell leaky boobs; hello office and adult conversations!' This, in reference to the end of her breast-feeding period and an imminent return to work.

'How is that gorgeous godson of mine?' I ask, smiling. 'You haven't shared any drool-over pictures in the group for a while.'

'He's still adorable. Teething now, so everything gets chewed and everywhere is wet!' She says this in mock annoyance but the adoration in her voice tells a different story. Who would have thought Kizzy would take so easily to motherhood? After fulfilling her dream of a stint working abroad, we thought she would return and struggle to settle, but her whirlwind relationship with Tom quickly led to a joint mortgage and not long afterwards, Cory was welcomed into the mix. She has taken to motherhood like a duck to water but now, after nine months at home, her maternity leave has come to an end.

'So, who'll be looking after Squidgy when you start back?' Lex asks, our nickname for Cory.

'Well...' Kizzy arches a brow. 'You know how both mums are competing for the Star Grandma award? Well, they've put together a rota for the three days that I'll be in the office. Tom and I can both work from home every so often, so between us, it's covered.' She raises her glass triumphantly.

We take another sip to salute Kizzy, then she asks: 'Last but certainly not least, what are you drinking to, Ren?'

I lean back in my seat, recalling our last get-together when I'd raised a glass to my single status and being back on the market (although meeting someone wasn't – still isn't

– on my list of priorities). I share out the little wine left in the bottle, sure that the waiter will appear beside us soon.

'I'm raising my glass to Redundancy, with a capital R, because I'm going to own it!' I say cheerily, adopting a fake American accent and a cheesy grin. 'And here's looking ahead to whatever awaits.' The clink of our glasses is dangerously loud, indicating the rising exhilaration and the brewing effects of the alcohol.

Following months of uncertainty – a hangover from numerous lockdowns – budget cuts, low student intake and a host of other points set out in a lengthy email, I have been made redundant from my teaching post at Upper Norwood College. Not a huge shock, and no real disaster; though if I'd been told ten years ago that I would be 'redundant' at the age of 28, I would have laughed out loud.

'Hear, hear,' Kizzy says. 'So, what's the plan? Must be quite exciting not having to deal with Sunday night blues and manic Mondays!'

'At the moment I'm loving it,' I say, honestly. 'Can't say much for daytime TV, but otherwise so far so good!' Although, truth be told, there is a part of my brain constantly flickering with the question: what next? A mortgage on a one-bedroom flat in Herne Hill, a decent redundancy package, careful with money (when I need to be) and still some part-time online tutoring work, by my reasoning I can survive for at least another six months before the pot starts to run dry. That's if I live within my means and ignore all those tempting deals that flood my inbox on a regular basis.

'I think this calls for another bottle,' Lex says, looking around just as the waiter approaches, both of us aware that the next bottle will be consumed mostly by the two of us. Although Kizzy is no longer breastfeeding, it'll be a while before she can handle more than a glass or two.

The waiter is beside us in a flash, and we use the opportunity to order some food as well. Antipasto to share followed by pizza for me and pasta dishes for Lex and Kizzy, making sure we save enough room for dessert. Our chatter continues non-stop, from the meaningful to the mundane and back again.

'So, how is that unruly sister of yours?' Kizzy asks, sometime later, once the errors of the world have been put right and our tasty dishes have been devoured, with dessert on the way. I'm sure Kizzy notices my darkening expression. 'She's okay, as far as I know. I'm sure she'll be in touch when the mood takes her.'

'Mmm,' Kizzy muses. They remain silent for a bit, knowing the fractious relationship that exists between Faye and me is often enough to crash my mood.

'Anyway!' Lex declares, slapping her palms against the table, changing the subject. 'Sounds as if we've all hit major points in our lives.' She relaxes back in her seat and counts on her fingers as she speaks: 'Kizzy's returning to the dark side, I'll soon be a divorcee and Ren is redundant!' We all laugh. 'Whatever you do, don't get too used to it,' Lex continues. 'You'll end up with Netflix-itis and Maltesers belly, then you'll totally scupper your chances of meeting some gorgeous hunk.' More childish giggling.

'Or falling back into the arms of delightful Denny,' Kizzy says, making dreamy eyes at me. So convinced they are that Denny and I will get back together at some point. Maybe it's the mention of his name that causes me to fiddle distractedly with my pendant – part of a matching diamond set he bought me for my birthday last year, my jewellery of choice most days.

'Seriously though, what are you going to do next?' Kizzy asks. 'You've got nothing holding you back. This is a great time to step out of your comfort zone; explore what's out there. Do you know how many people would love to be in that position?'

I spike a leftover olive onto a toothpick and pop it into my mouth, the sharp salty tang working well with the merry effects of the alcohol. I close my eyes momentarily then sigh. 'You know, the thing that's really pulling at my gut right now is getting back into my writing.' I use the term *'getting back into'* rather loosely, because, although I have a degree in Professional Writing, the closest I've come to using it in the last five years is writing feedback on my students' work.

'That's been your New Year's Resolution since we were at Uni, Ren.' Lex yawns, feigning boredom. 'You've always used work as your excuse, but now you're a bit of a layabout, what's stopping you?' she asks playfully.

I roll my eyes and throw my paper napkin at her. 'Well,' I say, breathing the word out slowly. 'I've got at least ten titles for my book; I've written my acknowledgements – which doesn't include you two by the way – and I've got a great idea for the front cover. I've even prepared my Novel of the Year speech.' I inhale deeply, dramatically. 'But I've got no idea what I want to write about.'

Lex and Kizzy snort loudly. 'You'd best put pen to paper, otherwise the only person you'll be giving your acceptance speech to is Cory when you come to babysit!' Kizzy giggles. 'Seriously,' she continues, her eyes gleaming with genuine interest. 'Grab the bull by the horns, Ren. Don't keep talking about it if you're not going to do anything. How much time have you actually spent trying to figure out what to write?'

I cover my eyes with my hands and peep at Kizzy through my fingers in embarrassment. 'You know me too well,' I say sheepishly. 'I haven't spent much time at all. Although two of my ex-students from Norwood would make really fascinating characters.'

'See, there you go!' Lex says excitedly, as if I've just

completed a first draft. 'That's how all great ideas are born. All you need is the pearl of an idea and then: POW!' She throws her arms wide, almost toppling off her seat. 'I tell you what,' she continues once we've stopped laughing. 'I'm going to set you a deadline. You've got a week to come up with some sort of plan of action. I mean, it doesn't have to be detailed or anything, just some idea of what you want to write about; what kind of story. A few rough notes will do.' She looks at me earnestly. 'Cos, seriously, Ren, if we are sat around a table on New Year's Day and you so much as mention—'

'Okay, okay!' Chuckling, I raise my hand, not allowing her to continue what I know will turn into a rambling lecture. And, rather than making excuses, because, in all honesty, there is so much truth in what she's saying, I accept the challenge. Accountability and all that.

'And don't either of you forget.' Lex wags an unsteady finger, squinting at us drunkenly. She's on a roll now, becoming more voluble, the topics shifting wildly the more she consumes. 'I'm not joking about having a divorce party, you know.' She had mentioned this several times in our WhatsApp chats, and now with the divorce almost signed, sealed and delivered, it seems that she's seriously up for it.

'Saturday. Four weeks' time. Put the date in your diary. It's going to be the bomb!' She squeals, wiggling excitedly in her seat. 'Have to celebrate getting that slimy no-good tosser out of my life for good. I need some ideas for a buffet though. Tan's promised to make some cupcakes, there'll be cocktails on tap, I might even be totally unsavoury and hire a stripper!' She flutters her eyelashes flirtatiously, while Kizzy and I listen, smiling. As desperate as she is to eradicate Phil from her life, we know that his behaviour and the subsequent fallout have left their scars.

After knocking back a jug of water, we settle the bill.

Hugs and kisses follow, along with the promise of a three-way call soon to discuss the divorce party in more detail. Then we part company. Kizzy, who lives not too far away in Clapham, is putting Lex up for the night so she can make the trip back to Wallington once she's sobered up in the morning.

Our conversation stays with me as I make my way along the main road towards my flat, glad that today's choice of venue was down to me. Ten minutes and I'll be home.

It's a mild evening, but with a nice breeze that sends a low whistle through the trees. The coolness is welcoming, fanning my face and helping to ease my tiredness. As always, my heart feels light after meeting with Lex and Kizzy. A significant tonic in my life. We've long said goodbye to the carefree days when life revolved around pubs, clubs, bars and assignments; living in each other's pockets. Now, our time together is even more precious and meaningful. Boyfriends, husbands, break-ups, motherhood, leaky boobs; and our friendship is still intact.

Tiredness aside, there is a spring in my step as I turn onto Braisley Road, key in hand to enter my sanctuary. Tomorrow, I will get the ball rolling on my quest to write my novel. It's time to be proactive.

Chapter 2

Seven weeks before the end

'You sound as if you're still asleep, Serendipity!' Mum's shrill voice threatens to puncture my fragile, fuzzy head. I knew I shouldn't have answered the phone.

'What do you expect, Mum. It's…' I force an eye open, a spark of pain piercing just behind my eyeball. Peering at the clock on my wall, I say in bewilderment: 'It's five o'clock on Sunday morning!'

'Not where I am,' she responds, far too lively for me to deal with at this ridiculous hour. How is this woman so oblivious and inconsiderate?

'Anyway, I just wanted to let you know that your dad bought a motorbike. Can you believe it?' She cackles. I know she's not expecting a response. 'He's trying to compete with the locals; they don't even wear helmets out here and he's only ever ridden a moped back in the UK.'

'Well, it sounds like he's enjoying himself. Maybe you should get one too,' I mumble, only half-engaged.

'You wouldn't see a woman my age on a bike in Indonesia!' She sounds appalled that I could even contemplate something so stupid. 'They're very conservative. The older women are anyway. Not that I'm old or anything.' A moment of silence.

'Are you listening to me, Serendipity?' As if she can see

that I've put the phone on loudspeaker and placed the pillow over my head, but it doesn't stop her voice from penetrating through cotton, feathers and down. The fact that she's calling me by my full name is an added layer of anathema, and I find my thoughts wafting away on a cloud of their own.

It's been said that your name defines you. During my younger years, I thought long and hard about changing mine: who wants to feel that they are here by accident? That the air they breathe and the space they occupy wasn't through careful planning; manic and obsessive checking of ovulation charts and the heart-stopping anticipation as the stick presented with two blue lines. No. At every opportunity, my parents are fond of reminding me – and informing anyone who does or doesn't ask – that I was an accident: an unplanned, misjudged error that threw their lives into disarray. Ironically, it didn't stop them from living the nomadic life they craved. With a baby in tow, in their mid-twenties, unmarried, but pledged to each other with matching tattoos, they packed up their few possessions and embarked on a two-year expedition across Southern Asia – developing a profound connection with Indonesia and Malaysia.

For two very different individuals who had met in a squat in South London amidst a fog of weed and cheap cider, it's quite a feat that their relationship has endured two children, a myriad of cultures and times with no one else but each other for company. The first two years of my life, unbeknownst to me and only verified by a photographic trail, were spent in a sleepy fishing port, Kuala Terengganu, Northeast of Malaysia, a place little known to anyone apart from the locals – who apparently fell in love with me and my parents. We only returned to the UK when mum became '*ill*'. Only to discover her mystery ailment was an eight-month-old foetus in the form of my younger sister. They didn't name her Serendipity Junior, but legend has it they initially named her Fate, until someone pointed out that the name might prove injurious to her life as she got older. They settled on Faye.

'…And it literally fell out of the tree and put its arms out for a hug. I'll have to send you a picture.' Mum's voice interrupts my reverie.

'What fell out of the tree?' I ask, not even trying to pretend I know what she's talking about.

'The monkey!' she exclaims loudly and then tuts. 'You're obviously not listening, Serendipity. I would have been better off calling your sister.' I actually wish she had.

Our relationship is often erratic, at best tenuous. Whilst I hankered for the stability and security that comes with more conventional parenting, I've been saddled with this impulsive, sometimes immature, duo whose idea of '*helpful*' parental advice is encouraging me to settle down '*with anyone who'll have me*' or discouraging me from going to university. 'What's the point?' was Dad's invaluable contribution. I don't dislike them; in fact, I find them rather intriguing, but I think they would have been happier living their lives without the burden of children and having to make grown up decisions from time to time when Faye and I were younger.

Mum and Dad's offbeat style of parenting has certainly had a bearing on the shape of mine and Faye's lives. I'm sure a psychologist would have a field day mapping some of our peculiarities to our childhood encounters. A total of thirteen primary and secondary schools behind me, with an education so splintered I didn't make any real friends until I met Kizzy and Lex at Uni, maybe that attests to the reason why a relationship breakdown has never left me broken-hearted, and the thought of ever having children fills me with dread. Whilst I've found the mettle to follow a relatively linear path, I am not filled with that passionate, hard-edged ambition that Lex, Kizzy and most of our other friends have. I'm happy coasting along, but that doesn't mean I can't be a tenacious lioness when I choose to be.

And then there's Faye. Poor, displaced Faye, who has never been able to get a foothold on life's ladder. Faye who blames Mum and Dad for all her shortcomings; for not being '*proper*' parents and giving her the anchor that she needed. I can empathise with her to an extent, but Faye does tend to blame everyone for everything, never one to take responsibility for any of her egregious decisions. She's spent most of her adult life drifting from one saga to another: an unsuccessful year abroad, back and settling somewhere near Exeter with a guy she met on the return flight, only for that relationship to come to a miserable end. She's back in the Southeast now, flat-sharing with some friends near Brighton.

Faye and I haven't been able to maintain the close relationship we had as children. Spending time with her leaves me with a feeling of infinite breathlessness, like being caught up in some sort of whirlpool of drama, and in desperate need of a glass of something strong and neat. Her regular chorus to me is: '*Well, it's alright for you.*' How she arrives at that conclusion, I'll never know. As if I spend my time trying to dismantle my wishing wand or wrestle the genie back into its bottle.

I love my sister, but from a distance. The current state of our relationship: she's still pissed off with me for declining her offer for us to '*bubble*' together during lockdown. Interestingly, she wasn't offering for me to stay with her, quite the reverse! An evening with Faye is hard work; an entire day is just about tolerable; bubbling together, in my flat, for an unspecified amount of time, that would have been enough to destroy our already flimsy relationship. I'd either emerge the other end a raging alcoholic; one or both of us in body bags, or me in a colourless jumpsuit, wrists handcuffed, shackled at the ankles. Some of her choices have left me stunned, and I often wonder how I've been able to forgive her for some of the things she's done to me.

Thoughts of my flawed family send me back to the depths of sleep. When I wake again, much later in the morning, I can't even remember if the conversation with Mum came to a conclusion or if she prattled on and hung up when she realised she was, indeed, talking to herself.

Hangover Sunday turns out to be quite fruitful. After polishing off a full English breakfast and now onto my third cup of black coffee, I complete my lesson reviews and log off from my laptop. Working from home suits me more than I thought it would. I've always loved the vibrant and diverse energy that comes from working in a college, and I do miss it, but having the flexibility to set my own schedule with my online tutoring work is brilliant. Granted it doesn't pay a huge amount, but it gives me some time to take a step back. No more nine-to-five, frantic lesson planning, interminable weekly meetings, contacting errant students, dealing with challenging behaviour. For now, at least, I'm out of that game.

I cross to the sofa and curl my legs beneath me, marvelling at the simplicity of my current set up. I've lived in my one-bedroomed flat for three years now. Ground floor, in a converted Victorian terraced house. London is a tightly compacted place: neighbours rarely ever more than a stone's throw away – on top, opposite, beside; the constant sounds from traffic, people, pets. But it's something I love. Had I not spent a fair number of years shuttling around various London locations, I would probably find this way of living extremely claustrophobic. But what I find most fascinating about London living is, despite being surrounded by so many people, everyone seems to live comfortably in their own little world. Some of my neighbours are ghosts: their presence is felt or heard, but I've never, or rarely ever, seen them. Prime example is Sonja who lives upstairs. She's lived here longer than I have, but I could probably count the number of times I've seen or had a conversation with her. Good-natured and polite, like most of the dwellers around me, she keeps herself to herself which works fine for me.

My phone chimes. An incoming email:

Dear Ms Shephard,

Thank you for signing up to Insight Academy's Writing Course: The Creative Journey – Accessing Your Imagination.

We are currently processing your payment. You will receive a link with joining details for the course within the next 48 hours. Please be aware that this is an online course. Only registered participants will be permitted access.

I skim through the remainder of the email, a languid smile spreading across my face. Step one: check! Lex and Kizzy come to mind, and I cannot wait to tell them that I've set the proverbial ball in motion, way before the one-week deadline Lex set me.

***

Thursday takes its sweet time to arrive. I'm restlessly anticipating the start of my course, like an excited five-year-old waiting in the audience to witness their first live pantomime. There is still something unidentifiably bizarre about the virtual world. A staple part of our existence that doesn't quite have an anchor, like some sort of twilight zone. Even with the essence of lockdowns hopefully behind us, it's as though parts of our lives have been unable to transition back to a tangible reality. I doubt I would have been so quick off the mark signing up for an online writing course if remote learning wasn't such a big part of my life now.

So, on this dry, mild morning, with the sun and clouds engaged in an inane game of hide and seek so that I am constantly oscillating between drawing and opening the blinds, I sit at my desk, in the corner of my spacious living room counting down the minutes until I click the link to connect me to my first Creative Writing Zoom session. A knot of anxiety sits in my stomach. Entering any online realm for the first time, those harrying questions loop together: Will my computer suddenly crash? Will there be a power cut that disables my internet connection while everyone waits impatiently for me? What if my laptop starts buffering and I miss important parts of the session? I know my mind will continue working ten to the dozen, until I'm comfortably settled in the session, camera and mic fully operating and no glitches to show me up.

Earlier in the week, an email had been sent out giving a detailed outline of the course, including instructions to keep mics switched off, unless speaking, and to keep cameras on. With this in mind, and with the certainty that I will only be seen in portrait view, I'm in a plain white t-shirt, my thick hair packed into a bun and I'm wearing specs. Not that I need them, but Lex always tells me I look intelligent and professional in them. A quick application of Ice Sparkle lip gloss, I check my reflection (no one will see the knee-worn, saggy jeans or slipper socks) and I'm ready. My mug of coffee sits on a placemat beside me; I've put my phone on silent and I've got my brand-new spine bound A4 notebook, ready to immerse myself in what I hope will be an inspiring first lesson. All I need to do now is '*join*' and wait for permission to enter.

At 9:58am, I '*arrive*' at the session just in time to catch the tail end of a sentence: '…help us determine what happens next.' And I imagine the tutor is engaging in small talk with the eager students already in class.

Someone else starts to speak before my laptop visuals have a chance to catch up with the sound: 'I haven't written anything since my children were toddlers! And that was twenty-something years ago. I'm not quite sure what I'm doing here!' The shrill voice makes it sound as if every phrase should end with an exclamation mark. Her voice has a sing-song quality to it, I almost feel like swaying along as she speaks. Laptop now fully engaged and in gallery view, I see that the sing-song voice belongs to Alison. She sits in what looks like a garden room, far too much sunlight in the background, causing her to squint uncomfortably at the screen. While she continues to elaborate on her reasons for not being worthy of a place on the course, I do the equivalent of a quick visual sweep around the room to get a brief measure of who my new classmates are.

Interestingly, our tutor (host) doesn't have his camera on, but as the time changes to 10:00 he informs us that he will switch to shared view so we can see both him and his presentation. While he does this, I click on the participants' icon, although, what are the chances I'll see a familiar name? Well, nothing wrong with looking, and I can also get an idea of how many of us have decided to embark on this creative journey. There are ten names in total. Not sure what I expected but that seems like a good number. Enough members to allow me to get lost in the crowd when I choose to, and hopefully a small enough group so there won't be an overload of discussion, interruptions and endless annoying anecdotes!

Back to gallery view just as TSJ, our tutor and host, appears on the screen. First impressions count, so we are always being told. And the first impression I get of TSJ will remain with me for a good many years to come. The first thing that strikes me is the kaleidoscope of colour that he brings to the screen, like one of Chagall's most vivacious paintings. Let's start with the background. There is something about filtered backgrounds on visual communication platforms that is super obvious. Whether outlandishly garish or a neutral wallpaper-style background, any movement makes it look like some sort of dodgy special effects. Ergo, I can tell straight away that the wallpaper that adorns TSJ's room is real. Splashes of angry, vibrantly coloured lines, like slash marks in a horror movie, overlap at varying angles across the wall, on a pale green background. It's as if a hundred pre-schoolers, high on fruit shoots and gummy bears, have been let loose with paintbrushes. This really isn't a computer-generated background chosen for effect. This is real. Above him sits a bookshelf with three books either side of a healthy-looking aloe vera plant – the only part of this set-up which seems normal.

TSJ's outfit is the next thing that accosts me. Put simply, he has come dressed to dazzle! It's difficult to tell, but his oversized shirt looks like it's made from a crepe de chine-type material; it hangs shapelessly but kisses his skin in places. I can only describe the colour combination as awkward. Grey collars with gold studded tips; breast pockets – one orange, one green; swirly blue circles adorn the sleeves. If not for the snippet of conversation I had caught, I would be justified in thinking I'd mistakenly joined an online children's activity session with the host about to introduce a puppet show! TSJ looks more like a children's entertainer than a creative writing tutor about to set us on the path to producing our own masterpieces. And then, as if his appearance couldn't throw up any more comical effect, I spot the comb-over. The wispy strands have been delicately positioned, but it doesn't hide the fact that he needs a trim. The slightest breath will blow that hair right out of shape, and only God knows what lies beneath.

I give myself a quick shake and ticking off. *Stop being so mean, Ren! This is not what you're here for. Time to starve your distractions and feed your focus!*

As if TSJ has been waiting for me to complete my unsolicited appraisal of him, his introductory slide pops up on one side of my screen.

Welcome to The Creative Journey:
Accessing your imagination
An Introduction.

'Hello, and a warm welcome, my Seedlings!' The exhilaration emitting from him is enough to set my laptop on fire. 'It's wonderful to be with you today, to start your creative journey into the unknown.'

Seedlings… Did he just refer to us as seedlings?

'Before we start with the introductions, just a very brief run through our Zoom etiquette. I would like to ask that you all mute yourselves. I can see you all have your cameras on. Fabulous. What a beautiful bunch you are!' He squints at his screen, his head making little jerky movements as he looks into the faces of each of his tutees. I immediately detect the Cockney accent, hidden beneath the plummy voice he adopts.

'Indeed, a gorgeous bunch,' he confirms, rubbing his hands together heartily.

I grit my teeth, wondering what everyone else is making of this. He's using the exact tone of voice and the exaggerated exuberance I would use to engage with my godson, Cory! Absentmindedly, I move my mouse to hover over the '*leave*' icon: Can I really spend three hours every week, for the next seven weeks, being called a seedling and having to listen to this irritatingly, fake voice?

I remove my hand from the mouse and again reprimand myself. I'm being very judgemental and defeatist. After all, not only will that be £200 flushed down the pan but I haven't even taken so much as one footstep of this journey. As if to confirm this, I look down at my notebook, open to the first page, the date and time neatly written in the corner of an otherwise blank page. I return my attention to TSJ, mentally pinching myself and promising to stay on track and focused for the remainder of the lesson.

'Soooo,' TSJ says, eager to move on to the next stage of his performance. 'For the next seven weeks, this will be our space to create, explore, connect and share. You've all signed up to this course for your own individual creative undertakings and it would be great to find out what they are. But first.' He pauses dramatically and raises his index finger, placing an imaginary tick in the air. 'Let me introduce myself to you.'

I take a sip of my now lukewarm coffee and reposition myself on my chair.

'My name is Tarquin St John.'

Well, that is it. Any chance I had of becoming a model student and focusing on my lesson slams forcefully against the window. Thank God for mute, is all I can say, as my mouthful of tepid coffee does an uncomfortable jig in my oesophagus, rises and splutters across the screen. I can only hope that everyone is busy focusing on Tarquin St John and no one has seen my calamitous exploit.

I just have to pause and deal with this before I have any chance of re-engaging. Everything about this man is anomalous. There are certain things in life that just do not work in harmony: a bed of nails, double-denim, oil and water. The name, the profession, the styling. Everything is off; nothing interlocks. Most names come with some prejudgment. I know mine does. When I think of Tarquin, I visualise a preppy, Eton-educated professor, with a tweed jacket and a trendy eye-glass. Someone professional, who wouldn't refer to a roomful of adults as '*Seedlings*'. Nothing at all like the Tarquin St John in front of me. I can only wonder if his name is really Tarquin.

Discreetly, I dab at my screen where the caramel-coloured drips race towards the bottom, leaving wet splotches that will need a proper screen wipe to restore it to cleanliness. This is turning out to be quite an eye-opener and the course hasn't even started! My mind is a law unto itself, engaging in all sorts of dishonourable conduct. I'm in recalcitrant student mode; the only difference between me and some of my ex-students is that they would have voiced these indelicate opinions out loud.

Tarquin continues in his faux accent: 'You may be familiar with my work already. I'm the author of the novel *In the Morgue*.' He pauses for the recognition that doesn't come, pride emanating from him all the same. I can almost see his forehead glowing. At this, I glance above him at the conservative collection of books on his shelf. It's difficult to see anything clearly and I make a mental note to google him later; though it sounds like a pretty macabre read, and not really the kind of literature I would be drawn to.

'I've been a university lecturer in creative studies for a number of years and I've also worked in publishing, newspaper editing, and the list goes on. Be it not for me to brag, but I have set many a new writer on the road to success.' He leans in close to the camera, his countenance now serious, voice a steady hum. 'All it takes, all it really takes, is an ability to be at one with your imagination; really open yourself up, let the seeds be watered, nourished and nurtured. You will live your work, you will breathe it, it will be with you all the time, as long as you constantly tap and tune, tap and tune…'

As quirky as he is with his expressions, I actually get it, and despite my disparaging, mean-girl thoughts moments ago, I'm quite enrapt. This is what I've been missing. My attempts to write have never consumed me, instead they've been nothing more than wishy-washy, jumbled ideas that have never gone beyond first base. I can sit and ponder over an idea which I think has some weight and five minutes later I'm wondering if I have any chocolate bars left in the cupboard. Maybe, just maybe, Tarquin St John is the magician I need to set me on the right path – I may even be able to put up with being called a seedling.

'Anyway!' The serious tone of a moment ago is abruptly released. 'That's quite enough about me. I want to know all about this wonderful bunch in front of me. Let me just take this away.' With that, he fiddles around with his mouse and turns off the screen share, which hasn't really served much purpose up to this point.

Movement and twitching signify that we're all a little uncertain how to proceed with this information-sharing section, so we all sit quietly waiting for Tarquin to single someone out to start us off. I spot Alison's mic symbol blinking and seconds later her voice takes over my room.

Alison (*but call me Ally*) reiterates her nervousness, in that self-flagellating manner I'm sure we will all become familiar with. Maybe she wants us to think she's completely rubbish and then blow us away with some incredible pieces of writing. Ally succeeds in setting the get-to-know-each-other wheel in motion. Next up is Stella Gibbs. Dressed smartly, as though about to give a formal presentation, I quickly get the impression that she's working her way through the Insight Academy handbook. 'I made a pact with myself some time ago that I would broaden my knowledge and get out of the humdrum routine I'd fallen into. I've learnt British Sign Language; I've done an online flower arranging course, basic Spanish and Accounting, all in the space of eighteen months. I was tempted to try crocheting next but I thought writing would better suit me. I've always kept a journal and I would love to turn it into a story.'

We would have heard a lot more from Stella, had Leonard

not interrupted her. He comes across as a bit of a smug know-it-all. A *'serious journalist, with more years' experience than some of us have been alive'*. He holds up a newspaper taken from a huge pile behind him and offers up an example of his work: an opinion piece for the Guardian online about the growing number of middle-aged men returning to education. Fascinating. Leonard tells us that he has worked all over the world, but having decided to take early retirement he wants to try his hand at writing fiction.

Gillian introduces herself next. She seems like someone I would get along with. Modest, smiley and straight to the point, I find myself nodding along as she speaks. Like me, she has found it hard to get to grips with her writing and needs some motivation and guidance to set her off. I follow on from her, expressing much the same sentiments.

Rusco, I'm sure that must be an alias, gives the quickest introduction in history. He mumbles a few words to the group, most of which I would politely ask him to repeat if I felt for a moment he wanted anyone to hear what he had to say. He looks unkempt, slightly bewildered, his long unbrushed hair partly covering his face, eyes never looking directly at the camera.

The introductions continue with Michelle Mac and Phina, then Tarquin reclaims the baton.

'So, as I expected,' he says, 'different walks of life, different motivations, all which will be explored. Is there anyone we've missed?' He inclines his head towards his screen.

Two virtual hands go up; one of which belongs to Mary H. I would put her in her mid-fifties, chin-length hair, moulded around a chubby ball of a face. She's easy to miss in a crowd. Her camera frames her from head to waist, so that her full figure encased in a shiny blouse is clear to see. Mary looks as if she bakes the most incredible Victoria sandwich. Not only that but her old-fashioned, flowery blouse radiates comfort; it says hugs and all things grandmotherly. I can picture her wardrobe, full of an array of blouses and a modest range of elastic-waisted skirts.

'I'm a carer,' Mary tells us in her soft, demure voice. But she doesn't go beyond that, so it's impossible to know if she cares for a family member or if '*carer*' is her employment status. 'I love jotting things down,' she continues. 'My thoughts, descriptions of things I see, anything really. But I would love to write short stories.'

The last member of the group is Josh L. He has the appearance of someone who has smartened up for the occasion. Hair freshly cut, so you can see the precise fade and shaping. Fashionable in his Boss t-shirt, I would place him in his late twenties at most. The word that immediately springs to mind is '*chilled*'. I can imagine him on the radio playing rare groove tunes on the Sunday early evening slot; that point where you need a fruity voice to get you ready for the vagaries of a new week. Interestingly, he's a part-time primary school teacher at an East London school, and he would love to write action stories for young boys.

Thirty minutes later, introductions are all done. My new classmates seem like a mixed and keen bunch, I conclude.

'First task!' I'm quickly becoming used to Tarquin's unexpected and enthusiastic bellows.

'I'd like you to look out of your nearest window. Take an imaginary snapshot and come up with ten random words that come to mind. They don't have to be directly related to what you see, just whatever springs to mind. Don't overthink it… Just do it!' With this, he claps his hands and rises from his seat. His cue for us to get on with it? I assume so.

After two and a half hours of brainstorming random words, writing a description of the last person I saw in '*real life*', writing a dialogue between myself and my hero / heroine, I am feeling quite dazed and exhausted. I can't remember the last time I put pen to paper in such an unrestrained and, I hope, imaginative way. After setting us homework to write a 250-word story based on a specific character, place and setting, we wave enthusiastic farewells to each other and disconnect from the session.

Phew! That was heavy going. But, despite my initial misgivings, I have a strong feeling that I'm going to enjoy this. Contentedly, I stretch and uncurl my taut body that has been in the same hunched position for the best part of three hours.

Chapter 3

Five weeks before the end

The migraine is thunderous. Like someone is gnawing and knocking on my exposed skull, sharply and relentlessly. It's been months since I've had a migraine and even longer since I've had one as intense as this. Yet today isn't a day I can stay home feeling sorry for myself. As if summoned by osmosis, following my conversation with Mum a couple of weeks ago, Faye has been in touch. The reason? She's in trouble and needs help. What type of help it is, I don't know.

I try so hard not to care; to see her for what she is: a self-serving, insensitive leech, who really doesn't deserve my time or energy. I can trawl the depths of my memory and I would be hard pushed to recall a time when she has been there to support me. But, still, I find it almost impossible to turn my back on her. The image of Faye and I in our matching yellow cardigans, probably six and eight years old, our chubby arms wrapped around each other's necks, while she planted a thousand sticky kisses on every inch of my face, always comes to mind whenever she calls on me for help. I'm her big sister, and by default, I'll always struggle to ignore her pleas.

The raging dragon in my head continues to breathe fire; fresh air and a distraction is what I need. I swallow down two ibuprofen, certain they will be ineffective, but anything that offers some chance of relief, however minute, is necessary.

Late morning train journeys on Thameslink are usually stress-free, especially if heading out of London. I'm fortunate that the 11:05am from Clapham Junction is a semi-fast train to Preston Park – where Faye currently lives. On straightforward commuter routes like this one, I rarely drive, preferring the chance to observe the views as I head out of London: from huge, overbearing buildings, houses literally clinging to one another and random pockets of green to the more constant open spaces and less congestion.

But today's journey isn't one where I find contentment looking out of the window and engaging in thoughts of green space and leaving behind the bustling metropolis. There's an anxious feeling in my stomach every time I think of Faye and the conversation we had. It was clear from her hesitant and limited words that she was being cagey, but I could sense the desperation in her voice too.

I try for distraction. My mind takes me to yesterday's coffee and cake catch up with Lex and Kizzy, each of us cosied up in our respective homes on a three-way video call: our way of '*getting together*' without physically getting together. Both had been eager to hear about my writing course – session two having recently taken place. I was happy to accommodate them, regaling them with the weird and wonderful stories: Flamboyant Tarquin and his wispy combover; self-critical, validation-seeking Ally, homely Mary H, (the baker in the blouse) as well as my other new '*buddies*'.

'Did you actually do any of the work, Ren? It sounds like you spent your time appraising everyone,' Kizzy had sniggered. 'And daydreaming!' Lex had added. 'Tarquin sounds like quite a character though. 'I can imagine him in a comedy sketch.' We all giggled, even more when I did my impression of him clapping his hands together passionately and calling us *seedlings*.

But in the end, jokes aside, I said: 'I know I've been mocking him, but he was so good at simplifying things and helping us to dig deep to make that creative connection. I think he's probably great at what he does.' And I meant it.

Talk had moved onto Kizzy's preparation for returning to work and her increasing anxiety about leaving Cory with the competing Grandmas. Then there was Lex's excitement about her divorce and, more importantly, preparations for her party.

'So how far have you got with the preparations for this divorce party extravaganza?' I had asked Lex, now that it seemed certain her plans weren't just the drunken ramblings of a pre-divorcee. 'You've gone all American on us!'

'Out with the old, and all that.' Lex had waved her hand flippantly. 'A new chapter begins, and, what better way than to get a group of girls together to eat, drink and make merry?' She raised her mug of coffee to the screen.

As the connection began to frazzle, we drew our conversation to an end, with the promise from Kizzy that she would try to find a free evening for us to meet before her life went full throttle combining work and motherhood.

So back to my current location: just past Gatwick Airport, not long to go now. I check my phone. No further message from Faye, but from our earlier exchange, she knows what time my train is expected to arrive. No point messaging her again.

Before leaving home, I'd packed my notebook and pen. Writing is becoming my '*second skin*' as Tarquin referred to it during our second session: '*Take it with you, wear it, always seek opportunities. There are stories and ideas everywhere,*' he had enthused, eyes sparkling with energy. In a short space of time, I'm fast becoming used to his elaborate use of language and often idiosyncratic manner. The walls of my flat have disappeared beneath a wallpaper of post-it notes on which are written single words, phrases, short descriptions, names of characters, and anything else that springs to mind that may one day have a place in my novel. I also bought a sketch book, because: *'even if you can't draw, fleshing out a character or scene by drawing it and colouring it in, can lead to well-rounded, believable scenes and characters.'* The Gospel according to Tarquin. So far, my sketch pad consists of a dodgy drawing of a high-rise block, sketched from a bench in Brockwell Park. Within some of the box windows I'd drawn different coloured stick figures; my interpretation of the melting pot of disparate and intriguing residents occupying the spaces within. What riveting stories do each of those windows conceal?

Our *'seedling'* group is also throwing up some interesting blossoms and weeds. Michelle Mac currently holds the position of *'the student who doesn't listen'*, having to be told multiple times to switch her mic off – all that yelling in the background is a major distraction. Then there's Phina, struggling to understand any of the tasks that have been set for us. She mentioned right from the beginning that she wants to improve her English, this is probably not the right course for her.

Mr Primary School Teacher, Josh L, with the sharp haircut and fondness for designer t-shirts is very self-assured and always keen to share extracts of his work, some of which has been really impressive. But the person I've found most intriguing and at odds with this setting, (despite the group being quite an eclectic mix of characters) is Rusco. Whereas everyone else is switched on, willing to participate, he comes across as displaced and apathetic. Eyes constantly averted from the camera, as if the thought of looking directly at anyone will cause him to combust, he gazes around the room he is in as though unfamiliar with his surroundings. The room itself is eerie and looks window-less. A lamp sits nearby, focused directly and harshly upon him, so that certain times when he moves, I can see every angle of his gaunt face, along with the multiple ear and nose piercings. With his mic always muted, but his lips at times moving in conversation, I'm sure there's someone off camera with him. Someone who makes him feel unsettled, jittery. It's impossible to work him out.

I glance down at my notebook, but the pain in my head intensifies so that I quickly stuff it back into my oversized handbag. Even the few minutes reminiscing has caused my head to spin in tight circles, and my neck feels heavy from the weight.

'We will soon be arriving at Preston Park. Please remember to take all your belongings with you as you depart the train.' The mechanical voice emanates from the overhead speaker. I check my surroundings, making sure I haven't dropped anything, clutch my bag to my side and rise slowly, suddenly feeling desperate to disembark from the train.

Faye had agreed to meet me outside the station, and I check my watch to see that, as the train slows down, we are exactly on time. So far, so good. I can only hope that whatever has brought me here can be resolved in a manner as straightforward as my journey. The only place I want to be right now is horizontal on my sofa.

A small number of people leave the train as the doors open, no major stampede for the steps. I'm sure it will be different in a few hours from now when the city workers head home, weary, in anticipation of turning the key in the lock, one step closer to the end of the week. My steps are heavy and plodding as I make my way upstairs, trying to keep my sore head as still as possible; any quick movements will be most unwelcome. I emerge through the barriers and out into daylight, sunglasses providing some protection from the expanding sun. I look in both directions, no sign of Faye. Conscious of being in the way of anyone behind me, I move further along to the end of the station exit.

Then I see her.

Raging dragon forgotten for a moment, I have no choice but to raise my sunglasses above my eyes, just to be sure the migraine hasn't affected my vision.

Faye and I have always been able to fit into the same size clothes. I'm a size ten with a bit of a lockdown squeeze that I haven't yet got round to shifting. Neither of us has ever struggled to find clothes that look good on us and complement our average height. Faye has always carried herself with poise. Despite everything negative I've said about her, there is something in her demeanour and posture that says: *I'm independent; I'm not to be messed with.* Let's just say she wouldn't be someone you would instantly pick a fight with. But what approaches me is a figure that can only be described as wretched and much older than her 26 years.

She looks as if she's spent the last three months sleeping under a bridge with limited essentials. Fond of experimenting with a range of crazy hair colours, if there was such a colour as *dull*, this would be an adequate description of the tendrils that hang from Faye's head. Usually thick, lobe-length, with a natural under-curl her hair now sits on her shoulders, the ends scraggly and weak, so that with the current light breeze it appears as if the hair is floating behind her. She doesn't walk, she shuffles along, like an old man accosted by the weight of the world, not to mention arthritis and years of neglected grief that has suddenly come home to roost. The shabby beige cardigan wrapped around her does nothing to disguise the fact that she's lost more weight than is reasonable. Even from metres away, I can see the thinness of her face, as if the skin has been pulled back over the bone; just a single layer of gauze-like skin. I suddenly realise that I've been holding my breath and my mouth has fallen open. Everything around me is shadowy and faint; all I see is Faye. My feisty, truculent sister looking like a juggernaut has rolled over all her hopes and dreams, flattened her world beyond recognition. A gasp catches in my throat. I feel the tears on my cheeks before I even realise they've leaked out of my eyes. I blink the unshed ones away furiously. Whatever has happened here, and it doesn't take an expert guess, I need to show some restraint and not allow my true feelings to dominate.

Seconds later, Faye stands in front of me. There is a look of defiance in her eyes, as if she's ready and waiting to be chastised. But this is not the time for indignation or harsh words. She needs me. I encompass her in a gentle hug, worried that in her fragile state she will break or crumble in my arms. Over the years, I know Faye has enjoyed more than the odd tipple. Mum and Dad were never conservative when it came to alcohol being in the house. Booze was never taboo. If the drinks cabinet was full, as it often was, it was anyone's game. Both of us went through phases in our teens when every weekend centred around copious amounts of alcohol, regular weekend binges. I got over the novelty post-Uni but I know Faye can drink some grown men, twice her size, right out of the bar. I know also that she smokes weed, but I never had any inkling that she would, or does, partake in anything stronger.

'Hi, Ren,' she greets me. Her voice sounds flat, and in contrast to the fire in her eyes, defeated.

'Faye. What's going on?' I try, honestly, I do, but I can't stop the consternation from creeping into my voice. 'Do you want to grab a bite to eat somewhere?' I ask, at the same time releasing her from the embrace. I'm straight into fixer mode, but I know a simple meal isn't going to fix this one.

'Yeah. There's a café just down there on the left,' she says pointing. She links her arm through mine – something she hasn't done since we were in primary school. Maybe it's more for physical support than anything else. Nevertheless, I cover her hand with mine, feeling how cold and dry her fingers are, even though the sun is shining down on us, and the day is shaping up to be a sizzling one.

We walk a short distance in uncomfortable silence. Questions and thoughts pitter-patter in my head, but they are not ready to be released.

'Have you heard from Mum and Dad recently?' I ask, wishing as soon as the words are out that I can shove them back in again. Those words may well be kryptonite to her fragile state. But it's either that or the big pink elephant, which I refuse to broach until we're seated. So, the Mum/Dad small talk will just have to do for now.

'Angie called me a couple of weeks ago.' I often forget that Faye never refers to our parents as Mum and Dad. 'Al was riding around on his motorbike delivering something or other and Angie was on some yoga retreat with her friends.' She places emphasis on the word '*friends*', sarcasm in evidence. 'She went on and on about Al's new hobby, then accused me of not listening to her. Said she would have been better off calling you.'

I smile, blandly, and let out a little *humph*. 'I wouldn't take it personally if I were you,' I say. 'When I last spoke to Mum, she said something very similar to me.'

'Mmm.' Faye is distracted, or uninterested, and I can feel her thin arm, entwined in mine, trembling.

'Weather's better than it was this time last year,' I say, trying to keep the conversation afloat. 'Wonder how long it'll be before the forecasters start comparing it to the Caribbean?'

Minutes later, we enter Sweet Fillings. Carefully, we navigate our way around a huddle of expensive-looking buggies, a group of mums enjoying a light lunch and some adult company with their toddlers in tow. The smell of all day breakfast permeates the air, my meal of choice whenever I visit a café, but today my stomach feels slightly upended. I doubt I'll be able to manage anything more than a coffee. Thankfully, we find a vacant table at the far end of the café where it's quieter. The cushioned benches provide enough room to sit comfortably opposite each other.

Faye's eyes bounce around, obviously trying to find something to focus on that isn't me. I can't wait any longer.

'Bloody hell, Faye.' I don't mince my words. 'What's happened to you? I'm really worried.' My hands are gripped around the cushion; it wouldn't surprise me if my nails pierce through it.

Faye nibbles the tip of her index finger. I've never known her to bite her nails and I hope this isn't a new habit. I can see she is desperately trying to figure out the best entrance point to whatever it is she has to tell me. But nothing comes. I don't wish to make her any more uncomfortable than she is, but I know that if I whitter on or keep probing, we'll be arguing within minutes. So, I try a different strategy. I sit in silence and wait. She shifts around in her seat, scratches her head, bites her cuticle again.

'I owe someone money, Ren, and I need your help.' Blunt and to the point, but at least I now know the crux of the issue.

From the moment I'd set eyes on her less than twenty minutes ago, I knew that money would come into the conversation. Now, I'm almost certain that the money has something to do with drugs. Ultimately, I want to help her, that's what I've come here for, but I'm not going to be a pushover. I've bailed my sister out on numerous occasions, usually for help with rent or an outfit for a job interview but today, there will be no cavalier handing over of cash, until I know exactly what is going on.

I rest my elbows on the table and raise my eyes to meet hers. 'So, who is it you owe money to and why do you owe them money?' My tone is calm but firm.

'Isn't it obvious?' Faye spits, indignantly.

'Not unless you tell me,' I state, equally aggrieved. I am not letting her off easily.

The waitress drifts over to our table, notepad in hand, and I place an order for a coffee, a hot chocolate and two cheese toasties.

Faye closes her eyes briefly and massages her temples with her fingertips. She takes a deep breath and looks me directly in the eye.

'No judgement, okay?' Without waiting for a response, she continues in the same breath. 'I'm already in a shit place and I don't need to be told that my life's a mess.'

I shake my head slowly. 'No judgement.'

Faye runs her hand through her hair, stopping midway when she is unable to work through the tangles. She pulls her hand away and lets some of the hair fall to cover her face. 'My flatmate, Kerry, is into all sorts of drugs and stuff. I was only meant to try a couple of pills but then she offered me some coke while we were out. I was drunk, fed up, I'd just lost my job and I thought: why not? It just spiralled a bit from there.' She looks up at me, almost belligerently, waiting for me to comment, criticise, lambast. But I don't say a word, instead, I bite down on my tongue to a point of near pain, hoping that my poker face checks out.

'She started giving me the stuff I wanted at first, all I had to do was serve her and her friends some freebie meals when I was on shift at the restaurant. It was leftover stuff anyway, not as if we could reheat it and sell it.' She shrugs, haughtily, in justification. Something tells me her employer wouldn't have viewed it in the same terms.

'Anyway, I got more into it, then she started asking me to

pay.' Her eyes widen as if the idea of exchanging drugs for money is a new phenomenon.

'The guy she deals with is hardcore. He made out as if he was giving me a good deal, but before I knew it, he said I owed him £500, which included the drugs I thought were free at the beginning.' Faye pauses to bite down again on her fingernail. 'At the same time, I had a couple of warnings at work about being late, messing up orders, and stuff like that. I came in one morning and the manager asked me to clear my bloody locker. No warning.'

My poor head. No longer raging, but now a steady drumbeat, not at all helped by my screwed-up, intractable sister. I'm left wondering if Planet Irresponsible has a room to let. I mean, how many times should an employer pull you up for being late, messing up orders, *and all that stuff*, before they ask you to take the high road? Her ability to eject herself from every situation and lay the blame elsewhere is just perplexing. I'm tempted to reach out and shake her in frustration, but instead I reach for the coffee, which has just been deposited beside me, take a small sip, and remain silent. Cue for her to continue.

'Elis sent a couple of his thugs round to rough me up. They smashed up my place a bit, and one of them held me down and threatened to do all sorts if I don't get the money by the end of today.' Tenderly, she pulls down the collar of her high-neck t-shirt and I shake my head, appalled by the necklace of angry dark bruises.

'He's not the kind of person to make empty threats. I know I'm done for if he doesn't get his money today.' Faye looks off into the distance, contemplating her fate at the hands of this nefarious rogue, who I hate with a vengeance already. A whoosh of rage passes through me, and I clench my fists in my lap.

The rustle of the waitress approaching indicates that our

food is ready. Though my stomach feels as if it's been compressed to the size of ping pong ball, I need to eat. She places two neatly layered golden sandwiches in front of us, and I ask for some water which she goes off to get. Faye picks at the corner of her steaming toastie, pulling at a strand of cheese so it stretches like a melted elastic band. She pops a piece into her mouth and chews vigorously. Thankfully, she doesn't seem to have lost her appetite.

'So how do you put an end to this, Faye?' I ask directly. There is so much more I want to say, but I'm still fearful of rocking our delicate boat.

Her expression is one of bafflement, as if I've just asked the most ridiculous question.

'I'm not just talking about paying him off,' I say, to clarify my question. 'How do you make sure you don't get yourself into this situation again?'

She bites into her toastie. 'I've stopped taking drugs,' she says pointedly, her mouth full. 'I know I don't look at my best, but I swear, I haven't touched anything for weeks. I've been through a bit of a withdrawal but I'm over the worst of it now.'

I want to believe her, I really do. But this is such a typical scenario. Girl meets drug-dealer, ends up owing him money, gets pushed further and further into seedy dealings. Before the season changes, she's prostituting to feed her addiction, whilst said enterprising drug-dealer now doubles up as her pimp. I don't want this for my sister.

We spend over two hours in the café, our hot drinks and toasties followed by Diet Coke and Sprite. I've tried my best not to be judgy and pompous; it's not what Faye needs and neither will it undo the damage that has already been done. But I'm governed by a will of fortified iron, that if I bail her out financially on this occasion, I will not be doing it again. We're talking hard drugs, slippery slopes and the kind of end-stop we read about in the local and national newspapers. In the past, Faye has called me prissy and self-righteous. Labels have never bothered me, but drugs do. They scare the living daylights out of me, and Faye knows this.

While she pops to the toilet, I access my online accounts and make a couple of transfers. I don't want to come unstuck later in the month. In my presence, she calls Elis and we arrange a time – later this evening at his insistence – for the money to be handed over to him.

The next stop is to the bank which is centrally located on the High Street. Unfortunately, drug-dealers don't accept cheques or bank transfer, so with £500 drawn from my account, (it will take me a fair number of tutoring lessons to replace this) and with hours to spare, I accept Faye's offer to while away some time at her house. At least I will be able to see where and how she's living. Maybe it will give me some indication if she's telling the truth about being clean.

The semi-detached house is in a quiet cul de sac, just off a busy main road. From the outside, it looks like it could do with a bit of TLC, the paintwork cracked and peeling, but overall, it doesn't stand out or look any different from the surrounding houses. Faye opens the front door to a canvas of magnolia and a couple of paintings adorning the walls of the spacious hallway. I get the impression the front and dining rooms are being used as bedrooms. We head straight up the well-worn carpeted stairs and Faye's room is on the left, next to a toilet and bathroom. South facing, her room is lovely and bright, with large windows overlooking a compact, square garden. Even with the windows closed, so the room is airless, there is a light vanilla scent in the air, suggestive of a fragrance stick. It's a good-sized room with a ¾ bed in one corner, neatly made, a double sofa that looks like it has collapsed on one side, but it is semi covered with a bright orange throw. Faye seems to have made good use of the space. There's a fold-away table in the corner and an array of magazines stacked neatly on the floor. Nothing about the room looks sloppy or disorderly. Or to better interpret: nothing screams drug-addict in need of a fix. It goes a little way to reduce my apprehension.

'Make yourself comfortable,' Faye says. She seems to have perked up, just a bit. 'D'you want a drink?'

'A coffee would be great, thanks, if you have any.' I'm not in the slightest bit interested in drinking coffee, but thinking on my feet, I conclude that if she leaves the room, maybe I'll be able to have a quick nose around.

Faye heads off downstairs and the moment I hear her slow footsteps stop at the bottom of the stairs, I'm on my feet, beside the drawer that I've been eyeing up. A swift rifle through yields nothing untoward. Make-up items, a diary with nothing that piques my interest. There's also an unused cheque book and what looks like birth control pills. Nothing significant under the bed either. I scan the shelf, running my fingers along the back in case anything is stored behind the books and few ornaments. Still nothing. It doesn't help that I'm not sure what I'm looking for, but I feel certain that if Faye had anything to hide, she wouldn't have invited me back here – or she would have thought ahead and hidden it.

I feel around under the mattress and in the pillowcases. Apart from an open packet of rizlas and a cigarette lighter, I don't find anything. I can hear Faye clinking around down-stairs, and I'm sure she'll return soon. I tiptoe to the other side of the room and gently open her wardrobe; it creaks ever so slightly but sounds amplified to my attentive ears. Her selection of clothes is pretty sparse. She still favours dark colours with the occasional splash of orange or yellow. I sift through, pressing my hands together to pat down each item of clothing in case there is anything tucked away in the pockets. Again, my search is fruitless. There is a shelf above the rails where some chunky jumpers have been untidily placed. I feel around, as far back as my arm will allow while standing on tiptoe.

'What the fuck, Ren!?'

I squeeze my eyes shut, frozen in motion, not even attempting to turn around or think of an excuse why my right arm is lodged deeply in the upper recess of her wardrobe. Those footsteps I was listening out for totally let me down. Crap detective I would make. I release my arm and turn around slowly, guiltily. Then I make an automatic decision: I'm not going to feel guilty. My hard-earned £500 – which I'm highly unlikely to see again – deserves some sort of covenant.

'I want to prove to myself that I can trust you when you say you're not taking drugs anymore, Faye,' I state, frankly. 'I want to believe you're clean, you know I do, but if there's anything you're not telling me, if you're not being completely honest with me, now's your chance to tell me the truth.' I fold my arms, my feet slightly apart, ready for combat.

Faye places the cup of coffee on the pile of magazines, opens the foldaway table before placing the coffee onto it, a slight tremor to her hand. She comes over and stands directly in front of me.

'I swear, Ren. I'm clean. I've been feeling so crappy lately, it's enough to put me off drugs for life. I am not taking anything.' The last sentence is emphatic, with conviction.

'Okay,' I say resignedly. 'I believe you. Let's just get this sorted so you can move on.'

She nods slowly, contritely, and I can't help feeling surprised that my snooping around hasn't led to a full-blown argument. I look at her, standing in front of me, a thinned out, beaten down version of her usual self, and a wave of sympathy flows through me. It must have been hard for her to reach out to me with this, knowing how often I've told her she needs to sort her life out, and knowing my stance on drugs. For now though, I think we've said enough on the subject. I won't offer any lectures or words that may reignite the embers, we just need to deal with the situation at hand and get this Elis character out of her life.

We spend the rest of the day lounging around Faye's flat, half-heartedly flicking through TV channels. Time speeds by and before long it's time to meet Elis – or whichever of his thugs he plans on sending to do his dirty work.

The meeting point is a street about fifteen minutes from Preston Park Station. Since I'm not familiar with the area, Faye leads the way. The sun has long departed, and night-time is settling in. As we walk along, I find myself thinking how much easier it would have been if he had just agreed to meet us after my visit to the bank. He would have received his money and I would be back home by now. But street law dictates that drug dealers prefer to conduct their business under the cover of darkness.

I've already lost my bearings as we make our way down a road with houses that look similar in design to the ones on the street where Faye lives. It's quiet but well-lit with very little movement. The road has a slight downhill slope and I can see another row of houses parallel to the road we are on. Since leaving her flat, Faye has been extremely quiet, and I can almost feel the tension emanating from her like hot steam. She checks her phone just as the chiming sound indicates that a message has come through.

'He's just around the corner,' she says, her voice barely audible.

My body is rigid and brittle, I can just about order my steps. The small amount of food I've consumed today threatens to rise. Am I really doing this? Skulking around in an unfamiliar area, about to hand over cash to a drug-dealer? It's as if I'm caught up in some parallel universe. I can be fearless and a bit of a rebel when I choose to be, but this is so far from my reality. I pull my shoulders back. A few minutes and it will all be over.

Faye glances across at me as if she senses my rising anxiety. 'You okay?' she asks, her voice tight.

'Yeah', I mumble. I had asked the cashier at the bank for £50 notes, thinking ahead that it would be easy and quick to count.

As if from nowhere, he appears in front of us. Rock solid, with the demeanour of a rottweiler? Well, that's what I'd been expecting, but even though his frame is enveloped in a padded bomber jacket, he looks lean. More greyhound than rottweiler. The mask half covering his mouth makes it impossible to tell what he really looks like, but in the near darkness, the eyes tell their own story. It's like looking into a dark pit and seeing Lucifer staring back at you. Not an angry Lucifer, but one that senses your fear and wants to capitalise on it – just because he can. I have no idea what his position is in the '*dealer chain*' but he's not someone I can imagine having a friendly conversation with.

'Brought some back-up, have you?' he asks, taunting us. As if there is a humorous element to this situation. I doubt he's expecting a greeting or introduction, so I remain silent, awaiting instructions either from him or from Faye.

'You got my money then?' His voice is surprisingly youthful.

Faye nudges me and I try not to jump out of my skin. I pull the envelope out from where I've been holding onto it in my bag. '£500. It's all there.' I try to inject some hard-ness into my voice, but I fail miserably. Conversing with drug-dealers isn't a module I've ever come across on my aca-demic travels.

He snorts. 'Course it is.' He doesn't bother to count it, just shoves it into the inner pocket of his jacket.

We stand there, as if waiting to be released from detention.

'Off you go then,' he says flapping his hand dismissively. 'Nice doing business with you. Let me know any time I can be of assistance again.' He winks at Faye. 'I'm sure it will be sometime soon.'

Faye does well not to retaliate. This had better be it.

We turn round; no further permission needed. Faye walks quicker than she has done all day, both of us eager to put as much distance as possible between Elis and this episode. We get to the top of the road and I steal a backwards glance, almost as if I expect to see him behind us. A sigh of relief emits noisily from my throat when I realise the street is as clear as when we first approached it. But there is a car creeping along as if looking for someone or something. I hasten my footsteps, Faye does the same. I won't feel safe until we're out onto the main road where the lights are brighter, the traffic is flowing and there's more footfall. But the car sidles up to us and we peek across at it. Is it Elis? Does he seem the type that will indulge in this depraved act of intimidation? Or would he take a more direct approach if he thought he'd been ripped off? My mind spins. There was definitely £500 in the envelope. I mentioned the amount to him, and he didn't query it.

I'm going over all possibilities when I sense footsteps approaching from behind. With all my energy focused on the vehicle keeping pace with us, I hadn't realised that someone was running, almost upon us. Faye screams. She is shoved aside. Someone bounces into me, hard. I feel a sharp burn around my neck, heat in my ears. Then my arm is yanked. My bag! I try desperately to reach for it before my assailant runs off. But I grab at thin air. He runs at me again. A ferocious bull. I do a half spin, trip over my left foot and I feel the side of my head smack into the wall.

Chapter 4

Four and a half weeks before the end

I wake from a deep, absorbing sleep. The kind that is heavy and dreamless as though I've been residing at the bottom of a dark well, but I can't say I feel alive and ready to face the world. Instead, there is still that clayey feeling in my head which I haven't been able to shake since the dramatic conclusion to my trip to Preston Park three days ago. Apart from a gash to my head, and a throbbing shoulder from where my bag was violently ripped from me, I'm okay.

Faye, although nursing a black eye from where she had been elbowed in the face, was also, thankfully, free from serious injury. Elis's ode of farewell. Not content with payment of the money owed to him, his parting shot was to injure and frighten us; not to mention robbing me of my watch, my diamond pendant, and earrings – cherished gifts bought for me by Denny. All to show Faye that he's not a person to be messed with. If sustaining these injuries and losing my valuables were enough warning for Faye to stay clear and turn her life around, then I can live with it.

Faye begged me not to report the robbery. I listened to her anguished sobs of guilt and the recording of a threat made by Elis that if his name was so much as whispered by her, she would wish she had overdosed on her first ever coke fix. This was enough to convince me to reconsider what would have been an immediate trip to the police station with descriptions, locations and everything in between. As it was, and with some reluctance, we had to be examined at the local hospital and there was no way we could avoid revealing some of what had happened, to both the doctor and the police who were subsequently called. The edited version I gave made it sound like a random attack: a vague, general description of the perpetrator. In the melee, I wasn't even sure if it was Elis that had attacked us. On top of all that, my purse had been rifled through, bank card taken and £400 worth of items had been purchased using my card. I'd been in touch with my bank and started the lengthy process of trying to reclaim the money.

Dragging myself out of bed, I wrap my house shawl around me and open the curtains. As much as I love the sunshine, I'm pleased not to be met with a powerful burst of sunlight in my current heady state. The sky appears welcoming, and there is just a glint above to convince me that it's only a matter of time before the clouds are incapable of defeating the sun's desire to break through.

A quick gathering of my thoughts and I remember today is Thursday – three hours with my creative writing buddies. One of the pitfalls of changing my work pattern is the way my routine has been knocked off kilter. Sometimes I wake up and need at least five minutes before I remember what day it is, what I should be doing and if there is a need for me to rush to get out of bed. Working a nine-to-five job has its upside, I guess.

Thursday is the only morning I have an early breakfast alongside my morning coffee. I wouldn't be able to concentrate for the duration otherwise. Keeping up with Tarquin and his random, thought-provoking tasks is hard work, especially if I don't have my wits about me. A bit like today.

After a lazy, warm shower, with the jet spray delightfully

massaging my body; a hearty bowl of porridge with banana and honey, and firing off emails to set up some online lessons for early next week, I check the time. Twenty minutes before the session starts. Today, I choose a different position from my usual seat at my desk. Not excited about the sun making its imminent entrance, my sofa is a better option, with my mini laptop stand secured over my lap. My notebook sits on the sofa beside me and I open a Word document which I can type directly into, if needed. I am logged in and waiting for my screen to come to life, when my phone pings a WhatsApp group message.

Kizzy: _How are you feeling? Hope you've recovered after your run-in with the Mafia. Don't ever do anything so stupid again! We're still pissed off with you for putting yourself in danger. Next time, call for back up!!_

I poke my tongue out, as if Kizzy can see me. I knew her and Lex would give me hell when I told them what had happened. The sympathy lasted a day before they laid into me and let me know how foolish I'd been and exactly what they thought of my no-good sister. It felt wrong not to come to her defence.

'She's learnt her lesson,' I told them over the phone. 'Even if she was lying to me about being off the drugs, she's had the wake-up call she needs. I think Elis' behaviour has shocked her into sorting her life out.'

Now Lex's message flashes up:

And no daydreaming today. CONCENTRATE!!

This is followed by a laughing emoji and two kisses. I chuckle to myself, my mind going back to my lengthy anecdotes about my tutor and class members.

I send a thumbs up and settle down ready for the session to commence.

From the moment we are live, and everyone has popped up onto the screen, I sense that something has shifted.

The usual exuberant, dynamic greeting that welcomes us is much more subdued today, as if Tarquin has been substituted by his toned-down avatar. Perhaps everyone else is feeding off this dull vibe; an aura of boredom and listlessness hangs in the virtual air. I click to see the participants; only nine of us present today. It will take me a few minutes to work out who is missing.

'Your first task this morning is... to write,' Tarquin says. Straight to the point, no further instructions.

I can only assume that the blank expressions staring out from the square boxes are mirror images of mine.

'Just pick up your pen or open a document and write,' Tarquin reiterates. Then a little more guidance: 'Whatever comes from your heart.'

I struggle with these challenges. I would much rather be given a context, a theme, something I can grasp onto without trying desperately to yank one of the endless strings of ideas that float around unbidden. Ideas that refuse to line up in rank order, so I can select the first one in the queue. I'm tempted to switch my camera off, walk to the window to seek inspiration, but that seems to require too much effort, and maybe that will defeat the objective of the task. I think about my recent experience with Faye and that prompts me to open my minimised Word document. I close my eyes and recall the moment I was most afraid.

I begin to type:

The thing about fear is that it has no logic. It is ambiguous, strangely paradoxical. My legs are leaden but my head feels light. Heat and sweat dampen my skin, yet I am shivering in terror. Time stops, but at the same time everything happens in an instant. The inconsistencies make no sense at all.

But what if I can pause in the midst of the fear and ask myself a question: What was it that brought me to this point: naivety, stupidity or bravery? To understand my story, let me

start at the beginning. Late one night, along an isolated resi-
dential street in a part of town unfamiliar to me, I met with
a drug dealer to pay off a debt. I am lucky I made it out alive.

I stop and read what I've written. A bit dark. A bit inex-
plicit too. Not exactly something I would want to share
with the group. I hope Tarquin doesn't single me out to give
feedback, because I think I will have to swerve this one. I
minimise my screen and see the rest of my class, heads
bent, writing away; maybe doodling, procrastinating, who
knows?

Dispirited by my pessimistic choice of topic, I throw in the
towel and decide not to do any more for this task. Instead,
I use the opportunity, whilst everyone is preoccupied, to
scrutinise them. Tarquin, back straight with his chin resting
on his clasped hands, appears to be staring directly into the
camera, in a day-dreamy far-off kind of way. Is that a film of
sweat clinging to his forehead and upper lip? Sporadically,
he glances to his left as though some activity is taking place
somewhere out of camera shot.

Mary, head leaning slightly to the left, sucks her cheeks
in, deep concentration causing her lips to protrude. At this
angle, her chin folds into her puffy, exposed neck, while
her hair is unbalanced like a set of old-fashioned weighing
scales, heavier on one side. But even the sustained level of
concentration seems mitigated by the fact that she's moving
her pen backwards and forwards as though tracing across
the same three-inch line. Maybe she's contemplating what
delicious goodies to bake later. I can imagine her letting out
a series of deep, troubled sighs, as she repositions herself in
her seat and looks up at her screen.

I look away, not wanting to be caught staring.

Not in the usual designer t-shirt I have come to expect,
Josh L is buried beneath a thick ribbed polo neck top, pulled
up so high it meets his bottom lip. A bit incongruous with

the time of year, but then again, there is no telling where in the country – or in the world – he is. It suddenly occurs to me that Phina is the person missing from the group. The challenges she'd been having understanding the tasks were likely beyond the remit of the course. Maybe she'd spoken with Tarquin and he suggested a more appropriate study programme for her.

'Pens down, Seedlings!' Tarquin resounds through my built-in speakers. His voice is less sombre than before, but still short of its usual animation.

'The tasks I set are not always going to be conventional and I know some of you struggled to let go of your imaginations during that activity.' He strokes his chin, thoughtfully.

'Now imagine if you step out of your house for a run one morning, you might do so without a direction in mind, but, it could be a mile or two down the road, that you settle into your stride and the direction becomes less of an issue – before you know it, you have an idea where you're going. It can be the same with your writing. Sometimes you just need to run… let your stream of consciousness guide you and see where it leads. Don't be afraid.' Interesting words but delivered like a soliloquy.

'Does anyone want to share what they've written?' Tarquin asks hopefully.

I burrow down into the sofa, wanting to dissolve into the cushions. I don't want to be the person picked on if no one is willing to share.

'Yes, please,' Leonard responds. He delves straight in without waiting for the go-ahead. 'What I have written is based on a conversation I overheard on a train recently. An elderly gentleman was talking to a young lad about the first time he saw snow after arriving in the UK.'

Leonard goes on to recite the entire conversation before reading the page-long story he has written. Hard to believe he has produced this mini masterpiece in such a short space of time.

The lesson continues and my mind wanders off several times during each activity. My focus is back on Mary now, and the fact that she isn't wearing a blouse today. The rim of her polyester top is stretched and shapeless, revealing a peep of squashed cleavage. From the tuned-in, absorbed stance of a couple of hours ago, she now appears disengaged, fiddling with her watch strap absent-mindedly. Today's session isn't progressing that well, and I'm sure I'm not alone in thinking this.

We are fifteen minutes away from what I can only describe as wading through an uphill quagmire. I've just finished my character description based on an image which Tarquin shared with the group. Everyone appears to be beavering away, and I'm about to minimise my screen to have a quick look at my emails when my eyes are drawn towards movement in Rusco's frame. Out of all the participants, he remains the least communicative and has never seemed willing, or interested, to share anything about himself, let alone any of his work. I've only ever heard him speak once, and that was when he delivered his jumbled, unclear introduction in session one. His long hair, which in the last session was pulled back from his face, today sits loose around his shoulders. It looks clumpy as if he's parted it in chunks and used solid castor oil to twist the chunks together.

His position from previous sessions is unchanged – still giving the impression that he is in some sort of airless box room with a single light focused on him and his device. Observing him makes me wonder what his motivation is for joining the course and whether he is serious about writing. I am a fraction of a second away from taking my eyes off Rusco when I witness the most heart-stopping and horrifying thing I have ever seen.

The movement is fast, with the precision of something that has been rehearsed. And while my mind tries to compute and process what I have just seen with my very own eyes, just like that, it is over, and I am left staring at the three-inch box on my laptop previously assigned to Rusco. My heart has ballooned, about to explode painfully from my chest, as my brain seeks to replay the events in slow motion. The man who appeared behind Rusco was wearing gloves and a baseball cap. With agility and skill that could only have been planned, and possibly enacted by the hands of a professional, a clear plastic bag was yanked over Rusco's head; pulled taut at the neck, and the knife that pierced his throat was thrust with such force that a jet of blood sprayed forth, splashing gruesomely across the screen. Rusco jerked violently then slumped forward, appearing to slide to the floor. His screen flickered once before his world and his screen went black. At the same time all of this happens, I am furiously grappling with my mouse, desperately trying to guide my cursor to unmute myself and… do what? At least raise the alarm, call for help. Surely everyone must have seen what has just taken place. I know I didn't imagine it!

'Hey! Did everyone see that?' I yell, once my uncoordinated movements successfully locate the mic icon. 'Someone's just attacked Rusco! I'm sure he's been killed!' I'm on my feet at this point, the rising panic in my voice doing nothing to help the situation. I can feel myself beginning to hyperventilate, as I peer into the screen like a lunatic, trying, impossibly, to see what lies beyond.

Tarquin is first to respond. 'Ren? Are you okay?' he asks, a look of concern and confusion creasing his brow.

'It's not me you should be worrying about. It's Rusco. Something happened just now. Someone must have seen it!' I am jabbing furiously at the screen, directed at no one in particular. 'It was right there in front of us.' My voice continues to rise in breathless exasperation. On wobbly legs, I oscillate from one foot to the other, eyes like magnified circles, never leaving the screen.

I am met with perturbed and unsettled looks. My position in this embryonic group, precarious. I am fighting for my life amidst this flock of relative strangers. But right now, I don't give a damn what they think of me. We have got to do something to help Rusco.

'I was typing my notes on the computer. I'm so sorry, I didn't see or hear anything.' My bombshell revelation has left Ally looking distraught. But her response isn't what I want to hear. Then, a domino effect as mics are unmuted, high-pitched feedback, a jumble of sounds pervading my room through speakers unsuitable for this tuneless din.

'Oh, how awful!'

'I didn't see anything.'

'Goodness me!'

'What should we do?'

A volley of comments, exclamations; none of them useful. Until one voice breaks through the disorder.

'I saw it, Ren!' Leonard. His voice usually powerful, assured, is timorous and small. 'I looked at my screen just as someone came up behind him. My goodness, the lad's just been knifed in front of us!'

Shock and relief fight for dominance. I am not on my own.

'Please,' I implore. 'We've got to do something, Tarquin. There must be something you can do! Can you try to contact him? You must have his details.'

My quick-fire barrage leaves Tarquin looking like a fish out of water, totally at a loss, but I can't blame him. He signed up to deliver a writing course to a small audience, not to take charge of a murder investigation! But then, finding his ground, he takes control. 'Okay. I am so sorry about this, everyone.' He clears his throat, searching for the right words. 'I-I think it's best if we leave the session here for today. We need to deal with whatever has happened here.'

I glance at the faces on my screen, expressions ranging from disbelief to horror, eagerness for the session to come to an end, so they can shut the door on this inexplicably disastrous session. But what catches my attention is the expression on Mary's face. Even through the shield of liquid crystal display and the layers of plastic and glass separating us, the look of latent fear is there to see. Mary becomes aware that I'm looking at her and her eyes shift downwards as though staring at her keyboard. She glances up again, nervously. The look is transient but it is there. The look that says: Yes, *I saw something too*.

One by one, the boxes close until only Tarquin and I remain, side by side, closer than we have been before.

'Ren. I have no idea what happened here, but it's obviously shaken you pretty badly,' he says.

I raise my damp palms to my face, pressing my fingers into my eyes. 'I just can't believe it. I can't understand why... what...' My thoughts and words are disorganised. Several minutes have gone by since the incident, but my breathing is still laboured. I relate exactly what I saw to Tarquin, at times closing my eyes so I don't miss anything out, though the images trapped in my mind's eye are painful and distressing.

'You must have contact details for all of the students, Tarquin. There must be some way of tracing him, finding out his address? Shouldn't Leonard be here too. He saw what happened as well.'

'Okay. Slow down,' Tarquin interjects. 'Let's take it one step at a time. I'm only responsible for delivering the course, I'm not in charge of the enrolments or—'

Something suddenly occurs to me. 'Did you record the session?' I ask hopefully, knowing that Zoom is multi-layered in its user access and subscriptions.

There is a pause before Tarquin responds. 'No. Unfortunately, the sessions aren't recorded, for confidentiality reasons. But it doesn't mean we've hit a brick wall.'

'Okay,' I say, placing my hands either side of me on the sofa, trying to get a grip. Tarquin is right. I need to apply the brakes and think rationally. 'So who's responsible for the administration of the course?' I ask. I recall finding out about the Insight Academy through a Google search. I had to fill in an online form and give the usual personal details.

'Well, my contract for delivering the sessions is with Insight. They employ the tutors and deal with all the administration of the courses. So, yes, that would be the best place to start, I think.' He sounds hesitant, unsure, and his calm, measured approach is at odds with my desire to act immediately. My insides are flipping and twisting but I feel the need to take the reins.

'Well, you need to get in touch with them. Surely there'll be someone who deals with the student side of things, someone in HR that can send the police to wherever he lives.'

Tarquin appears to be tapping away on a phone whilst I continue to prattle on, certain that I'm in shock. I massage my temples, flinching when my hand makes contact with the exposed gash on my head. My entire body feels weakened, emptied out.

Tarquin completes whatever he has been doing on his phone. He looks up at me, eyes boring deep. There's concern mixed with perplexity, but I can't be sure if the perplexity is based on the thought that he is face-to-face with a deranged, unstable individual or that something so shockingly sinister has taken place on his creative writing course.

'I'd imagine the police will want to speak to me,' I say,

more to myself than as a statement requiring a response. 'And Leonard.'

'Yes, absolutely. I'm sure they will,' Tarquin agrees.

'I think Mary might have seen something too,' I add as an afterthought. 'She was terrified and shocked. I don't think she quite knew what to say or do.'

Tarquin nods, his eyes fixed on me. 'I think the best thing for me to do is to take your contact details so I have them to hand.' He leans forward, reaching somewhere unseen for a pen and pad. 'I will make some enquiries at my end, so we can try and find out what's going on.'

Maybe it's because I'm at the centre of this and still grappling with the images, blinking at me like giant Christmas lights, but I can't help balking at his tone. He sounds a bit flippant. Anyone would think we are dealing with something relatively trivial, like someone making an inappropriate comment or sharing a rude meme. Does he not understand that I have just likely witnessed a murder? There doesn't seem to be the same high-priority response you would get if it happened in a classroom. Is he doubting me?

I decide to take the high ground. 'I don't think I'll wait around for Insight Academy to get in touch. I'm going to contact the police as soon as we end this conversation.' The firm tone I aim for sinks like a well-used mattress. 'This isn't a situation that can be marginalised.'

'Ren, I can promise you, I'm not marginalising this at all,' Tarquin says attentively. 'As well as speaking to you, I will arrange to contact the other members of the group individually. It will be dealt with in a serious manner. I guarantee it. Now,' he continues, ready to bring this conversation to an end. 'I'll take your telephone number and email address so I can update you as soon as I find anything out.'

I give him the requested information, struggling to remember the last three digits of my phone number, before admitting defeat and looking it up. Then we exit the session.

Now that I'm totally alone, the full weight of the situation assaults me. The time is 1:25pm. Even with the truncated lesson, I have still exceeded the amount of time I would have spent online with Tarquin. 1:25pm and I'm in need of something strong to calm my nerves. Remembering the open bottle of wine I have in the fridge, I go to the kitchen and pour myself a large mug. I don't even waste time opening the cupboard to pull out a wine glass. Three gulps later, and with another wine-filled mug, I head back to the living room and sit heavily on the sofa.

What the hell was that about? It's going to take a lot more than wine to erase that sequence of images from my mind or to fully process any of this. Was it opportunistic or planned? Everything about it was just too proficient and clean for it to have been random. Whoever did it knew exactly what they were doing. The magnitude of this is so overwhelming that I suddenly feel desperate for air. I need to get out. Being here, right now, almost feels as if I haven't left the scene of the crime.

***

By the time I walk through the black iron gates into Brockwell Park, my heart rate is almost back to normal, and I tune into the early summer sounds that surround me. Toddlers in their element, birds too, the tuneful melody of an ice-cream van in the distance somewhere. Cyclists manoeuvre along the windy paths, punctuated by the range of joggers you would expect to see in a park this size. I've been walking at a similar pace with a couple who look to be in their sixties, swinging their arms rhythmically, sweat-shirts tied around their waists. We approach the fork in the path: right, steeping uphill, towards the pond and café; left, towards the lido and the exit that takes you onto the main road leading to Brixton. I veer to the left. I could have taken a shorter, more direct route to the Police Station, but my stroll through the open green, especially at this time of year, is refreshing and soothing.

The 1950s structure is hard to miss. Part of the fabric of Brixton, the substantial building stands authoritatively, set back slightly on the corner of the main road. Who can imagine the tales this building can tell and the secrets it holds? A building I have passed on so many occasions but today is the first time I have entered it.

It must be a slow day for reporting crime because there is no one at the main reception window, just some activity behind a screen further back in the office. I press the bell protruding from the side of the clear screen, and moments later a police support officer appears, whistling, cup of steaming tea in hand.

'How can I help you, Madam?' His expression is open, the floppy fringe giving him a boyish appearance.

I clear my throat. 'I'd like to report a crime I witnessed earlier today,' I say self-consciously.

'Okay.' He places his mug on a placemat then taps some keys on the computer in front of him. 'Let me take down some details and I'll get someone to have a chat with you.'

Thirty minutes later, I'm sitting in an interview room opposite Detective Constable Phillips, breathing in the smell of dirty mop and disinfectant. The room, although fitted with a small oblong window, feels as if it is deep underground.

'So, Ms Shephard, can you tell me, right from the beginning, what happened?'

I start by setting the scene for him, explaining why we were all online. Then, frame by frame, I describe exactly what I saw. The moment he realises the crime I witnessed was online, he places his pen gently on the table, listening and watching me intently. I don't leave anything out. I even tell him about Leonard, although I am unable to furnish him with any details other than his first name.

DC Phillips waits until I finish before he speaks.

'And this all happened in the last—' he looks at his watch '—two hours?'

I nod, gory images constantly invading my thoughts, so that I have to blink harshly to try to clear them.

The pause is long, as though he has forgotten his lines in a play.

'Detective,' I say, desperate to move this forward. 'I've never been a fanciful person; I've never had delusions or episodes of any kind. I don't drink excessively, nor have I ever taken hallucination-causing drugs. I know, without a doubt, that I did not invent what happened.' My right hand is raised, palm facing forward, and my left is flat on the table. I could well be in court, swearing under oath. 'I know it wasn't a TV screen placed in front of a camera or some sort of trickery. Everything I have just told you is exactly what happened. I know what I saw.' My speech is delivered with clarity, but the pitch is erratic, and it occurs to me that the two large mugs of wine I consumed before leaving home might be incongruous with my impassioned words. I honestly cannot make out what DC Phillips thinks of me.

'Right.' He finally picks his pen up again, drawing the notebook towards him so that it is only half supported by the table. 'I want you to go through everything again,' he says steadily. 'If there's anything that you may have left out, however small you think it might be, I want to hear it all.'

An hour later, with my statement read back to me, signed, and having been given a crime reference number, DC Phillips walks me back to reception. He shakes my hand, thanks me for coming in and moves onto his next case. I look briefly at the Victim's Support leaflet he gave me at the end of the interview, and I shove it into my bag before heading back out onto the main road.

I'm nearly home when my phone vibrates in my pocket. Immediately, I assume it will be Lex or Kizzy. In times of crisis, they have always been my confidantes, but the thought of once again reciting what happened, answering another 101 questions, leaves me feeling weary. I decide to hold off telling them for now.

Surprisingly, the display lights up with Faye's name. Since the incident with Elis, she has assumed the role of caring, thoughtful sister, checking in on me, either by phone or text message. Guilt, no doubt. But if guilt keeps her clean and out of trouble, then bring it on.

There must be some truth in the notion that memory links to pain, because the sound of my sister's voice causes an echo chamber effect in my skull, highlighting the pain I felt when I hit my head against the wall. I don't really feel like conversing with her, but after the usual pleasantries, she asks why I sound so despondent, and I find myself pouring out the events of earlier, my words tripping over each other as though I'm afraid the scene will fade away if I don't regurgitate it quickly enough.

'What-the-actual-fuck?' Faye remarks, disbelief evident in her voice. 'How the bloody hell does that happen? I mean… really? How? Do you think it was some kind of setup? I don't even…' Her voice fades out, at a loss for any words that can bring sense to any of this. It is small comfort to know that someone is as disconcerted as I am. Faye knows I'm not one to catastrophise; that is her arena.

'I've gone over it so many times, my brain feels like mush,' I say, my footsteps dragging. 'I know the brain can play funny tricks, Faye, but this was not a fake. It was so violent and the way the blood just spurted out everywhere…' I tail off, feeling dejected and slightly nauseous.

'I should have spoken to Leonard before he left the session,' I continue. 'How am I going to get hold of him now? I might not get to speak to him until next week – that's if the lessons are allowed to continue.' I keep up this outpouring of thoughts, while Faye listens patiently. 'Poor Rusco,' I sigh. Another image, high-definition, slow motion.

'I hope the police are onto it,' Faye says. I hear her ragged intake of breath. 'I don't want to scare you, but you've got no idea who attacked Rusco. What if they saw you? You could be in danger too.'

I'd been so caught up with my concerns about Rusco it hadn't struck me that witnessing this crime could have put my life in danger too. It didn't seem as if the attacker looked into Rusco's screen, but I can't know that for sure. Faye is right. I hope the police really are taking it seriously. Tarquin should have been more responsible and insisted I go to the police, even offer to accompany me. It is exactly what I would have done if something so serious had happened in a lesson I was teaching.

We talk for another five minutes. I ask how she is getting on, and if there has been any contact from Elis, to which, thankfully, she says no. We end the call, Faye offering some reassuring words and promising to check in with me soon. It's a role-reversal I have never experienced before, but it feels heartening – Faye being the one offering to support me.

Chapter 5

Four weeks before the end

It's four days after the incident, and by this point, I have put in three failed calls to DC Phillips to ask if there have been any developments. After being placed on hold, again, on my fourth attempt, I finally speak to someone, only to be given another number to call – the cybercrime unit, where the case has been transferred. My details are taken again and now it is back to waiting and hoping. Why they couldn't have given me a number for the cybercrime team in the first place, I'll never know.

I have spent hours scouring news channels and listening to the radio in the fading hope that something relating to the case will pop up. It struck me a couple of days ago that I had again made the sweeping assumption that everyone on the course was somewhere '*local*'. Rusco could be somewhere overseas, maybe this is the reason there has been nothing in the press.

And then I hear from Tarquin.

It's strange hearing his voice without seeing his image on my screen. As always, I am struck by the counterfeit veneer; the cockney accent that scratches its way to the surface the more I hear him speak, and today, it is more obvious than ever.

'I'll get straight to the point, Ren,' he begins. 'I can't go into detail, but it *does* seem that something untoward happened during the lesson last Thursday.'

The emphasis on *does* is not lost on me. He didn't believe me last week?

'Has someone found out where Rusco lives? Is he dead?' I ask bluntly.

There is a pregnant pause at the other end, as if Tarquin isn't expecting such blatant questions. I'm just about to ask the questions again when he speaks:

'I think we would be better off discussing this in person.'

Why do I suddenly feel unsettled? 'What is it you're not telling me, Tarquin? Have the police been in touch with you?' This would be a good time to be online. I could really do with seeing the expression on his face.

'It's not as straightforward as it seems.'

He outright refuses to discuss the incident any further on the phone and despite my reservations I arrange to meet him. The address for the Starbucks he gives me in Wood Green is one that I know will be easy to find. Desperate to know what it is that Tarquin is keeping from me, we arrange to meet the following day. I flick to tomorrow's schedule in my diary: two tutoring sessions, the second due to finish at 2pm. We agree to meet at 4pm – more than enough time for me to get to North London once I have wrapped up the session.

I force myself to stay on track during my Teams lesson with Robbie, Tam and Estelle, Year 11 students preparing for their upcoming English exams. They are great teenagers, likely to achieve high grades that reflect their tenacity and willingness to improve. The main task I set requires them to work individually on exam questions. It will mean a fair bit of time marking and I ask them to take pictures of their completed work and email this to me by the end of the day. I end the session without the usual chatty conclusion, feeling a tad guilty that they haven't had my full attention, but promising myself that I will be extra thorough with the feedback I give them.

Today's weather offering is as unpredictable as it has been for the last few days. It looks murky for a late May afternoon, and although today hasn't been particularly cold, I get the impression that I will need to take a jacket with me, at least for my return journey from Wood Green.

The commute passes quickly; no unforeseen interferences to disrupt my route on London Underground. Wood Green. I can't remember the last time I ventured to this part of London and I am impressed at how modern and spacious the high street is. Typical of a London high street with all the usual coffee shops, retail and fast-food outlets, estate agents, and as busy as I expected it would be. The Starbucks is centrally located, and with fifteen minutes to spare, I decide to head straight in and find a table for two.

Meeting someone face to face when you have spent the last few weeks liaising across the ether is interesting. My seat near the back of the coffee shop allows me the opportunity to assess him unnoticed. Tarquin is shorter, and at least five years younger, than he appears on screen, and the trendy, dark blue mac he wears is not quite the outdoor attire I would have pictured him in. A pair of thick squarish specs are perched low on his face, so they pinch his nostrils, and his comb-over looks more nourished in real life. That aside, he is still recognisable as the inimitable leader of our creative writing group.

Now he spots me and strides over, a thin smile on his face. I rise in greeting; not quite sure what level of formality is required here. However, I am taken aback when he draws me into an uncomfortable embrace, holding on for slightly longer than is virtuous. He holds me at arm's length as though appraising a family member he hasn't seen for several years.

'Good, very good,' he says enigmatically, shrugging his coat off and sitting in the vacant seat opposite me. 'I'm glad you could make it, Ren. Can I get you a tea? Coffee? Something to eat?'

After a ten-minute wait in the queue, he is seated again, with a cup of coffee for me, an espresso for himself and a large slice of carrot cake, a spoon at either end, despite me declining his offer of anything to eat. I ignore the cake, as moist and delicious as it looks. I hope he doesn't expect me to share it with him.

Tarquin gets straight to the point, much to my relief.

'Again, I'm so sorry you had to witness such an awful thing, Ren,' he says genuinely, shaking his head. 'It is the most bizarre thing I've ever experienced.'

'It certainly is a bizarre experience,' I respond, tempted to put air quotation marks around the word *experience*. I hate to seem as if I'm vying for points here, but what exactly did he experience? If I hadn't been so forceful and obstinate, he would have easily dismissed me.

'I'm sure you can appreciate there's no protocol in place for such a situation, so I've done everything I can to get to the bottom of it.'

I lean forward, resting my elbows on the table eagerly, as Tarquin fumbles around in the inner pocket of his mac. He removes a small notebook. 'We have a student enrolled on the course by the name of…' He flicks through a few pages: 'Richard Usco-Lewis. We have his personal details and I've informed the relevant bodies about the event that you and Leonard witnessed.'

'By relevant bodies, I take it that includes the police?' I ask candidly.

Tarquin clears his throat, and wriggles in his seat. 'Well, my obligation is to inform the organisation and they then take it up with the authorities. They are aware that we have two witnesses so it's likely you'll receive a phone call or a visit sometime soon.'

'Well, I've already been in touch with the police,' I say defiantly. 'They should be able to join the dots when they contact me.'

'Right, right,' Tarquin responds, nonplussed. He seems surprised that I have followed through with my vow from last week to contact the police. But then I suddenly feel guilty for acting unkindly towards him, adding to his obvious discomfort. I can't blame him for what happened. He is bound to feel out of place and, truth be told, if I were in his position, I may well be a bit incredulous too.

'So has anyone tried to get in touch with Rusco – Richard,' I say. It will take some time getting used to his real name.

'I'm sure they have, or they will do if they haven't done so already.' His words, delivered like a riddle, would have made me laugh out loud if the situation wasn't so grave. I get the distinct impression that Tarquin knows more than he is letting on and may be trying to distance himself from this. Is he worried about the impact this could have on his career?

We talk for a while longer. Every so often I sense that he wants to say something more, but the words never come. Once I establish that the information he is willing to share is limited, I'm quite eager to get going. I don't feel particularly comfortable in Tarquin's presence. Why we couldn't have had this conversation over the phone is a mystery.

'Another drink?' he asks eagerly when the conversation begins to wane.

I use this as an opening to take my leave, and I am about to make my excuses when he rises from his seat and, in a flourish, he dashes towards the counter. It would be rude to get up and leave now. Another coffee won't hurt. I look down at the carrot cake drying on the table in front of me, wondering why Tarquin bothered to purchase it. It has sat between us untouched.

I see Tarquin returning to our table and at the same time I feel the need to use the loo. A few minutes away will give my drink a chance to cool so I can gulp it down and be on my way. I smile politely and point in the direction of the toilets: 'Back in a sec,' I say. Tarquin nods and fusses about removing the used coffee cups and the uneaten carrot cake.

I loiter in the ladies for longer than necessary, retying my hair into its bun and checking my phone. I fire off a response to Kizzy's WhatsApp message in our group, letting her know I am good but have a lot on at the moment.

If I hadn't been looking up as I exited the toilet, and if our table hadn't been in my direct line of vision, I would have missed what Tarquin did. With his notebook in one hand, he reaches his other hand across the table and slips something into the mug opposite him: my mug of coffee. Was my mind playing tricks on me? Definitely not.

I reach the table and stand in front of my seat, astonished at his audacity.

'Did you just put something in my drink, Tarquin?' I ask, trying to temper down my rage.

'What?' I give him credit; he looks utterly bewildered.

I lean towards him and whisper, harshly: 'Please don't let me have to repeat the question because this time, it won't be just you that hears it.'

'Ren! Why would you assume something like that?' he asks, affronted, looking around in the hope that others haven't been alerted to our tense conversation. The indignation in his tone is almost enough to make me retract my accusation, but I am not backing down. I'm thinking on my feet now, because when you become frightened, you become inspired. 'So, you wouldn't mind if I ask the barista to pour that drink into a takeaway cup?' I ask, wrapping my hand around the hot mug and drawing it close to the table's edge.

The momentary look of trepidation could not be masked. For a second it's as though a different person has taken Tarquin's place, then in the blink of an eye, he is back. He takes his eyes off me, turning in his seat to shove his notebook back into his pocket.

'Ren, I think the situation with Richard is affecting you.' His voice is unruffled, placatory. 'I am not the enemy here. It sounds as if you're accusing me of spiking your drink. Why ever would I do that? Please.' He motions towards the counter. 'Ask for a takeaway cup. You can do whatever you need with the drink; get it analysed, whatever, I can promise you I did not put anything in there.' He points towards the mug. 'I simply put a sachet of sweetener down for you.' Without moving my head, my eyes trace downwards to the yellow sachet, partly obscured by the mug I have pulled in front of me. I look again at Tarquin, my eyes hooded, expression flat. I don't believe him.

I turn purposefully and head towards the counter. I tap my foot impatiently as the one customer in front of me engages in banter with the barista. I lean around him and signal the barista's attention. 'Can I have a takeaway cup, please?' I ask.

'Sure!' comes the enthusiastic response. As I grasp hold of the paper cup and thank him, I hear a clatter and a few gasps behind me. I turn instinctively and can only widen my eyes helplessly as my coffee mug smashes to the floor several feet away from me. But strangely, Tarquin is nowhere to be seen. I look around frantically, at the same time striding to the table. His mac is still draped over the back of his chair, and his notebook has slid out of his inner pocket onto the seat. I look towards the toilet, the only place he might be, and quickly I lean over and grab the notebook.

A hurried flick through reveals pages of notes, short-hand scribbles, but one particular page catches my attention. The title reads: '*Rusco – Ricky Usco-Lewis*' – slightly different from the name Tarquin revealed to me. I don't focus on the rest of the words on that page. I glance up again. Someone emerges from the toilet area, but it's not him. I whip my phone out, unlock it, and snap a picture of the page then continue flicking through another three or four pages of what look like work-related notes. Then I come to a page that has my name on it. For a second, I freeze, but realise time is running out. Tarquin will be back soon. I take another picture and slap the notebook shut, leaning over the table and almost throwing it back on the seat. One of the baristas is busy mopping up the murky brown puddle and carefully picking up chunks of broken ceramic. How the hell did my coffee end up on the floor?

I grab my coat, just as Tarquin emerges from the short passage leading from the toilets. He stops suddenly when he sees the mess, then looks to me quizzically. 'I've got to go now,' I say hurriedly, brushing past him. He reaches out to grab my arm but thinks better of it. 'Ren,' he says imploringly. 'I'm sorry if I upset you, but honestly I haven't done anything wrong.'

'Fine,' I snap. Another few steps and I am outside, the cool air wrapping welcomingly around my flushed and sticky body. I zig-zag my way to the station, glancing behind me every so often, making sure Tarquin isn't following me. A couple of times I almost bump into people heading in the opposite direction, such is my eagerness to see the back of Wood Green.

It's only when I'm on the overhead train heading from Victoria to Herne Hill that I open my phone. There is a stream of messages in the group from Kizzy and Lex. Seems they've been having a WhatsApp party without me. I ignore them for now, more interested in the pictures I have taken of Tarquin's notebook. I pinch and expand the first one with Rusco's name. Below it there is an address. I swipe to my next picture. This one has my name in capital letters at the top of the page. I lower my head closer to the screen, annoyed at myself for failing to get a clearer image. I can make out a picture of some sort, as if it has been sketched very faintly. It causes my heart to stop momentarily, because the drawing is obviously me: the wide brown eyes, frizzy hair up in a bun with loose strands either side of my face. A ball of lead forms in my gut when I read the words beneath the picture: *Untainted beauty, the taste of caramel, mouth-watering. What does she desire? What would make her scream?*

My blood runs cold.

Chapter 6

Three and a half weeks before the end

My dream that night is vivid and unearthly. Clawed hands tear at my face and body, hands covered in clumps of thick, dark hair. The sound of sirens come from all directions, whirring, ominously, a merry-go-round in my brain. I see people I know, and I call out to them, but everyone ignores me, looking through and beyond me as they journey on their way, leaving me in this state of purgatory. Alone and afraid.

I exit the world of horrors violently and abruptly, jerking out of my sleep. I yell something out loud, but the moment I am back in my body, I cannot quite access the words. I pick my phone up from where it lies on my bedside cabinet, and I have to rub the sleep from my eyes to see the time: 9:15am. I've slept for longer than I usually do. The memories of the last week nudge and poke through, producing lacerations that threaten to do irreparable damage. I'm in desperate need of a shower and a coffee. A shower that I wish could jet wash this period of horrors out of my life. I'm clammy and shivery, even in the stuffy warmth of my bedroom. It is at the point when I'm sitting in my living room, fresh, and holding a cup of coffee, that the fog in my head begins to clear, bringing some clarity to my thoughts.

I open a new page in my notebook, swallow the lump in my throat, and begin to write:

- *Rusco was violently attacked – most likely killed.*
- *Leonard also witnessed it*
- *Mary H – horrified and scared expression – did she see it too?*
- *Rusco's name is Ricky Usco-Lewis <u>NOT</u> Richard – did Tarquin know this? Any significance?*
- *Tarquin says the situation is being investigated: By management? Police?*
- *I have given my statement to the police.*
- *Tarquin spiked my drink?? Why does he have a sketch of me and that creepy description??*
- *Does Tarquin know more than he is letting on?*
- *<u>I have Rusco's address.</u>*

I underline the last bullet point. Twice. Then I read through the notes so many times that I feel hypnotised. Tarquin's image invades my mind. Already it feels like days ago that we were sitting opposite each other in Starbucks, but it was only yesterday. One day is merging into the next as if I'm being dragged along an endless path. But I refuse to sit around and let my thoughts implode when there is a gaping hole that needs plugging.

I start by googling Rusco's name: I can't imagine Ricky Usco-Lewis being a common moniker. Nothing comes up, so I try different arrangements, feeling a frisson of excitement when I come across a *Ricky U-Lewis* linked to a Facebook account. After several password fails, I successfully log onto my Facebook account and find Ricky U-Lewis. His profile picture is a man sitting under a tree, holding a newspaper so all that is revealed are his eyes and a patch of messy brown hair. There is no way of knowing if this is the same person. I scroll down. A number of birthday messages on 19th February: this year, last year, the year before… but nothing in between, or by way of responses. Ricky U-Lewis isn't a fan of Facebook. I consider sending a friend request, but that seems pointless. A flick through his personal information, no workplace listed but his hometown and current town are listed as Watford. The address in Tarquin's notebook is also in Watford. I doubt it's a coincidence.

My next step is to contact the police again, maybe they are in a position to share something with me, especially now that Insight Academy have (or should have) contacted them. It is another laborious task getting through to the relevant person, and the proverbial brick wall makes it seem as if I'm the criminal, rather than the person trying to report a crime and make sure someone pays for it.

There is a tone of scepticism from the female voice at the other end of the line. Her drawn out '*Ookaay*,' when I explain who I am and the reason I am calling, sets my teeth on edge. I hear her clacking away on the keyboard, probably asking herself how Lady Luck has matched her up with this indefatigable, neurotic witness first thing in the morning. '*Yes, we have received additional information, but there has been no further progress. Yes, it is still an open case, and we have your details if we need to get in touch with you. Is there anything else I can help you with?*' A summary of our conversation.

The next hour is spent trying to speak with someone at Insight Academy. Aware of my increasingly garbled words, as I explain for the third time what my query is about, I am not surprised by the dubious sounding voice I am met with. When I finally get through to Jean Fleming in HR, she tells me that the incident has been reported, apologises for what must have been a traumatic sight to witness and confirms it is in the hands of the police. I breathe a small sigh of relief, but there are still so many unanswered questions.

One of these unanswered questions: *how do I deal with Tarquin?* On my way home yesterday, in my frenetic state, I had made the decision to report him to Insight Academy, and the police. Attempting to spike someone's drink, drawing pictures of a student, and writing suggestive words surely constitutes assault and harassment. But today, with my head clearer and the heat and intensity dampened down, I ask myself if I have demonised him. There is certainly something about him that I find distasteful, disconcerting, but would he really try to spike my drink in the middle of a busy Starbucks, on a busy high street? Could he really have been placing the sweetener beside my mug? On top of that, he is always encouraging us to sketch our characters, flesh them out, ask questions about them. As creepy as it is, he might be characterising me. Maybe others in the group too. I didn't have time to look through every page of his notebook, maybe there are sketches and similar details about everyone.

The doubts remain, but for now I can put Tarquin on the miscellaneous pile, to be revisited. However, there is one thing that has been swirling around the periphery of my brain; lying in a blind spot, ready to be accessed if I allow myself to go there. I open my phone and go to my pictures, making a note of the address from Tarquin's notebook. My fingers trace the name of the road as I go through various scenes in my head. The perfect, but unlikely one, being that I knock the door and Rusco opens it, stunned and annoyed at the stranger standing there – a stranger who the only thing he has in common with is that we share online space once a week. But at least I will know he is alive. Scenario two: the place is a crime scene, cordoned off with a police officer standing sentry on the doorstep. I know they wouldn't let me near the place, but I might be able to find out a bit more. Scenario three: Rusco has a flatmate, a partner, or parents – someone who can shed light on what is going on. Scenario four: if no one answers, I can pretend to be a concerned friend and knock on the neighbours' doors, see what they can tell me about Rusco's whereabouts. With each mini play taking on a life of its own, I feel less like a cog in a stuck wheel. Briefly, I consider contacting Lex and Kizzy, maybe I shouldn't be playing detective by myself, but the thought of trying to explain this to them sits like a lead ball and I wouldn't feel comfortable getting anyone else involved in this. Not yet anyway.

The things I know about Watford: It's in Hertfordshire, somewhere out west of London. It has a football team. A famous, and very good-looking, boxer has put the town on the map. I'm sure it isn't too far away, and when I google the postcode, I am pleased to see that the drive is estimated at only an hour and ten minutes. My rarely used car will be in for a treat today. Apart from my fortnightly shopping trip to Sainsburys, I've hardly driven it since I was made redundant.

I scroll through the options the AA route planner has given me, deciding to take the M4, via Heathrow, a route I am marginally familiar with. With traffic, I am hopeful I will make it in around an hour and a half, if I time it right. Taking a couple of things into consideration – a lot of people work office hours, perhaps the best time to catch most people at home is in the evening – I decide to leave home at 4:30pm and stop to fill my tank on the way.

The customary pockets of traffic hinder my journey. Not surprisingly, heading towards Heathrow is the most problematic. At one point, I am stuck behind what looks like a fleet of taxi vans, as if a 30-strong rock band and entourage are heading on tour. Once this passes, I navigate my way to Watford without major issue.

The Satnav directs me past the town centre and then through a new build estate. A few turns and roundabouts later, I enter a narrow road with a neat row of terraced houses, just outside the centre of Watford. I slow down, pleased that the street is quiet and there is no impatient driver behind me eager to get by. Just as the Satnav informs me that the address is on my left, I spot the house that I'm looking for: Number 43 Barcourt Road.

The uniformity once present on a street like this has long vanished. Houses have been customised or modernised in some way. Acrylic rendering in a variety of colours, UPVC front doors, a couple of recently paved drives, chipped paint in need of repair; it is a distinct blend which adds to the character of the street and probably reflects the diverse people that live here. Immediately, I can cross Scenario two off my list – there is no police presence, no crime tape sealing off the area.

I reach the end of the road. Now that I know which house it is, I can look for somewhere to park. I decide to turn right and go down the adjacent road, sure that a couple more right turns will bring me back onto Barcourt Road. I passed a few vacant spaces when I first entered the road, so hopefully I can double back on myself and slot into one. I complete this mission successfully and find a convenient spot at the bottom of the road, step out of the car and after a quick stretch, I lock the doors. Now I begin to feel nervous.

Despite building my portfolio of scenarios, I haven't given any thought to what I will say if Rusco opens the door, or if I'm faced with a flatmate/partner/parent. I take a deep breath and head towards the house, mentally preparing my speech as I walk.

Number 43 is in a decent condition. The shrubbery at the front is slightly overgrown and the deep burgundy wooden front door stands out sorely from the houses on either side, but overall, it looks occupied and cared for. There is a low iron gate leading to the front door which I unlatch and push. It scrapes the ground with an annoying squeak, so I only open it with enough room for me to pass through.

I step up to the door and ring the bell. I hear the internal chime, a shortened version of a popular nursery rhyme.

A minute passes. No response. This time I rap firmly on the door and tap the gold letterbox.

Still nothing.

I look behind me, checking that my movements aren't being observed by the Neighbourhood Watch resident on duty. There are no curtains twitching and no neighbour suddenly needing to put the rubbish out. I turn back to face the door and peep through the letterbox. The air inside is warm and stale. Thankfully, (and I can now address what I was fearful of) I don't detect an odour that might belong to a dead body.

My eyes dart around through the small rectangular opening. There is what looks like a gutter cleaning leaflet on top of a pizza brochure lying on the rug, but no pile up of mail. I can see straight to the back of the house; the kitchen door is open. Everything seems neat, in its place and lived in. I quickly retreat and stroll back to my car. It is still early evening, so before I go knocking on the neighbours' doors, perhaps I should wait a while and see if anyone comes home. Finding a comfortable position in my driver's seat, I notice a car indicating to move away from a parking spot further up. This would put me in a vantage position should anyone enter or exit number 43. I put the car into gear, drive forward and reverse park into the vacated spot. Now to sit and wait.

I'm glad I checked the time on my phone before I reclined my seat because the next thing I am aware of is the double beep of someone's vehicle door being opened. I flip the seat into an upright position, shaking my head and blinking hard to clear the haze. It feels as if I have been asleep for at least an hour, but only fifteen minutes have passed. I look around, half expecting to see several curious faces gazing in at me. There is no one. I can see a couple further down the road, they must have walked past me less than a minute ago. Somewhere nearby I hear a dog yapping followed by the commanding voice of its owner. Nothing seems to have changed at number 43 and I am reluctant to risk drawing attention to myself by sitting here for much longer. Besides, I would rather not undertake my return journey to South London in the dark.

I check my reflection in the rear-view mirror. My eyes are a tad puffy; I look tired and just a bit frayed around the edges. The gash on the side of my head, when I move my hair to the side, although healing quickly is noticeable, discoloured.

I check my driver wing mirror for any approaching passers-by, getting ready to step out of my car once again. At this point, I notice movement on the other side of the road. I swing round in my seat to get a clearer look. It is a woman, carrying what looks like a heavy shopping bag. I decide to wait until she is out of vision before I do my door-to-door interrogations. She may even be one of the neighbours I could target.

As she gets nearer, I have a tingling sense of familiarity. I don't know anyone who lives in Watford so maybe she just reminds me of someone I can't place. One of the canteen staff at Upper Norwood College comes to mind. Eleanor? No, it can't be. But as she draws level with my car on the other side of the road, my heart flips and a dull pounding reverberates through the upper cavities of my chest, followed by a deep clunk in the base of my skull. She puffs on by, all attention on the heavy bag she is carrying. She doesn't make it much further before she is forced to put the bag down and take a rest. She looks behind her, perhaps to make sure she isn't blocking anyone's pathway, and I get a full and clear view of her. After a quick massage of her left wrist, she picks up the bag and with renewed energy, trots a few more paces and unlatches the gate to number 43. The same gate I unlatched a short while ago. She turns again to secure the latch. I don't even realise that my phone is in my hand and I have opened my camera to snap a quick picture. From the pocket of her buttoned-down cardigan, she whips out a set of keys.

Shopping bag still in one hand, Mary H opens the door and enters the house.

***

A little after 10:30pm I arrive home, grateful that my usual parking space isn't occupied. It takes four attempts before I successfully squeeze into the spot, and even then, I'm not as parallel to the pavement as I should be. I am desperate to be indoors, enclosed safely within my four walls. The drive home was a total blur, my thoughts running amok, diving, fighting, no structure or sequence. Now, I am bone tired and all I can do is take off my shoes and jacket before flopping down lifelessly onto the sofa. I switch on the TV, in need of some mindless distraction to bring balance to my unsteady world.

How do I begin to unravel this craziness?

I press my thumbs into my neck, trying to loosen the knots that have clamped down, threatening to crush the life out of me. My mind back-pedals over the events of earlier, the disbelief still enshrouding me like an invisible cloak.

I had sat in my car, staring at the closed door of number 43 Barcourt Road for at least twenty minutes, trying to fathom exactly what could be going on. This was definitely the address Tarquin had for Rusco. The *Ricky U-Lewis* I found on Facebook comes from Watford. Yet no rational or feasible explanation came to mind. The one thing I recalled was the look that crossed Mary's face the day the attack happened. I was right. She knew something. But I had assumed her look was a result of witnessing the same horror I had seen. Mentally, I ran through the bullet-pointed list I had created earlier, realising that things had become murkier and even more complicated. After some time, I concluded that there was no way I could simply return home without confronting Mary. What could she possibly do? I didn't see her as some axe murderer despite what may have happened in her home. I had to get some clarity on the situation.

With my heart thudding, and for the second time that day, I rang the doorbell. The jolly chime now seemed at odds with what this house stood for in my mind. I imagined a baffled-looking Mary opening the door widely, a myriad of emotions crossing her pudgy features before she… raged at me? Slammed the door in my face? Invited me in? But after two more attempts, I realised that none of these possibilities were likely. I lifted the letterbox. 'Hello?' I shouted. 'Can you answer the door please? I just want to talk to you.' The guttering and pizza leaflets had been moved from the doormat. I could still see that the kitchen door was open, but there was no sign of Mary. I crossed to the front window, placing my head close, hands cupped so I could see beyond the solid white net curtains. Everything visible was contoured. A table, a cabinet in the corner and some oversized sofas. I knocked on the window, gently but firmly. No movement; nothing.

What now? I couldn't stand there banging all night, nor did I feel comfortable knocking on the neighbours' doors.

Feeling more confused than ever, I eventually gave up, walking back to my car, head constantly turning towards number 43. Now that darkness had begun its stealthy approach, the house had a deadness about it – no pun intended. No lights, no shadows, just a deadness. That was when I decided it was time to head home.

Chapter 7

Three weeks before the end

The next few days pass in a grey mist. I find myself going through the motions, doing nothing more than I need to, ignoring calls, messages, emails. Rusco's case is like a leech, sucking away greedily at all my energy until I feel as if I'm floating; awake in a relentless, mysterious nightmare.

Before I can catch my breath, it's Thursday again. Thursday, and I still haven't come to a conclusion about the writing course. I have toyed with the idea of quitting, putting it all behind me and refocusing on other things. In a short space of time, the default setting of my life has switched from uncomplicated to volatile. There is no way I will be able to concentrate on creative writing with everything that is going on. I struggle enough to focus as it is.

Less than ten minutes before the session is due to start, I come to a decision. The only decision there is for me. I have to put myself back in the midst of where it all began. It may offer some further insight or revelation. Not to mention, this is my opportunity to try and communicate with Leonard. Maybe he knows more than me in terms of the investigation. With our shared experience, we could offer each other a bit of support through this, although I am sure he hasn't made it his mission to go on a crime-solving spree. I have no idea how I will single him out in the lesson, but I am determined to find a way. I suddenly find myself missing the traditional face to face, classroom setting. Things would be very different.

Thoughts of Tarquin have also been slithering through my mind, gaining strength the closer we get to our fourth lesson. Neither of us will feel comfortable being in each other's presence and I wonder if he will say anything to me about our encounter or if he will continue as if nothing untoward happened between us.

And will anyone mention Rusco?

The thoughts and questions keep aiming and firing, and at 9:55am I am perched on the edge of my seat, like a bird about to take flight, waiting to be admitted to the session. My mind flits to Mary. Did she know it was Ren from the creative writing group knocking on her door earlier this week?

The pen, held between my unsteady fingers, flips backwards and forwards. My feelings have fluctuated between stoicism and dread, determination and agitation, to the point where I am coiled tightly like the wire inside my pen.

I am let into the session at 10:04am. I appear to be the last member of the group to join, and I can't help but wonder if Tarquin has done this deliberately. Maybe he is doing whatever he can to keep distance between us, even across the ether. Faces pop up on my screen, and though it is difficult to tell, I sense that they are all staring at me, wondering what drama I might witness in today's lesson. I search the screen, half expecting, half hoping, that Rusco's name and image will appear. It doesn't. Is that enough evidence to tell us that he is dead? I click on the participants list. Definitely no Rusco.

There is some initial chatter in the group as everyone settles down, but I remain quiet, unobtrusive. One by one, I take in the names of the group members in the participants list. I move my mouse to scroll further down, but it won't allow me to go any further. Yet there is one name that I need to see which isn't there.

Where is Leonard?

Back to gallery view and I am overcome by a wave of disappointment. I abandon my thought of finding a way to communicate with him in the lesson. How the hell am I going to speak to him at all? The only thing I know about him is his first name. Not even the initial of his surname.

I sidestep this obstruction for now and focus on Mary. I search for a change in her demeanour. A look of guilt, anything that tells me she knows I have connected her to Rusco, but she seems fully absorbed in the introductory part of the session; everything about her unchanged – even her blouse is similar to the one she wore in the first lesson. I zoom in on her surroundings, not quite sure what I am expecting to see. Besides, I didn't enter her house, so there is no way to tell if she is inside 43 Barcourt Road. The wall behind her is a light modern grey, bare except for a small, 3D picture frame that looks like it contains a pressed calla lily.

'Are you okay with that, Ren?' Tarquin's voice interrupts my thoughts. Everything about him seems to have lost colour, metaphorically and physically. His usually quirky attire is replaced by a dark, collarless shirt which hangs in a way that make his shoulders appear less upright. His facial expression doesn't yell: *teacher trying to engage and inspire students,* more like: *how long till break time?* Even his voice seems enervated; an entertainer fed up trying to impress his booing audience. It's as though a façade has slipped or been stripped.

'Err, sorry, I think I missed that,' I stammer.

'I've put you into breakout rooms to work on the task we started last week,' he says. 'You'll be partnered with Josh.'

He switches his focus back to the group. 'So, everyone.

Once I click the button, you will enter your breakout room. We'll reconvene as a group in about thirty minutes.'

I have no idea what I am supposed to be doing in the breakout room, but I am suddenly alert. This is the first time we have been asked to work in pairs or small groups. Being partnered with Josh will be a chance to speak to someone on a one-to-one basis. Apart from brief group discussions and sharing bits of our written work, it doesn't feel like the group dynamics have manifested beyond polite greetings and the odd words of praise for the work shared.

Seconds later, we are in a '*room*' together and Josh is grinning at me expectantly.

'Hey Ren. How are you?' He sounds chirpy, pally, giving the impression that we are old and close friends.

I smile back. 'I've had better days but I'm okay. You?'

He ignores my question. 'Yeah, it really kicked off last week, didn't it? Were you able to get to the bottom of it with Tarquin?' he asks. 'Well,' he corrects himself, 'I doubt you can get to the bottom of something like that. But I hope he took it seriously?'

I decide not to mention my encounter with Tarquin. 'The police are dealing with it, so that's something,' I say.

Josh nods, approvingly. 'Well, I hope they do whatever they can to find who did it. You and Leonard were clearly shaken up. Must have been really traumatic.'

'It was. What about you? I take it you didn't see anything?' I ask.

'No. Much as I would have loved to…' He quickly catches himself. 'Not in a gruesome kind of way, but just so we could all back you up. I could see how petrified you were when it happened. I had my head down writing away at the time. I only looked up when I heard your voice. What a horrific thing to witness.'

I smile, sadly, seeing genuine concern in Josh's expression.

Hearing a sympathetic voice is reassuring. 'I've had to convince myself I'm not going mad. I mean, who logs onto an online course and witnesses someone getting brutally stabbed? It's so ridiculous it's almost laughable… until the images start playing around in my head.'

'Mmm,' Josh murmurs. 'It's a shame they don't record these sessions, isn't it? At least then the police would have something solid to go on.'

I nod. If only. I decide to try my luck.

'You don't happen to know anything about Leonard, do you? Apart from the fact that he's not here today,' I ask, hopefully.

'Sorry, I don't,' Josh responds. 'Maybe he couldn't cope with coming back after what he saw. Can't say I blame him. I think everyone feels a bit uncomfortable about it, even though nothing's been said.'

'Yeah, I know I definitely feel odd. And you're right – I think we've all lost a bit of momentum.'

Josh strokes his chin and raises an eyebrow conspiratorially. 'I hope you don't think I'm speaking out of turn, but I tell you who I think is a bit odd.' He looks around, almost as if we are in the same physical space and there is a danger of us being overheard. Clearly, we are so far off track from the task we are supposed to be doing.

'Mary,' he continues. 'I can't quite put my finger on it, but sometimes I can't help watching her. Still waters and all that. The witch in Hansel and Gretel comes to mind – lure the children in under false pretences.'

I let out a forced chuckle, but at the same time I stiffen. Until yesterday, my perception of Mary H was favourable. Benign, humble, the giver of warm, encompassing hugs. The kind of hugs that flush away all things negative, transport you to the promised land. Mary H who knocks on the neighbours' doors with offerings of freshly baked scones, home-made preserves, lollipops for the children, just because it's a nice thing to do. What has Josh been able to see that I totally missed?

At the point when we are reunited with the rest of the group, Josh and I are only five minutes into the thirty-minute task. I feel like a naughty schoolgirl, but at the same time, the conversation has helped to assuage some of the heaviness that has been weighing me down.

Josh has an impishness about him which is easy to warm to, as well as a wry sense of humour. It felt like chatting with a friend. I appreciate that, although he didn't witness Rusco's attack, I can tell he believes me and genuinely wants me to be okay. During the activity (that we didn't do), we exchanged email addresses. At some point, we are going to have to catch up on the work we've missed.

The remainder of the session goes by without incident. The only problem being that I haven't taken in any information at all. Apart from a few copied notes and mindless squiggles, I may as well have been lying on a blanket, headphones on, looking up at the sky. I am tempted to speak with Tarquin at the end of the session, but what more is there for me to say to him?

***

Later in the afternoon, I'm in the middle of doing some overdue housework when my phone pings to alert me of an incoming email:

Hey, Ren.

Nice buddying up with you earlier. Attached is my offering for today's task. Perhaps when you've completed yours we can 'change the perspectives', as directed.

Get back to me when you're ready.

JOSH

I feel warmed by his message. I'm glad we were buddied up too. I click on the Word document he has attached, and speed read through. A section of it reads:

You pressed the rewind button on your apology, so please don't say the word again. That would be the greatest most unimaginable insult. Sorry has a heart. It breaths gently and wantonly… Your sorry has been ruined. It was chewed up in the spool when you pressed rewind. Again.

He has an interesting way with words. My task now is to write the 'apology', as well as a character description of the recipient of Josh's letter. I email him back:

Hi Josh,

Thanks for your 'offering'. You've set the bar high!

I'll crack on with some writing later today and email you once it's done.

Enjoy the rest of your day.

Ren

With a load of washing spinning away, carpet vacuumed and my flat smelling of citrus and bergamot, I flick through the pages of my notebook and search for the bullet pointed list I made a few days ago. I make some additions:

- *Leonard was absent from the lesson – how am I going to get in touch with him?*
- *Mary didn't appear ruffled or affected – did she know it was me at her door?*
- *What is the relationship between Mary and Rusco?*

My mind starts to purr again. I contemplate putting in an anonymous call to the police – get them to search Mary's house. Surely there will be blood or some trace to indicate that a crime has taken place? Then I picture myself creeping into the house when she's out, trying to identify a room that resembles the windowless, eerie one that Rusco occupied during the Zoom sessions. What am I thinking? I'm completely out of my zone to even consider such a thing, as if I'm some maverick investigator. Whatever is going on, I have to trust that the police are carrying out a thorough investigation.

There is no doubt about it, I have totally lost myself in this saga. A cruel, twisted brainteaser that only two people have the answer to: but one of them is more than likely dead.

When I next look at the clock, it is 4pm, and aside from my earlier spring clean, I cannot for the life of me work out what I have done with my day. Unless I count the time spent thinking about Rusco and Mary. I revert to Josh's email and quickly bang out my own half-hearted contribution to our paired activity. He emails back almost immediately, enthusing about my work but also pointing out a couple of spelling errors. We engage in a bit of backwards and forwards banter, a great distraction, and at the end of his final email, he includes his phone number, underneath which are the words:

Just in case…

***

During the early hours of Saturday morning, I bolt awake, my curls slightly damp at the base of my neck. I dart out of bed and feel blindly for my dressing gown, the chill of the early hour seeping through my thin nightdress. I stumble out of the room and switch the hallway light on. It provides enough light for me to enter the front room and pad my way to the table where I left my laptop earlier in the evening. I can't be sure if the image came to me in a dream or what, but I recall the first writing session when we introduced ourselves to each other. Leonard told us that he had been doing some freelance writing and he even went as far as sharing an article he had written for the Guardian online. I search through the corridors of my brain, trying to recall what it was about: something to do with men... Just as Google opens up in front of me, a thunderbolt arrives out of nowhere. *The growing number of middle-aged men returning to education*. Or something very similar!

The internet is my saviour. It can't be difficult to trace Leonard with the pieces of information I have.

An hour later, I'm reading an article : *Middle-Education: Why a growing number of middle-aged men are returning to the classroom*, by Leonard Sharpe. And right at the end of the article is an email address.

For the remainder of the night, sleep evades me. I am fully awake when the birds begin their sweet yet persistent chirping; when the darkness reluctantly gives up its reign, and when the distant slams of car doors signal that the weekend workers are on their way to earn their crust. By the time the postman whistles his way to number 12 Braisley Road with the loud slap of mail hitting the mat, I have already used up the equivalent of a day's brain power.

A brief, courteous email to Leonard, which for all its limited content took me forty minutes to construct, is the high point of my restless morning. I am sure Leonard wouldn't have been up reading emails at the ridiculous hour at which I had sent it, but that didn't stop me from checking my phone every two minutes for a response.

For want of some distraction, I spend the rest of the morning mindlessly scanning through the Guardian and TES job pages, just to get an idea of what is out there. Putting together some resources for my upcoming tutoring lessons takes up a bit more of my morning. The nagging discomfort in my stomach is a reminder that I haven't eaten properly for a few days now. The snack cupboard has been my go-to for meals lately, but crisps, energy bars and peanuts can only sustain me for a short amount of time before I fall ill. I rummage around in the fridge and freezer, mentally listing the items I need to buy from my visit to the supermarket. For now, an egg and cheese bagel will do perfectly. I wolf it down, feeling better, more awake, with each mouthful.

Shopping bags littering the kitchen, I'm back home from the supermarket before the Saturday crowds have been let loose. This is usually my ideal start to the weekend: up early, shopping done and the prospect of a long, lazy Saturday ahead of me. Today feels different though. I'm restless and, despite my lack of sleep, I feel hyper. There has been no response from Leonard, but my detective skills have buoyed me. I am confident he will be in touch, even if I have to wait till after the weekend.

Restless, hyper and buoyed. Probably not the best combination of feelings to make a snap decision. If I stop to think it through and weigh up the pros and cons, I will find 101 reasons not to throw caution to the wind but to spend this Saturday afternoon catching up on the soaps or sitting in the park.

So, in less than a week, I make my second trip to Watford. This time, the journey is more cumbersome with several patches of slow-moving traffic, reminding me of exactly why most of my journeys are made by public transport. Heart FM keeps me company along the way; the late afternoon phone-in competition throwing up some interesting responses to the '*name that tune*' segment.

When I arrive at Barcourt Road, there are fewer cars than were there on my previous visit. I envisage families and couples packing into the car for a Saturday adventure, possibly a weekend away, making the most of the pleasant weather. Mary's house, just as I left it, unassuming, no intimation of the horrors that may lie behind that burgundy door. The only thing that contrasts it with the surrounding houses, is that the curtains are pulled firmly shut, as though desperate to keep the world at bay.

I park in a different place this time, but still with the house in sight. My plan? I won't be winning any rookie undercover awards anytime soon. My plan is to sit, observe and wait. The answers haven't presented themselves, even though I've been asking the right questions, so further action is needed. This is the mantra that has been drumming a beat in my head throughout the journey to Watford. I have to do more than sit around waiting for the police to tell me what's going on, because at times during the past week, I've felt as if I'm teetering somewhere close to the edge.

In my rucksack, I packed two bananas, energy bars and just enough water to ensure I won't be needing a loo, at least not for the next few hours. I pull out a magazine, brought along to while away the time, although I will be hard pressed to concentrate on anything apart from number 43.

At 9:15pm, when daylight has dwindled to nothing, I get the first indication that someone is home. A light comes on in the room at the front, shards visible through the dark thick curtains. I uncurl from my slumped position, squinting in the hope I can make out a figure, but the curtains are opaque. However, I don't have to wait long before the hallway light comes on. Through the obscure glass panel, I can make out the distorted figure of a person, but it is impossible to tell anything other than the fact they are moving around.

So acute is my concentration that it is only when the reverse parking lights of a dark blue Ford van illuminate part of the street that I am aware of its presence. It pulls up two houses away from Mary's, and the driver switches the engine off. I wonder which of Mary's neighbours has arrived home and whether it is someone who knows her well.

My eyes dart between Mary's house and the van. No one has emerged from either. The noise of raised voices to my right momentarily distracts me. Three lads, late teens or early twenties, engage in care-free, fatuous banter, play-fighting their way along the street. Their uniform of slim jeans and crisp pale shirts suggestive of a night spent clubbing and imbibing far more bottles of lager than they can manage. I almost wish for that care-free feeling.

There is more movement at number 43. The twisty and distorted shapes I can see through the glass indicate that someone is moving close to the front door. And then it opens; the light goes off at the same time.

It is the distinctness of her heavy, slightly diminutive figure that makes me certain this is Mary. Shrouded in black, her coat reaches her ankles, not quite what you would expect to see with the weather being so mild. Her usually bouncy hair is covered by a scarf, tied loosely under her chin. A stealthy look up and down the street, as though checking the coast is clear. She attempts to heave something onto her shoulder, but realising it is too heavy, she drags it out of the front door and closes it behind her. From my vantage point, I can just about make out what looks like a large, hessian sack tied securely at the top.

What could be in there? Rusco – out of place and fidgety in our Zoom session – comes to my mind. It's difficult to estimate someone's height when they are sitting down, not least in a box on a screen, but let's imagine he's an average five foot nine inches. It couldn't possibly be him in the sack. Mary would never be able to lift that dead weight by herself.

With what is clearly a great effort and strain, she manages to hug-lift the sack using both hands, so the item is wrapped firmly in her grasp, clutched securely against her vast chest. Then there is a clumsy battle to put one foot in front of the other, but she adjusts her grip, even managing to open the gate before stepping out and turning left along the street. My hand grips the door handle; mentally calculating how long I should wait before I attempt to follow her:

she can't be going far. But there is no need for me to exit my car. She stumbles along a few more paces and then, as though by magic, the back doors of the blue Ford van open. Mary hauls the weighty sack into the van, almost toppling in with it, before slamming the door, looking around cautiously, and sliding into the front passenger seat.

I am totally flummoxed by this scene. I start my engine at the same time I see the lights of the van switch on. Hopefully, the driver will be busy getting ready to drive off and won't notice me. I reverse slightly and carefully manoeuvre my way out of my spot. I see the taillight of the car, winking a left turn at the top of the road, and I make my slow move in the same direction. Another left turn followed by a right shortly after and we are onto a busy road with a steady flow of traffic. I should be able to follow without drawing attention to myself. My heart is thudding a tune of misadventure and warning. The rational part of my brain questions why I would put myself in this situation, and there is an almighty temptation to put my sat nav on and head home to safety. But curiosity is the bird perched on my shoulder, eyes gleaming in anticipation of what is going on.

I settle comfortably behind them, keeping my body as low down as possible without compromising my safety. It is a straight road ahead with possible turnings at every junction, so I hope they aren't going to make any complicated deviations. In the distance, I can see approaching traffic lights, just turning green. At a guess, we should both make it through. But as the car ahead of the blue van approaches the lights, they begin to change to amber. I am hopeful Mary's driver will slow down and stop, but they reach the traffic lights and suddenly speed up leaving me at a red signal. There is no way I can jump these major lights. I keep my eye on the taillights, praying they continue in a straight line.

To my right, the drivers are given the go-ahead to progress with their journey, and cars either go straight or turn right, putting further distance and obstacles between me and the van I am following. It seems like a never-ending wait before I can move again, and I feel like a stray cat in a dark maze, not knowing either my location or which route to take.

I continue onward. By now there must be at least eight cars between us, that's if they haven't turned off in another direction. For now, I can only hedge my bets and continue on this main road. I lean my head against the window and peer ahead. There is no telling if the blue vehicle I glimpse some distance away is the one Mary and her driver occupy. I have only been driving for five minutes, yet it feels like a lifetime. I have no idea where I am going: the last thing on my mind is paying attention to road signs. I slow down; another set of traffic lights approaching. Now I am about fifth in line, in the left-hand lane. Up ahead the occupants of the right lane can only turn right, whereas my lane is ahead only. There! I spot the van, in the right-hand lane, at the front of the queue. I check my rear-view mirror. There are several cars behind me, and alongside me. I am boxed in; but not caring for the onslaught that is bound to come, I indicate to switch lanes as the green traffic arrow gives the go-ahead for those turning right to continue their journey. I edge out slightly, but the driver of the white jeep in my side mirror isn't having it. He leans on his horn and speeds up. I sense him looking at me as he passes, but I don't make eye contact with him. I am not spoiling for a fight. Two more cars pass by before there is a small gap. I've edged out enough that the person in the silver Honda Civic has no choice but to wave me ahead impatiently. I squeeze in, flash my hazards to show my gratitude, and speed forward, almost butting the car ahead. I just make it through as the lights begin to change.

I am now on a less well-lit road than the main road I have just left. The two cars ahead indicate to take another right down a narrow lane. Thankfully there are no cars coming towards us in the other direction, so they turn with ease and speed. I keep going, glancing ahead, left, right searching out the van that has to be somewhere within sight. I look to my left, just in time to see the van moving along a tree-lined street.

'Shit!' I have just missed the turning. A quick glance in my rear-view mirror reveals that I am too late to reverse, as someone is right behind me. I decide to take the next available left, in the hope that this road will be adjacent to the one Mary is now travelling along. A sharp left turn which sends my rucksack flying off the front seat and I am racing, quicker than I should be, along this darkened part-residential road. I get to the end and do another left, slowing down to look, as I approach the top end of the road. No sign of them. I keep going. I can see lights ahead, but as I approach, it is a totally different vehicle. What now?

There are several inter-connected roads, and a few lights from moving cars. I crawl along, my head swivelling in every direction. From my position, I can see a car further down the road; its lights fade to black before it turns right. I decide to go in that direction. I have to wait a moment for the car ahead of me to reverse into a spot in front of a house. This slows me down and by the time I get to the end of the street and take the right, there is nothing but a silent street. This is fruitless. I swing into a spot beside a streetlamp. My vice grip on the steering wheel and my tight, arched position haven't ceased since I started following the van. My lower back and shoulders burn from the pressure. I guess it is time to switch on my sat nav and head home, I think despondently.

I'm waiting for the sat nav to calibrate my return journey

when I see movement further along the street. My eyes are alert. I can see a figure dragging something along the ground. If I start my engine and drive forward, I will draw attention to myself. Throwing all caution to the wind, I get out of the car, onto the quiet street, closing my door softly. I cross the street and walk stealthily towards the action. The dark, squat figure belongs to Mary. It's the same huge bundle she left home with that she is now relocating to this small, terraced house with the black door. I am twenty metres away on the other side of the road, crouching behind a car. I try hard to peer into the van, wondering if the driver is still in there. Mary completes her challenging task. With one final effort, she is swallowed up into the darkened cave of the house. The door closes with a soft thwack but no light comes on. I sneak out from behind the car, edging closer to the house and the van. Opening my phone and zooming in, I take a picture of the registration number.

I hear a rustle behind me and look up sharply. No one there. Fear embraces me, and I know it is time to leave. I jog back to my car and as I am doing so, commit the name to memory: Milicent Street. My headlights come on automatically when I switch the engine on, so I hastily deactivate them and edge out of my spot. As I approach the van, I slow down to a near crawl. Holding my breath as I pass parallel, I am surprised to see that no one is in it. They must have stepped out before Mary. But why didn't they help her with the sack? I look at the door – number 30. It would be foolish of me to try anything else. Just like a build-your-own-burger, the layers keep being added. I either need to step away from the counter or come up with another plan. I let out a huge sigh and head home.

Chapter 8

Less than three weeks before the end

I dream again. This time it's barbarous. Shady and mysterious underpasses, like intestines wrapped steadfastly around the bowels of the earth. The sounds are ghastly as if the whole world is being painfully disembowelled. Invisible arms reach out to drag at my limbs: a ragdoll being torn apart by vicious dogs. I open my mouth to scream but a ball of hessian is shoved down my throat. From the distorted images that are beginning to blur at the edges, a face begins to form. The deadened, evil eyes are the first things to come into focus. I know who it is but the image is in ghostly motion, refusing to be still. The pallor of the face is such that his skin looks translucent. I try to spit out the material, but with every shallow breath I am able to take, it forces its way, deeper and deeper. Shutting everything down. It is at the point when I am about to lose consciousness that the face becomes limpid.

Tarquin.

I jump out of my sleep, the battle between reality and fantasy in full operation. I'm spiralling, trying to claw my way out, to raise my head above the dungeons of hell. It's another twenty minutes before I feel strong enough to stumble out of bed. My entire body feels wrong, as if I have lived in it for 100 years; even my footsteps are cumbersome and painful like walking across jagged stones.

The sofa beckons. I lower myself onto it, knowing that it will take some sort of mass evacuation to move me from this spot. And even then, I will leave reluctantly. Thankfully, the remote control is inches away on the dining table. I reach for it and switch on the TV. The unified and triumphant strains of the choir cause my brows to knit in confusion. How is it even possible that a choir is singing on TV? That only happens on Sunday. Sunday. The day after Saturday.

Thick sludge continues to seep through the channels of my brain. A sludgy festering swamp. I've missed something. But the effort to clear the lumps from my brain is too great. I pick up my lifeline – my mobile phone – though I can't recall the last time I checked it. Not surprisingly, the battery is dead. The thought of rising from my horizontal position to locate the charger is a task I don't relish. Thankfully, I spot a wire sticking out from my laptop on the table in front of me, so I reach out to it, my arm flaccid and uncooperative. After a few clumsy movements, my laptop is on, and my phone is charging. It will be at least a few minutes before there is enough juice to bring it to life.

I use the waiting time to tune back into the service. The priest is giving his sermon, advising the fervent congregation that they should be living a Christ-like life. Life here on earth is only preparing us for eternity where the true benefits and rewards are. I've always taken a rationalist approach to religion but I find his sanguine voice and words comforting, soothing my fevered mind.

I drift off, this time peacefully, my breathing deep and rhythmic. When I wake up, there is a nature programme on, highlighting some of the many species of fish that reside in the Mississippi River. The remote control is lodged between my ear and the crevice of the sofa. I turn it off and flip my mobile over, now fully charged. Before I use my fingerprint to open it, I scroll upwards getting a snapshot of the slew of correspondence that I've missed: emails, WhatsApp messages, text messages, phone calls, notifications. An endless stream from the last 24 hours. The only thing my brain can confirm is that it's now Sunday afternoon. It feels as though a chunk of my life has been cast into purgatory. Is this a natural reaction to witnessing a violent crime?

The recall is like an unexpected firework. A sudden bang that jolts me and launches me straight off the sofa.

Yesterday was Saturday. Lex's divorce party! I missed Lex's party.

I open my phone and flick straight to WhatsApp. 30 unread messages in our group chat. The guilt soars through me, it swirls around and settles uneasily in my chest. How could I have missed the party? Lex has raved about it, outlined a plan in my presence and though Kizzy and I have teased her, I know this party is symbolic of her emergence on the other side. Like the antidote for a scorpion sting, this party meant a lot to Lex. What kind of a crap friend forgets something like this? Chasing answers to Rusco's attack has robbed me of my ability to think about anything else.

The messages started yesterday with the usual chit-chat and banter. Then Kizzy asked:

Why the silence, Ren? Ditched us for your new friends. Followed by laughing and heart emojis.

They continue the two-way banter – banter that I'm usually entrenched in. The conversation turns to Lex's party. She shared a screenshot of the list of invitees: ten names, including Lex's two sisters and a couple of mutual friends. Lex being the devilishly organised person she is had even sent us the menu: ringless finger buffet; free and single cup-cakes and an inviting cocktail selection, appropriately named: *flying solo*. I know this would have been the focal point of the night. Not only does Lex have a fondness for cocktails, but she also fancies herself as a bit of a cocktail bartender.

Kizzy had sent a response, informing us that she would be at Lex's in the afternoon to help with the decorations and she had asked me to bring along my party lights, assuming I was also putting in an early, helping-hand appearance. All of this I had missed. The final message, from Lex, was sent at 2:45am. All it contained was a sad face emoji.

I'd let my friends down.

The missed phone calls and voice messages were also from Lex and Kizzy. Turns out Kizzy had stopped by at my flat on her way to Lex's and, seeing that my car was missing, had assumed I was on my way there already, or something more interesting had come up.

Where would I start with the apologies and explanations?

***

We meet in Clapham, close to Kizzy's house. If my friends weren't so amazing and forgiving, I would be ostracised right now, cast aside like an item of unwanted clothing. But, guilty though I am, there is no rebuke or bitterness. Not to mention both Lex and Kizzy are in need of fresh air, copious amounts of water and a chance to clear the fog from the over-indulgent excess of the previous night. This is the reason we settle on Tortilla Treats – comfy sofas, hearty, healthy food, and the closest thing to alcohol is the zest of lime on top of my spicy three bean wrap. Lex looks completely done in; Kizzy, two or three paces behind. On my way to meet them and after having sent a lengthy voice message dripping with apologies, I remembered that Kizzy will be returning to work later in the week. The fact that they are both willing to meet me on Sunday, early evening the day after a heavy night, is testament to our friendship. I owe them a full-blown, unedited explanation.

'Wow, Ren. I thought I looked rough. What's happened

to you, girl?' I fall into Lex's embrace, relishing the sound of her drunken giggle, and her frank honesty. Truth be told, I hadn't even looked in the mirror before I left home.

'Tell it like it is,' I respond, trying to keep my tone light. 'Don't worry about hurting my feelings.' My voice sounds croaky to my ears.

'I'm surprised you weren't escorted off the train looking like that,' she continues relentlessly. 'Come on. Let's grab that empty booth.'

She sashays ahead of me to the vacant area with the padded seats, and I catch a glimpse of myself in one of the mirrors behind the counter. Lex does have a tendency to exaggerate, even in jest, but her reaction to my appearance is justified. I usually pack my hair up or back in a bun, often achieving a look that is naturally but stylishly simple. Today, however, the bun is loose and wild. Where I have let a few curls hang loose to cover the wound on my head, they don't lie flat, instead they stick out at odd angles, giving me the look of someone who has recently been in a fight.

We are just getting settled in our booth, having ordered some juices and water, when Kizzy arrives. Thankfully, being less candid by nature than Lex, she doesn't mention my appearance, but I can tell by the way she looks at me that she is taken aback. I guess that means I usually scrub up well.

I give Kizzy just enough time to sit down and remove her jacket before I jump back on the apology train.

'I really am sorry, Lex. You know how much I was looking forward to the party. I wouldn't have missed it for the world.' I fiddle with my earring, twisting the silver stud round and round in my ear, looking for any sign that she might be angry at my no-show. 'I've had a lot going on lately. I won't even lie – the party completely slipped my mind,' I admit.

Lex purses her lips, looking at me through slitted eyes.

'Mmm. Be a while before I find it in my intoxicated heart to forgive you.' She slaps the air. 'Honestly, don't sweat it. Just glad you're here.'

Kizzy reaches over and tucks one of my many stubborn curls behind my ear. 'So, what's going on, Ren?' she asks, concern creasing her brow. 'You don't seem yourself.'

I insist on hearing about the party first and I'm entertained with all sorts of raucous tales of karaoke, wild, drunken games and cocktail making competitions. It sounds like just what Lex had in mind for her exit party, and I'm so pleased she enjoyed herself, although deeply upset that I missed it.

Then it is my turn to take centre stage. In unison both sets of eyes turn to me, the anticipation palpable, broken only by our order being placed and the food being delivered.

I take a gulp of my orange juice and launch into it. I start at the beginning of the grisly Zoom session and let loose an avalanche of words until I get to the part where I sat-naved my way from Watford back to South London…. for the second time. Not a word is spoken by either Lex or Kizzy until the end. The food in front of us sits plentiful and untouched.

'Bloody hell!' they exclaim at the same time.

I play with a chunk of lime, squeezing a small amount onto the tip of my exposed bean wrap. 'It sounds completely unreal even to my own ears, but everything I've told you is exactly as it happened,' I affirm, my teeth biting into my cheek, seeking moisture.

Kizzy is first to proceed beyond the initial shocked reaction. 'I wouldn't doubt you for a second, Ren,' she says. 'I can see the effect it's having on you.' She shakes her head in wonderment. 'I'm just at a loss for words! I mean, what sort of evil nutcase does something like that?' The question is rhetorical. None of us has an answer.

Lex's myriad expressions that have ranged from disbelief to confusion, now changes to irritation. 'But Ren, I can't believe you're telling us that you went all the way to Watford – with no idea what you were looking for, or what danger you might have been in – by yourself.' Her slightly blood-shot eyes are wide, dark marbles glaring at me. 'How bloody reckless! And not once but twice! What exactly were you planning to do?' Her fury and frustration are undisguised; emotions that have never before been directed at me.

I look at her, contrite. Nothing to say in my defence. 'And after what happened with that drug-dealing turd who almost took your head off. Have you got a death wish or something?' she continues.

I can see her point, so I sit quietly and allow her to unleash a flurry of impassioned reprimands.

Kizzy, still in shock, but clearly in agreement with Lex, re-joins the conversation once the volley of bullets have ceased. 'Do you think the police are taking it seriously?' she asks. I can sense her internal battle now that she has had time to think.

I shake my head sadly. 'The police haven't been exactly forthcoming with information; it's been so hard trying to get any updates from them,' I say. 'But they seem to have all the information about what happened, and not just from me.'

Kizzy finally bites into her chilli laden burrito, and I do the same with mine, nibbling lightly at the soft doughy wrap. 'I mean, could it be some really unfunny, morbid joke that someone is playing? Maybe this Rusco chap set the whole thing up?' Kizzy continues.

'I've gone over every scenario, Kiz,' I respond, once I've chewed and swallowed. 'I wish it was a prank, despite how tasteless it would have been. But between me and Leonard, we saw it all; right there in front of us. There is absolutely no way it could have been a prank.'

'Have the police interviewed Leonard too? Has he responded to your email?' Now she has taken a few generous bites of her meal, Lex's anger has subsided.

Throughout my journey to meet them, phone in hand, I had resumed the constant checking of my emails, hoping for a response from Leonard to pop up, but he remains silent. I tell this to Lex and Kizzy.

'I just can't get it out of my head,' I say, glumly. I abandon my wrap: spice and dough making a thick, sluggish journey to my stomach. 'I would love to be able to leave it alone, let the police carry out their investigations – whatever that consists of – but it's consuming me. Even when I'm sleeping, I'm bugged out by it.'

Lex and Kizzy nod their sympathy.

I address my rash decision-making. 'I know it was foolish of me to go on a solo mission to Watford. I've been so caught up, like my head is going to explode if I don't get to the bottom of it. I thought maybe I would be able to find something out…' I tail off and sigh in frustration. 'But everywhere feels like a dead end.'

It's fleeting, but all the same, I notice the brief look that passes between Lex and Kizzy. Unspoken words I'm unable to interpret.

'There's got to be a way to find out exactly who Rusco is,' Kizzy strategizes. 'You've got his name and his address. You couldn't find much from a Google search, so let's try something else.'

We spend the next 45 minutes playing internet detectives, heads close together, fingers dancing across our phone pads. We search sites like Pipl and YoName. We search address finder for 43 Barcourt Road in Watford, identifying that Mary Harris is the registered homeowner. The address I followed Mary to, 30 Milicent Street, is owned by Andrew Shales.

I sign up to Car Registration Checker and pay a small fee to find out who the blue van belongs to. Again, the name Andrew Shales comes up.

'But whoever he is, it doesn't mean he's involved in anything shady. She could be his laundry lady for all we know,' Lex states.

It would be remiss of me not to have considered the possibility that what I witnessed on my last trip to Watford was just an innocent encounter. There is every chance the meeting between Mary Harris and Andrew Shales was a simple, straightforward interaction; nothing to do with Rusco's death, but now I have Mary on my radar, she is the only person that can possibly shed light on what has happened.

I have an idea and decide to test the waters with Lex and Kizzy. 'What if,' I begin tentatively. Two co-ordinated heads look up at me expectantly. 'What if I make an anonymous call to the police. Tell them I saw something brutal happen at 43 Barcourt Road. Do you think they'll investigate?' I look haltingly from one friend to another. They both seem uncertain. Kizzy's nose twitches; one of the idiosyncratic things she does when a complex situation presents itself to her.

'This is all very odd,' Lex says contemplatively. 'I can't believe we're even talking about doing something so audacious. What if she's totally innocent and a fleet of police cars turn up on her doorstep?' She looks from me to Kizzy and back again. 'How is that going to affect her? It might ruin her relationship with her neighbours, her health, her life even.'

Kizzy agrees. What neither of them understand, because I'm the one caught up in this nightmare, is that I'm so convinced of Mary's complicity, the thought of ruining her life doesn't bother me.

We spend another hour going over it all. Every angle,

every possibility. But no resolution. Lex and Kizzy are sympathetic but adamant that I should step back, try my best to put it out of my mind and trust that the police are doing what they can. Maybe take DC Phillips' advice and get in touch with Victim Support for some counselling? After all, I'm likely suffering some sort of trauma.

Our Sunday catch-up ends on a light note with Lex and Kizzy giving me the third degree about Josh, ribbing me about our burgeoning friendship. Although I reiterate to them that we have simply exchanged a handful of messages, mainly in a student-to-student capacity, there is still an unexpected flutter in my tummy when they mention his name.

Kizzy makes me promise to check in with them regularly and keep them updated if there are any more developments.

'No more maverick escapades to Watford,' she says wagging her finger, only half-jokingly, in my face.

'No more ignoring us on the group chat either,' Lex adds her tuppence worth. I clasp her hand, still not over my dreadful failure at forgetting the party. The guilt must be written all over my face. Lex pinches my cheek affectionately. 'You know I love you. You'll be okay, Ren. If you need to talk, you know where we are.'

I nod, unable to speak in case the floodgates open. I give my word that I will have an early night and get back on track tomorrow; back to my life before I got caught up in this whirlpool. We part company with good luck wishes for Kizzy. No more tot's TV and toddler clubs but back to the adult world of work.

Relieved to have been forgiven, I return home feeling happier, less anxious than I have in a while.

Chapter 9

Less than three weeks before the end

The email exchanges between Josh and I quickly turn to text messages and then phone conversations, not many of which relate to our creative writing course. He tells me about his job as a part-time primary school teacher. It's a job that suits his character down to a tee. He is witty, unassumingly intelligent and has an equable disposition that is very easy to warm to. Not to mention his ability to listen without interruption.

My decision to entrust him with my recent exploits is not a difficult one. I feel more at ease talking to him about it than to Lex and Kizzy, probably because of his indirect involvement and his familiarity with the people involved. I even share with him my plan to make an anonymous phone call – contrary to the conclusion I had reached with my best friends.

'There's definitely something off key about this whole thing,' he says in one of our phone conversations. His voice takes on a curious tone: 'If you're planning to make an anonymous tip-off, how will you know if the police actually visit and search the property?'

I had vague thoughts of watching from a distance, but I hadn't really thought it through to be honest. But Josh is one step ahead of me. 'What if we take a trip down there together, make the call and see what happens?'

I could have kissed him through the phone.

So, our first face-to-face meeting (I wouldn't go as far as to call it a date) is Operation Rusco/Mary: a journey to Watford on a mission of discovery. What has happened to Rusco and is his body festering and decaying at 43 Barcourt Road? This really feels like an alien out of body experience.

Josh informs me that Wednesday and Thursday are his days off, then kindly offers to drive. I decline his further offer to pick me up from my flat. As sweet as he is, and as ironic as it is that I am undertaking this mission with someone I hardly know, I wouldn't feel comfortable sharing my address with him.

I don't go out of my way to impress, but I take my time getting ready. My favourite jeans, a pale green Bardot top and a light jacket suitable for the changeable weather. I carry my oversized leather handbag and match it with a pair of flat open-toe sandals. At my insistence, and conscious not to inconvenience Josh more than I already have, we arrange to meet in Tottenham Hale, easy enough for me to get to and it marries well with his journey from Wapping.

He picks me up from the station in an electric blue Toyota Rav 4, the scent of newness filling the air the moment I open the door. It feels awkward at first, clambering into the front passenger seat of a car belonging to a person you've become familiar with, virtually, but have never met in person. He looks and sounds like 'Josh'. No surprises, other than his boyish grin and even teeth are more conspicuous in '*real life*'. He is dressed casually in faded jeans and a t-shirt that, from the side, has the hallmark of something designer and expensive.

'Ren. Very nice to meet you,' he says, adopting a posh voice and sticking his hand out for me to shake.

I giggle, shyly. 'Nice to meet you too, Josh.' I settle myself into the seat, pleased that I made the decision to wear jeans

– this is not the easiest car to manoeuvre my way into. He waits patiently as I strap myself in and then we are good to go.

'How crazy is this, eh?' I ask rhetorically. 'I've been asking myself all the way here if I've entered some mad alternate world. Are we really actually doing this?' I am blathering, clearly nervous, but Josh doesn't seem to mind. And it's not long before we're chatting away like old friends, which makes the hour-long journey to Watford go by relatively quickly.

We discover a few things in common, not least our career of choice. Like me, Josh's family set-up lacks the usual rigours and conventions. One of three, with an older brother and sister, his parents were more interested in shaping and enhancing their careers than devoting time to their children. Much of Josh and his siblings' formative years were spent shipped between a mercurial, domineering auntie (his mum's sister) and a nonchalant, dismissive uncle (his mum's brother); neither of whom gave the impression that they were fulfilling this obligation out of love or loyalty but, as Josh discovered in later years, a financial transaction. I'm touched by his openness and impressed that he hasn't allowed this early lack of stability to blight his relationship with his family.

Josh seems to have come up with a plan and I feel grateful that he is sharing this burden with me, even taking the lead. There is a scintilla of excitement in his voice when he tells me about the throwaway phone which we will use to call the police. As we turn onto Barcourt Road, I point out the house to Josh. We find the first available parking spot and he switches off the engine, swivels round in his seat and takes a long, intense look at number 43.

'Just an ordinary street, isn't it? Can only wonder what goes on behind closed doors,' he says pensively, his thoughts mirroring those that I had on my previous visits.

'Nothing is as it seems right now,' I muse. 'I always thought I was a good judge of character. And then Mary came along.'

'Mmm. I agree. Things aren't always what they seem,' he says, repeating my words. 'Neither are people.' We are both lost in thought.

Josh slaps his palms on his knees, snapping us out of our respective trances. 'I say we find somewhere away from here to park the car. We can go for a stroll, make the call and then wander back in this direction.' He looks to me for approval and I nod, happy to go along with the plan.

'Do you think the police will come immediately?' I ask, having no idea what sort of priority police give to anonymous calls. 'What if they don't think it's important enough for them to come out straight away – or even at all?' I'm asking these questions as if Josh has all the answers when we are as inexperienced and ignorant as each other.

'I guess it all depends on what the caller says to them,' he says, winking boldly at me.

We find another spot about three streets away, close enough that we can walk to Barcourt Road in about three minutes. We use Google maps to locate the local police station so we have some idea of the direction they will be coming from. The road we are on is not too far away from the High Street, so we head in that direction to grab a bite to eat before we put our plan into action.

Another revelation that my judgements are not quite on point – Josh's six-foot plus stature dwarves me; he is much taller than I imagined and a bit on the lean side. I have to quicken my pace to keep up with his long strides.

Being on foot provides a much different experience of Watford, and I am pleasantly surprised at the vast indoor shopping centre; a steady flow of shoppers moving between floors and shops. We skip through all of this and make our way to the top floor. Café Gee is our eatery of choice, though neither of us has the appetite for anything more than coffee and a pastry. I whip my card out and insist on paying before Josh has the opportunity to, and then we perch on a couple of high stools in front of a long bar-style table.

'Feeling okay?' Josh asks considerately, as if he can sense the tightness settling in with every second that draws us nearer to the deed.

'I'm good!' I respond, tearing off a piece of my flaky almond croissant. 'But let's think about something else for a bit. My brain needs some time away from sinister thoughts, especially if I want to enjoy this.' I hold my pastry up in the form of a *'cheers'*.

Josh dives in too, washing down a chunk of pain au raisin with a gulp of hot coffee.

'So, tell me what you love most about teaching children, and why you only teach part-time – I take it the two aren't mutually exclusive?' I ask, genuinely interested. 'Actually,' I say changing tack, 'more importantly, what made you want to become a teacher?'

'Simple answer,' Josh responds, brushing crumbs from his t-shirt, 'I had crappy experiences at school but loved learning. There's got to be synthesis somewhere, so that's what I want to create. A happy balance.'

I find his response inspiring. 'And have your young charges found that happy balance?' I ask.

'Mmm; it's a work in progress but I think I'm winning. And I was born to win,' he says, beaming with confidence and positivity. 'Must be ten times harder teaching teenagers.' He switches the attention to me. 'At least my students are still malleable; haven't yet been scorched by the kinks in the system.'

I tell him about the high and low points of teaching teenagers, realising how much I miss some of my lively, dramatic students. We exchange anecdotes about some of the funny encounters we have had in both the classroom and the staffroom.

Fuelled with enough sugar and caffeine to shake off any negative thoughts, we stroll away from the town centre, back towards the car. We are about to turn onto the road we are parked on when Josh pulls out his phone. I look up at him, but he doesn't so much as glance at me. He slows down, fingers tapping on the pad, then puts the phone to his ear. Seconds later, it's as though he has transformed into a different person right in front of me.

'Police! Can I have the police please?' his voice has taken on a breathless, urgent tone.

A slight pause.

'Yes, yes, you can. I've just seen someone violently attacked in my neighbour's house. There's someone in there and I'm sure he's dead!' I look around, afraid that someone may overhear this dramatic performance. Josh sounds so credible. There is no way the recipient of this call can doubt him.

'No. I cannot tell you my name. You just have to trust what I'm saying and send the police now! They are dangerous people... 43 Barcourt Road. Watford.' Josh terminates the call and we both quicken our pace. He begins to dismantle the phone, completing the task as we reach the parked car.

'Wow, that was genius!' I enthuse. 'Are you sure you haven't done something like this before?' I ask, trying to lighten the intensity of the moment. My heart is in my mouth.

'When you work with kids, you learn to take on different personas,' he says casually. 'Wait till you see my Ogre impression!'

Josh redirects our footsteps, taking us past the car to the end of the road and round a corner. We do a round-the-block slow walk, and it's as we approach the car again that we hear the distant sound of sirens. We look at each other, the air palpable between us.

'No need to get into the car then,' he says simply.

He falls in step beside me, placing his arm lightly around my shoulder as we walk, giving the image of a local couple out for an afternoon stroll, oblivious to what may be about to unfold. The sound of sirens draws nearer, and it's not long before we see the flashing blue lights. Two police cars and an ambulance. They whizz by at the top of the road adjacent to us. We continue walking, heading to the location where they will pull up imminently. I move closer to Josh; my Trojan horse to the rescue. I'm anxious, but confident that this is the smoking gun I've been holding out for.

A minute feels like an inordinate length of time, but that is all it takes before we turn onto Barcourt Road to witness the hive of action already in motion. Curtains are slightly parted; doors open and people walking by have stopped to look. Just what we need to help us blend in. I relax slightly. By the time we have number 43 in sight, police officers have already entered the property. A couple more, who both appear to be wearing bullet proof vests, speak into walkie talkies beside their car. I spot a female officer, engaged in conversation with the neighbour to the left of Mary's house. I am holding my breath, almost certain that the next thing I see will be Mary being led from the property in handcuffs, but it seems we are a long way away from that. Josh and I remain at a distance, across the road. The moment the police begin asking for names, addresses, witness statements, and everything else, we may need to make a swift exit.

I glance across at Josh, noticing the look of intensity on his face. He seems to be as invested in this as I am.

'Do you think they'll find anything?' I ask, not quite sure why I'm whispering.

'Well, they obviously took the call seriously, which is just what we hoped,' he responds, looking at me closely. 'Are you okay? You look like you're about to have a panic attack.'

'Feels like it too,' I reply truthfully, feeling the unpleasant prickles of sweat throughout my body. 'I just wish I'd followed up on this last week when it first happened. What if he's been moved already? Or what if I could have saved him?' My mind flits back to the scene I witnessed: Mary heaving the hefty bundle into the waiting van. Then I'm accosted by an overload of uncontrollable and heinous images of Rusco's body, hacked to pieces, unceremoniously stuffed into the large sack.

Josh seems to get my line of thinking.

'If anything's happened to him in that house, they'll be able to work it out. There will be traces. We just have to trust they do their job thoroughly.'

I have a sudden thought. 'What about the address I followed Mary to? What if it's connected? Maybe the police should be searching that property too.' I look to Josh for approval. Perhaps we should make a second anonymous call.

His expression clouds over in a way I can't quite read. Then I follow his line of vision. Emerging from the open door of number 43 is a police officer leading someone out. The culprit, head down, has a dark shawl or sheet covering them. I try to work out from the height and physique whether it's Mary, but they are bent so low, it's impossible to tell if it's male or female let alone anything else. They are led swiftly into one of the awaiting police cars. There is a buzz of voices and indistinguishable conversations both over the walkie talkies and with the police officers present. A van has turned onto Barcourt Road and is slowing as it nears number 43. It stops in the middle of the road, parallel to the offending house. At the other end of the street, at least two other police cars have arrived, blocking that end of Barcourt Road. More officers emerge from the cars. Then I see it. The line of red tape being used to cordon off part of the road.

The doors of the van open and two figures emerge. Like astronauts preparing for a moon expedition, the scene of crime officers create a solemn sight as they exchange a few brief words with one of the officers, then make their way into the house.

By now, doors and windows are wide open as people gawp in awe at the scene unfolding in front of them. Officers, like ants, are suddenly everywhere, notebooks and pens to the ready as they converse with residents, knock on doors and begin what will probably be a long and thorough investigation.

In situations like this the sense of unity is tangible. Residents – who have probably never exchanged more than a nod to each other in the past – clutter together, keen to conduct their own investigations and post-event analysis. The gossips at the ready with insightful, more than likely flawed, revelations about what they saw, thought they saw or knew about the residents of number 43. But, as someone whose presence here is more than a passing opportunity to gape and engage in conjecture, I tune in to a conversation taking place a few feet away from where Josh and I stand.

'I said it, didn't I? Something's happened to that poor chap. He was never alright, was he? Kept him hidden away they did.' The recipient of this one-sided conversation lets out a regular stream of 'Mmms seemingly aware that her response isn't required.

'Didn't see much of him at all, did we? I only ever caught him looking out of the window when she was out. God knows what he went through in there.' She tuts loudly, eyes never leaving the scene. The police are now galvanised into action. From the middle of the road, they fan out in a wave, requesting that everyone move away from the scene and re-enters their homes. It appears they are keen to cordon off the entire street. The car containing the suspect is still parked in front of the house, the engine now running. I squint, trying desperately to get a final look at the person, but they are snugly disguised beneath the dark sheet, not to mention the shaded windows of the police car.

'Might be time for us to make a move,' Josh says, drawing me out of my absorbed state. 'I think our work here is done.'

Part of me is reluctant to leave; I would love nothing more than to see this through to the end. Does it matter if we are questioned? After all, today's development started with something I witnessed which, up until now, I couldn't be sure that anyone was taking seriously. Josh, however, is insistent that we leave, assuring me that the incident will probably be all over the news by morning, and I will more than likely be contacted to give a proper statement. I am doubtful for a moment, thinking about the lack of communication from the police so far. That is until I feel Josh's sharp elbow nudge. I look at him then follow his gaze. Emerging from the house is one of the scene of crime officers. Even from some distance away, the sealed black bag, resembling a miniature body bag, carefully cradled in his arms tells its own story.

With an unanticipated sense of triumph overshadowed by a deep melancholy, I follow behind Josh, keeping my head turned in the direction of number 43 until we reach the end of the street and turn left.

'Are you okay?' Josh asks. I'm touched by his constant concern, and I can't begin to thank him enough for being here with me. Even though the situation looks grim, at least there may be some sort of closure on the horizon.

'I'll be fine,' I say. 'Thanks so much for being so supportive.

Most people would have either run a mile or written me off as bat-shit crazy.'

'Mmm, I haven't concluded on the second point yet,' he teases. 'But really, don't sweat it. I'm glad you didn't have to go through it on your own.'

This time, he takes my hand and we stroll back to his car, leaving behind the pulsating lights and the air of unfettered activity that is likely to prevail over this area for some time to come.

Chapter 10

Just over two weeks before the end

I half expect to wake up the following morning to the sound of urgent thumping on my door: a senior police detective eager to hear my invaluable statement again, along with every news channel reporting on a serious incident that has taken place on Barcourt Road in Watford; a desperate call for any further witnesses.

This is not the case.

I emerge from the most contented and trouble-free sleep I've had in a while. Apart from feeling light-headed with some tension in the base of my skull, there is a discernible feeling that a weight has been lifted. I've spent the last fortnight chasing my tail, trying to get to the root of a heinous crime that has been committed, way out of my depth, and now the blur is lifting.

I have been channel-hopping for the last thirty minutes, but so far nothing emerges. I imagine the police trying to keep a lid on things until they start to piece together the story, or at least find the unknown witness who made the anonymous call.

My mind wanders back to the time spent with Josh. After our eventful day, he was insistent on going out of his way to drive me back to South London. To the point that his insistence made me a touch anxious. Maybe it was the swirling agitation and unease that had encamped itself around me since I witnessed Rusco's attack, affecting my usual gaiety and even temperament. But also, as wonderful as he is, baby steps work best for me, and I certainly wouldn't rush to invite anyone to my flat. I insisted he dropped me at the station so I could stop at my local Sainsbury's to pick up some milk. We spent another 30 minutes in the car, de-briefing after our eventful day, before going our separate ways.

'Next time, Miss Adventure, maybe we start again with a proper date?' Josh's cheeky statement disguised as a question.

I couldn't help smiling… and blushing. 'I think I can manage that,' I said diffidently.

'On one condition,' he continued, as if the stipulation was his to set. I raised my eyebrows questioningly.

'I choose where we go.'

'Ha-ha! Fine by me,' I said, more than happy for him to make the decision. 'A date of your choosing will probably turn out a lot better than mine! In the meantime, same time, same place tomorrow,' I remarked, referring to the next instalment of our creative writing course, wondering how that would play out.

That had been our parting conversation. An hour later, he had sent me a message to ask if I was tucked away safely indoors, and to let me know that he had arrived home.

Back to my morning. I leave a protracted voice message for Lex and Kizzy. (I know they will be shocked and mad at me for going against my word.) I fill them in on everything that happened the day before, and not forgetting to ask Kizzy how her first couple of days back at work have been. Within the hour, there have been a stream of messages and I respond to the onslaught of questions they have. Not surprisingly, they are aghast at the situation, give me a bit of a ticking off, but at the same time they're eager for me to let them know when the police make contact.

I spend a short time catching up on some admin, remembering that I haven't sent off my invoices for my latest tutoring sessions – well overdue now. I'm supposed to be exercising thriftiness, not forgetting to bill for my services. I'm already £900 lighter than I should be after bailing Faye out, and still awaiting word from my bank regarding the fraudulent purchases made from my account.

True to her word, Faye has kept in regular contact with me. Her messages to enquire about my healing head and the situation with Rusco's case have been appreciated. But, no surprise, there has been no mention of paying back my money. She seems to be back on track though. Maybe everything that has happened can act as a springboard to rediscover that bond we had as children. I send her a message, letting her know what has been happening and telling her that we'll speak at the weekend.

I make some notes in preparation for my lessons and download a job spec for a teaching job I've come across a few times which I need to look at in more detail. At the same time, I'm constantly checking the time, refreshing my emails and glancing at my phone. Nothing from the police, no breaking news online… and still no word from Leonard.

After another hour faffing around and with increasing butterflies diving around in my stomach, though I'm not sure why, I log on for our lesson. I don't know what to expect today, other than some level of certainty that Mary will be absent.

One by one, faces pop up on my screen as we come together for another session. Ally and Gillian are engaged in a two-way conversation, giggling loudly at something the rest of us aren't privy to.

Tarquin dons another jazzy shirt, the colours clashing

luridly with his garish wallpaper. He must have a window open nearby because strands from the comb-over yield to the movement in the air. He sits silently for a while, observing as members of the group greet each other. Ally, self-deprecating as usual, commandeers the chat with a detailed explanation about the challenges she experienced completing her homework. Apparently, the chairperson for her local fundraising committee came down with a bad case of gastroenteritis so she had to step in at the last minute and co-ordinate an activity evening. She would have gone into further detail if Tarquin hadn't politely interrupted.

'Welcome Seedlings! Good to see you all again. We are breezing our way through the course!' His changeable nature is truly disconcerting. Today's personality and tone correspond with the Tarquin we met on Day One – flamboyant and excitable. Maybe the choice of clothing has some reflection on the mood, or vice versa.

'Great work, great work,' he continues. 'We're closer to the end than the beginning. Sooo, it's time to step it up a gear. I hope everyone has polished their creative hats today.' He beams in expectation; his exposed teeth conjure up an image of the wolf in Red Riding Hood. My skin crawls just a bit.

While he continues by outlining today's session, I switch to participant view. The usual members are present, but not surprisingly, no Mary, and sadly, still no Leonard. Back to gallery view, which I enlarge and take a close look at Josh. It doesn't feel like just yesterday we were caught up in a scene so remarkable, it could have been straight from an episode of a police drama. His eyebrows are fused together in concentration, one hand stroking his chin, and he appears to be making notes as Tarquin speaks. I am surprised he can focus with such intensity on the lesson, while I struggle to disengage my thoughts from yesterday. I feel it already, this is not going to be a productive session for me. I wonder what my classmates would think if they knew what we had been up to.

Reluctantly, I tune back in.

'So, whether your central character is to be a superhero, a reclusive farmer or a successful florist, they have to be multi-dimensional. You create that by living through them. What motivates your character? What annoys them? How would they react to different situations?' Tarquin's hand gestures are in overdrive. 'Character focus will be the emphasis for the remaining lessons,' he continues. 'Remember the follow up courses will be your opportunity to pursue a specific line of interest, whether it's writing a novel, short stories or exploring genres. Insight Academy has a great range of courses.' A bit of sales patter before we are set our first task, which is to respond to a questionnaire that will help us better shape and identify with a potential character.

After taking a picture of the slide Tarquin uploads to the screen, I make a snap decision. I minimise the lesson and log onto my emails, composing a new one.

Hi Leonard,

I hope you are keeping well. I'm following up on my previous email regarding the incident during our creative writing lesson. I know it was traumatic to witness – well, it definitely was for me. I hope you're coping okay. Sorry you haven't been able to attend the last two sessions.

There has been a further development, which I discovered yesterday, but it doesn't appear to be public knowledge yet. Perhaps we can have a chat about things? Or at least, it would be good to know that you're okay.

All the best,

Ren Shephard.

I skim read what I've written, decide to add my mobile number, and press send. My phone beeps unexpectedly and my head snaps towards it. With everything happening, I am still wound up tightly, whether I choose to acknowledge it or not.

The text message is from Josh: *You seem a bit distracted. Struggling to focus?*

I look up at my laptop, maximise the lesson. He appears to be looking at me. He confirms this with a stealthy wink and a lopsided smile which I return.

Very distracted. Finding it hard to get back on track with the course. All seems different now, I fire back quickly.

A minute later: *I get it. Maybe you need a proper distraction. How about we meet for that date tomorrow evening?*

A small fluttering in my chest. I force myself to remain straight-faced. It's weird knowing he can see my reactions as we exchange messages.

Sounds good, I respond. *Seeing as you're responsible for choosing the venue, I'll await further information.*

All will be revealed... This time, I can't stop the smile from spreading across my face. But it takes just an instance for a boulder of trepidation to settle painfully in my gut, turning my smile into an agonized frown. The gallery view of faces blinks twice, and another face pops up on the screen.

Mary.

The high-pitched gasp that emits from my throat is similar to that made by a frightened cat. The saving grace is my muted microphone. For a second, I expect everyone in the group to point at her accusingly, a silent unified gasp behind their respective screens, to match mine. But the virtual world continues, oblivious to the giant rock that has pinned me to my seat.

She unmutes herself: 'Sorry, Tarquin, sorry everyone. I had a bit of a carer crisis first thing. All sorted now.' She sounds cheerful and earnest, no hint that she is the main suspect in a serious crime! The only person I can picture her caring for is the devil.

'Ah, no problem, Mary. Good to have you with us. I'll just revert to the previous slide while everyone's busy.' Tarquin clicks away.

'Thank you. That's great.' Mary beams.

I'm watching this exchange with my heart pumping erratically. I am a millisecond away from unmuting myself and calling her out. She shouldn't be here! I may not have seen who the police arrested yesterday, but it was her! I know it was her!

Flabbergasted, I seek out Josh just as his camera goes off. I imagine he has been blindsided by this, just as I have. I open my phone, my fingers bulky and awkward as I struggle to send a coherent message to him.

What's Mary doing here?!

I wait. It's ten minutes before he responds.

??

Is that really all he has to say? Surely he has more than that. I put out an urgent plea to myself: Calm down. What exactly am I expecting him to say? This is a huge shock for both of us. But would the police really have released her so soon? Is she out on bail? If so, isn't it a bit brazen of her to attend the lesson as if all is hunky-dory in her world? Questions and errant thoughts cannon around in my head, the equilibrium I had struggled to regain threatening to topple over like dominoes.

Just like Tarquin reverting to his style of outfit from lesson one, Mary wears a patterned blouse with rounded collars and a slight frill around the tips. Back to the kindly carer; the self-appointed '*grandma of the community*' who rounds up the local kids, sharing out sweet treats. Except, I know, this is not who she is. I stare at her, sending a telepathic message for her to look at me. I want her to see my expression. I want her to know what I have seen.

Look at me, Mary. Look at me! The words are spoken only

in my head. But they don't communicate to her. She has her head down, scribbling away trying to catch up on the task she has missed, unaware that I am shooting daggers at her through the screen. The monster is yet to be slayed.

I don't know how long I sit staring at my screen, willing something to happen. It's like being in one of those silent discos when the music is so infectious you expect everyone else to dance to your rhythm, be in sync with you. But no one engages. I'm all alone, the music only exists for me.

'So my final words for today: You must let the characters inhabit your world. Live with them, live through them. When they reach out to you, nurture them. Speak to them; question them. And respond to them.'

Three hours have passed by already. What have I achieved apart from taking a few incoherent notes?

Mary asks Tarquin if she can have a word with him at the end of the session. He seems keen to usher the rest of us out of the virtual room. Curious though I am, I can't wait to exit the lesson.

I want desperately to speak with Josh, but I sense his reticence to engage with me. Maybe he's busy trying to construct and assemble his own theory; maybe he doesn't see it as a big deal. I pick up my phone but decide against messaging him. I'll leave it till later. Instead, I call Lex, catching her on her lunch break. I know the conversation will be rushed but anything is better than the voiceless, unrequited conversation I'm having with myself.

'What could she possibly be doing in the lesson, Lex? This woman is responsible for a murder. How is she walking the streets?'

Lex listens quietly to the bombardment before addressing me coolly. 'First, you need to slow down. Yes, it is surprising that she's not in custody, but there could be several reasons for that. Remember, whatever happened to Rusco, she wasn't the one that harmed him. She was online, on camera, at the same time you saw it happen.'

'Yes, I know, but—'

This time Lex doesn't let me finish. 'Calm down for a minute, Ren. Simply because you've charged and convicted her, it doesn't mean she's guilty. Yes, there's a high chance she's involved somehow – I don't doubt it – but if the police have released her, they must be sure she's not a threat.' Lex's voice of reason resounds through the phone. 'She might be out on bail. They may have arrested someone else which puts her in the clear. Tying yourself up in knots isn't going to solve this, it's just going to cause you unnecessary stress.'

I rest my head on the arm of the sofa, allowing her words to penetrate and put the brakes on the rollercoaster.

'I know Kizzy and I weren't keen on you stoking the fire with the anonymous call, but it's probably a good thing Josh teamed up with you to contact the police. Whatever they weren't doing before, they are doing now.'

I re-examine the scene from yesterday: police presence, scene of crime officers, crime tape, gossiping neighbours, the miniature body bag. I can't argue with what Lex is saying.

I force my rampaging brain to be still, wishing I could bubble wrap it and preserve it from the headache that will soon make its presence felt. I hear voices across the line and I know I'm keeping Lex from her work. I thank her, agree to message later, and terminate the call.

By the time Josh messages me later in the evening, I have taken on board Lex's words and barricaded all negative thoughts; anything to do with Mary/Rusco is firmly held at bay. The mellow sounds of 'Music to unwind to' emits from my laptop speaker while I give myself a mini manicure and pedicure.

What a weird day! What on earth is going on? Looking forward to seeing you tomorrow.

I only focus on the latter part of the message:
Me too!

***

We meet in Covent Garden. True to his word, Josh texts me the details of the venue for our Friday evening '*date*'. With the world back on course after pockets of lockdowns, it's nice to be in this part of London again. The central square is buzzing as expected: tourists, Friday evening revellers, after-work drinkers, a delightful mix of people all with important business to attend to. I see Josh before he sees me, walking in my direction. Tall, lean and very hard to miss. His smart trousers, dark brown brogues and slim-fit shirt an indication that he has headed here straight from work. Well put together, clean lines, all evidence that he takes pride in his appearance. His satchel is slung casually across his shoulder and one hand is firmly in his pocket. I could easily take a picture of him as he walks towards me and send it to Lex and Kizzy. Somehow, I think they would be impressed.

He spots me waiting and seconds later he is in front of me, greeting me with a friendly hug and a peck on the cheek.

'Hi Ren,' he says in his familiar manner. 'Hope I haven't kept you waiting?'

'Hiya,' I respond enthusiastically. 'Not long got here myself. I haven't been to Covent Garden for ages. Great choice of location, I must say.'

'Well, that's a good start then. I thought we could head to Maxim's for a drink first. Okay with you?'

'Yes, of course. Lead the way!' We stroll along, dodging and ducking our way through the eager crowds, side by side, to avoid getting separated. We don't engage much in conversation, just savour the warm air and the vibrant atmosphere.

Five minutes later, we are seated opposite each other in Maxim's wine bar. Its stainless-steel decor, mirrors and clear glass, give it a very modern and cutting-edge feel, as though trying to attract twenty-something year olds with a decent disposable income. At this time, there is still a good choice of places to sit, so we choose a table for two with a view of outside, high-backed chairs designed more for style than comfort. I shrug out of my light summer jacket and place it over the back of my seat. Josh looks at me admiringly, a little twinkle in his eye.

'What can I get this lovely lady to drink?' he asks.

I don't need to browse the drinks menu. I settle for my usual drink of choice. 'A glass of medium Rosé would be perfect, thanks.'

Josh hangs his satchel over the seat and goes to the bar, returning minutes later with my wine and a pint of lager.

'Thank you, and cheers,' I say, raising my glass and clinking it with his. 'Let's drink to Josh choosing the venue,' I tease.

He joins in with the banter. 'To Josh's choice of venue! Hopefully, this is the first of many more.'

I raise an eyebrow coyly. 'The first of many more of your choosing, or the first of many more dates?'

The air sizzles with chemistry and flirtation. 'I have to give you a chance to redeem yourself, don't I? It'll be interesting to see where you take me next.' He chuckles at the irony. Then he adopts a neutral expression. 'I'm curious to know why someone as gorgeous and intelligent as you is single though.'

I feel myself blushing. 'No great story, really.' I reveal the bare bones of my relationship with Denny. 'We were just heading in different directions,' I conclude.

He nods his understanding and outlines the ending of his most recent, two-year relationship. I learn more about his Year 6 class at Wayland Primary School. He entertains me with interesting and funny stories, stories that illustrate the peculiarities amongst children of that age. He seems like an adored and well-respected teacher, the kind of male presence missing in many primary schools today. Curious, I ask him again what he does with his days off from the classroom. Apart from knowing his job is part-time, I'm not sure if he does other work. I discover that his family run several residential homes across the Southeast and he is responsible for the management and administration.

'Keeps things varied and keeps me out of trouble,' he affirms.

We nibble our way through two rounds of table snacks and a couple of drinks each, as I share stories about my wanderlust parents, and my wayward sister. I draw short of telling him about Faye's recent foray into the shady world of drug debt. I don't want him to think that my life is surrounded by drama and danger.

Around us, the number of drinkers is increasing. So caught up in our non-stop conversation, I hadn't realised all the seats are now occupied and people are lounging around the bar, seeking out any vacant position to stand or lean.

Josh glances at his watch. 'Is that the time already? I made a dinner reservation not far from here. We're about five minutes late, but that should be okay. Ready?'

I drink the last of my Rosé. Josh helps me into my jacket and we prepare to make our way through the throngs, our seats taken the moment we rise. It has cooled considerably since we entered Maxim's but the hit of fresh air is appreciated.

La Bras is a French a la carte restaurant with a heated outdoor terrace, perfect for an evening like this when the sun has set, and summer nights aren't yet balmy but are still very temperamental. I'm already feeling a touch light-headed after two glasses of wine and not enough food to absorb them. We both opt for the signature starter of scallops, whilst for mains, Josh plumps for the ginger and soy salmon and I go for the lamb with cognac Dijon cream sauce. Josh orders a bottle of Rosé, which I hope he plans to share with me.

Conversation turns to our creative writing course and it's not long before I steer the conversation to Mary – going against my earlier resolve not to broach the topic unless Josh did.

'Are you still worrying about it all?' Josh asks me, feasting heartily on the meal in front of him.

'It feels as if it's back to Square One,' I say, trying not to throw a dark blanket over what has so far been a perfect evening; the food and company both thoroughly enjoyable.

Josh's response is quite offhand. 'She's not in police custody. Doesn't mean that's the end of it.' He shrugs.

'Yes, but considering they brought out the red police tape, they had the forensic team in, and they arrested her.' I point out these three significant points, using my fingers as markers. 'It seems a bit soon for her to be out and back to her normal Thursday routine.'

'Ah, but we don't know if it was her they arrested,' Josh advocates.

The conversation is following a similar path to the one I had with Lex. I recall what she said about convicting Mary and finding her guilty, and this is exactly what I can't seem to stop doing. Josh continues as if reading my thoughts. 'Somewhere along the line, we have to stop speculating. The police are onto something – I think we can say that for a fact. Whether or not Mary is involved and to what extent, we just don't know.'

He looks at me, expression sober. 'Promise me you'll put the whole thing out of your mind. Let's leave it for a few days and if nothing comes up, we can think of another plan of action.'

'I can't promise not to think about it… and I'll try my best not to do anything rash,' I say.

His expression darkens for a fraction of a second. The firm nod seems to signify that this conversation has been bookmarked. I can only imagine he's had his fill of this incident.

'Pudding?' he asks. We are back on terra firma, but my mood has been dampened, and I'm ready to call it a night.

'I think I'll pass,' I say, stretching out in my seat. 'If I try and fit anything else in, I'll have to roll myself home!' I try to regain the easiness that has framed our time together.

'I think I'm with you on that,' Josh agrees, patting his flat, compact stomach and signalling for the waiter. He pays the bill, refusing to allow me to contribute, then we gather our possessions and prepare to leave.

'It's been really lovely,' I say sincerely. 'Thank you for paying for everything; that's very generous of you.'

'Wouldn't have had it any other way,' he says magnanimously.

We wander back towards the square, the underground station beckoning. I'm looking forward to getting home, but pleased that the date has been successful. We enter the station together and locate the separate directions we need to travel in, our footsteps slowing in unspoken agreement. Josh turns to me and takes hold of my face tenderly. His gaze is intense as he looks unblinking into my eyes, face millimetres away from mine so I can feel his warm breath gently caressing my face.

'Ren Shephard, I've loved being in your company. Let's do it again soon, please.'

The moment is magnetic. Everything else seems to slip away, except this arresting, absorbing moment. He kisses me in an unhurried and delicate way that sends ripples of longing through me. And then, just like that, it's over. Our time together ends, and he steals away like a figment of my imagination.

It's a hard task to control the smile that lights me up the entire journey home. Contentment from good company and food, the tingle on my lips from where Josh kissed me, a sure sign that I like him. He is very easy to like. Home within an hour, I curl up on the sofa, a welcome place to wind down from a delightful evening. But first, and not that I've ever been a cyber-stalker, curiosity gets the better of me.

Wayland Primary School. I google it and scroll through the menu. There is a link that takes me to the staff page. I scroll past the Head, Deputy, non-class-based staff and then down to the teachers. It is set out by year groups, and it doesn't take me long to find Class 6JL: Class Teacher Joshua Lee, followed by his email address. There is a miniature sized picture of him surrounded by a gaggle of beaming children, as though the picture was taken in the middle of a lively activity. Josh's smile is the biggest of all: the pride in his young charges evident.

***

It's little wonder that he invades my dreams, floating in and out of my sub-consciousness. From across a room he smiles at me, beckons me over, but the closer I get, the further he moves away. I call his name and he ignores me. He is unpredictable, enigmatic. My tireless attempt to unite with him, rescinded. And then he responds, open-armed and yearning, but at the same time devoid and taciturn. Mutating constantly so I'm caught up in a dizzying and insecure cyclone.

I'm rocking gently, cradled between a lullaby of fantasy and the fringes of reality. I bounce between the phases of sleep. A thought, somewhere in my brain, is grasping, clambering its way to the top, and trying to make sense of something that is just out of my reach. Handsome, funny Josh. My sidekick, my partner in an attempt to unearth a crime. He entered my world virtually, and I have unlocked the door for him. His warmth and charm drawing me in, taking me in a direction I would love to explore. Why then are the tentacles of doubt inveigling their way into my psyche? As I turn down the passageway that leads me deeper into dreamworld, where my brain activity is heightened but my body creates the chemicals that render me temporarily paralyzed; it is then that a sudden thought confronts me. So caught up was I in our trip to Watford, I overlooked a simple yet salient point: How did Josh know exactly where in Watford we were going? I didn't give him Mary's address.

Chapter 11

Two weeks before the end

I'm pottering around on Saturday morning, immersed in my thoughts. The inimitable voices of cartoon characters provide the backdrop to my morning, but I don't really hear them. I'm trying for a semblance of normality, and that means laundry basket, vacuum cleaner and furniture polish. In my house-joggers and frayed vest, it's clear as day that I've lost weight; the drawstring bow of my bottoms hanging limply from where it has been pulled to accommodate my shrinking waist. The mental ordeal of trying to wrap my head around recent events has left me with a fatigue that goes beyond the norm. I regret signing up for the online course. All it has succeeded in doing is bringing an unhealthy, noxious disturbance into my life. Unread emails, letters flippantly cast aside, most of them unopened, voice messages I haven't accessed, not to mention missing my best friend's party. So invested am I in this situation, I'm even losing track of my days. Something has to change.

I toy with an idea that has been formulating since waking up this morning, but I know it's a last resort. What I need right now is a distraction; something that will anchor me and go some way to supplant the tribulations of the last few weeks.

Al and Angie. The turbulent force that is my parents. I

would have to dig deep to remember when it was that I had that conversation with Mum, or where exactly in the world she said they were. Thank God for social media. Not a great fan myself, but with the sudden urge to see their faces, I know their joint Facebook account will provide me with some photographic footprint of their recent escapades and their current location.

Sure enough, there is a stream of pictures and video clips: most recent ones are of Dad on a motorbike, bare-chested, tanned, with a cushion of grey hair covering his chest. Another set shows Dad fishing with what looks like a group of locals, most of them clutching bottles of beer but no fish. There are some of Mum and Dad together, eating at a roadside diner. The food looks healthy and in abundance.

Not to be outdone, Mum, her figure lending itself to the outdoor living and fresh local food, looks slender in her bikini, contorted into one of her yoga poses. I have to turn my head to the left to work out where her right foot is. I'm sure that pose would finish me off. I remember now, Mum said they were in Indonesia, but they haven't mentioned this on their post.

I scroll through my contacts – four numbers listed under 'Dad'. Dad #4 is likely the most recent. My finger hovers over the number. Speaking to Mum and Dad is sometimes on a par with prodding a wasps' nest, usually best left alone unless you can deal with the aftermath. In my state of mind, I'm certain Mum and Dad's theatrics is just what I need. I can always hang up if it gets too much.

The single continuous ringtone that indicates shores afar greets me. Almost immediately, and much to my surprise, Dad's familiar voice resounds in my ear, as if he's in the house with me.

'Now, this had better be one of my daughters. If it's not my favourite one, I'd like to speak to the other one; if it's the other one, she's also my favourite!' No one starts a conversation quite like my dad.

'Whichever daughter you'd like it to be, I will assume the role for you,' I say, trying to match his humour.

'Sweet Serendipity. Hello, love!'

'Hi, Dad. How are things? It's been a while.'

'Can't say I noticed. But things are good. My skin's a bit on the leathery side from all the sunshine but why would I complain, eh?'

'Worse things to complain about, I guess. Where in the world are you then?' I ask, curiously.

'Recently out of Indonesia, now in Thailand,' he says, as if he's just meandered from one end of the West End to the other. 'Home for us at the moment is Ko Lanta. Your mother's choice. I would have preferred somewhere less deserted and slightly more salacious,' he laughs, devilishly. 'Anyone would think we're geriatrics the way she behaves sometimes.'

I can just imagine my 54-year-old father raising his eyebrows in consternation. Clearly, Al isn't ready to slow down just yet. 'But your mum's taken up crocheting AND her eyesight is deteriorating. I might have to trade her in for a younger model!' Off he goes again, laughing uproariously, a joke at every opportunity.

'As if anyone else could put up with you,' I rib. For the next ten minutes, we engage further in this mostly one-way dialogue with a few interjections from me. According to Dad, they've recently settled in a not-so-touristy part of Thailand, trying to immerse themselves in a local way of life. Dad gets around on his trusty motorbike and they're staying in an *'upmarket'* hostel called Peacocks, while they decide on their next adventure. Apparently, Mum is teaching yoga and lifestyle (whatever that means) to local women, and to the tourists who wander to this quiet side of the island. Dad refers to the work he does as *'selling stuff'* and *'a bit of building work here and there'*. The transient world of my parents never fails to amaze me. I sometimes wish I could live my life with that same effervescence and impulsive manner, often attributed to those under 30.

'Sereny!' I hear Mum's sparkly vocals in the background, referring to me by her favoured pet name, which is only a touch better than the full version. Dad must have switched the phone to loudspeaker.

'What's your dad been saying about me?' she asks.

'Don't be so paranoid,' Dad jumps in. 'I didn't get to the part about your greying hair and your mid-riff getting softer.'

'Oh stop it, you silly bear!' Mum chastises, knowing full well there isn't an ounce of excess fat on her taut stomach. 'Says you, who can't keep up with my yoga class.' The two of them together; incorrigible. There isn't room for anyone else.

'What's up with your sister?' Mum asks, out of the blue. I'm silent for a moment, my mind swinging back to the ugly encounter with Faye and Elis. It can't have been more than a few days ago that we last exchanged messages and she seemed fine.

'Why? Have you spoken to her?' I frown, feeling ill at ease.

'She called me out of the blue a couple of days ago. Never calls, does she, Al? Slurring her words, she was, couldn't string together a proper sentence. Asked us to send her some money for a debt she owes. Is she doing drugs? She was very evasive.'

Mum doesn't give me the opportunity to respond, just a torrent of commentary and questions. My heart does a painful slow-dive causing my shoulders to slump. Bloody Faye! Hasn't she learnt a lesson? After the scare we had at the hands of Elis, has she gone back down that slippery slope? It seems that paying Elis off was just a temporary bracket for a much deeper problem

'How much has she asked you for?' I query, certain that my parents are not in a position to honour Faye's request. And even if they were, they wouldn't.

'£500!' Mum sounds incredulous.

'And she was none too pleased when we told her we didn't have it,' Dad chips in. 'I told her to ask you, but she mumbled something about you not caring enough to help her out.'

My mouth falls open in fury. The absolute cheek! Just when I thought we were turning a corner in our relationship. I sigh heavily. This is typical Faye behaviour: she is ungrateful and opportunistic. Forget the fact that I put myself in harm's way, parted with hard-earned money to rescue her – money she will likely never mention again. And then she has the audacity to give Mum and Dad the impression that I don't care.

I decide against sharing any of this with them. What would be the point? They won't lose any sleep over it and they certainly won't be rushing around raising funds for their delinquent daughter. In fact, once our conversation is over, they will simply switch back to their self-absorbed lives, until we speak again at some point in the future.

The conversation ends with the sounds of chanting in the background: Mum's yoga session is about to commence. I hang up, not even offended by the fact that neither of them bothered to ask me anything about my life.

Unsettled and fired up by the conversation with Mum and Dad, I scroll through my phone to locate Faye's number. I must be the epitome of naivety to have believed any of her twaddle about turning over a new leaf. Even with my limited experience in this area, wisdom should have prevailed. Is being roughed up by a drug-dealer enough to stop an addict from the irresistible allure of their drug of choice? The depraved lengths that people go to for the sake of a quick fix; a little beating probably pales into insignificance.

Elis, cocky and arrogant, is probably awaiting my next visit with another £500 to rescue my sister and further line his pocket. How can Faye be so stupid? She has taken liberties with me many times over the years and her lifestyle has always left a lot to be desired. But this? This feels like an inoperable tumour. Extricating herself from this mess will be like trying to climb out of a vat of treacle.

I hate myself for letting it worry me; but my conscience won't allow me to sidestep the conversation I've just had with Mum and Dad. Who else can Faye turn to? A visceral anger brews away deep inside. This should be Mum and Dad's responsibility. I know Faye is an adult, accountable for her actions, but she is their daughter, a by-product of their flaky attempt at parenting. Why should the burden fall on me? She is so off-track and struggling to find a place in the world, largely because of them.

Reacting in anger is never advised, but I disregard that thought and for the second time this morning I call Dad's number. No response, so I leave a rambling message expressing my disappointment at their selfishness and crap parenting skills and sign off by asking them why they bothered having children. This done, I turn my attention back to Faye.

I try to rebalance my emotions. Faye needs a firm hand; I can't allow sympathy to dominate otherwise I will be just as much an enabler as her drug-dealer. Such is my reluctance to get involved that I sit gazing at my phone for another thirty minutes before I muster up the energy to call her. The least I can do is speak to her, shout at her and beg her to get help.

***

An hour later, I'm stuck on a slow-moving train heading towards Brighton. A signalling fault along the way has impeded the journey, and I only hope there won't be a further announcement asking us to leave the train. The refrain that has been playing on repeat in my head since I hung up the phone from Faye iterates resoundingly: *I will not give her any money. I will not meet with Elis. I will not... I will not... I will not...*

Hearing my sister slurring her words, speaking volubly and incoherently at 11am on a Saturday morning propelled me into action. There are some situations where, try as I might, every resolve goes right out of the window. I close my eyes and inhale, recalling our earlier exchange.

'I'm not taking any drugs!' she had yelled, her slurred, hiccupy words throwing shade at her defiant tone.

'Well, are you drinking then?' I had asked. 'You certainly don't sound as if you've been sipping tea and eating cornflakes.'

'No, Ren, I am not drinking either,' she responded, sounding bored. 'I just need some help to get back on my feet. I haven't got anywhere to live. I slept in a flipping car park last night.' As if it's my fault.

'I haven't got any money and I need... I need...' Had she been halted by confusion, or had she stopped short of admitting that she needed a fix? From the hoarseness of her voice and her incoherence, I would take my chances on the latter.

'What's happened to your room in the house?' I recalled the neat, cosy space she had created for herself.

She didn't answer directly.

'I've been to the council but they can't even give me a room in a hostel until all my paperwork comes through.

I've even lined up a job but it doesn't start until next month. I really need some money to tide me over until I can sort myself out.'

I was sure her tale of woe had been redacted for my benefit. Two things I was certain about: I would not hand money over to anyone; and I couldn't allow my sister to sleep in a car park. She had begged me to meet her. I couldn't say no.

For most of the travellers on the train with me, the excitement of the weekend and all it promises overshadows the major delay we are experiencing. They chatter and babble away, reaching a crescendo just as the announcement comes that we will shortly be continuing with our journey. It doesn't take a genius to work out that the busy train is packed with those either heading to Gatwick Airport or further along to spend a day at the beach. Suitcases, large beach bags, picnic hampers are interlaced with the scores of people, most with various body parts on show, ready for their sojourns to sunnier climes or dressed to reflect the forecast that today will be a hot, sunny day.

My handbag lies across my lap, as I gaze out of the window. My body language reflective of my feelings: closed and implacable. I can sense that if I so much as move my head to the left, the grandfatherly-looking gentleman beside me humming softly to himself will engage in conversation. On a normal day I would be fine with this, I would likely pre-empt small talk, especially as he has a placid and lonely look about him. But today, absolutely not.

My earlier conversation with Faye has sent down a thunderstorm of rocks, making me feel as if I'm being buried alive. I've been straining to draw an even breath since hanging up from her. Today, right at this moment, is the first time I've allowed the painful and frightening encounter with Elis to come at me as more than a zephyr moving through open plains. Now, the memory hovers and lands, leaden and tortuous. My head throbs, concentrated on the area that made contact with the wall, as if revisiting the memory has induced an illusory reaction to it.

I feel his malevolent presence, as if he's here in front of me. What had been the point? I had already parted with the money Faye owed him. Anyone could have seen how scared we were. I wouldn't have resisted if he asked me to take off my jewellery and hand over my bag. Why did he, or one of his goons, attack me? I recall Faye's yelp of shock and the feeling of her hovering over me, dragging me, as if trying to pull me up. I catch a ragged breath, feeling the emotions beginning to build. If I allow myself to go back there, I will fall to pieces. Now is not the time to relive this trauma that I haven't properly dealt with.

The train pulls up at Preston Park just as I'm feeling over-whelmed to the point of claustrophobia. I contort my way to the doors, stepping around my fellow passengers while avoiding obstacles, bags and body parts. In a minute or so I'm out of the station and standing in the same place where I met with Faye only a few weeks ago. I look from left to right, hopeful that Faye will be on her way, if not there already. No such luck. Despite all the thoughts that have accosted me on my journey here, I haven't stopped to think what exactly I plan to do. I *will not give her any money*, especially if there are any obvious signs of drug-taking. Maybe I can meet with her flatmates and beg them to give her another chance, especially if she has secured a job for herself. (If there is any truth to her words). Or maybe we can find a hostel or B&B for her to stay for a few days. It would mean parting with money but at least I wouldn't be putting it directly into her hands.

I'm going through all possibilities and solutions, com-fortable in the position where I stand leaning against a wall, I don't even realise that time has passed by quickly. Faye still hasn't arrived. A glance at my watch tells me she is twenty-five minutes late. Feeling restless now, I take a slow stroll backwards and forwards, the length of the station, as I retrieve my phone from my bag. No missed call. From my recent call list, I dial her number. The phone rings for a while before going to voicemail but I don't leave a message. I will assume she is on her way.

Forty minutes later – and far longer than I would have waited around for anyone else – I finally call it quits. I leave a short voice message and send a text. If she can't be bothered to answer her phone or call to let me know where she is, she's hardly desperate, is she? Feeling frustrated at my wasted Saturday afternoon, I make the spontaneous decision to spend some time in Brighton. It's been a while since I've inhaled sea air and walked along Brighton's pebble beach. The thought of dipping my feet in the water and sitting on the rough stones with a bag of chips is enough to temper my annoyance. And it turns out to be just the tonic I need.

Though crowded, I find a spot on the beach with enough space around me that I am not forced to listen to anyone's conversation. I rest my head on my folded jacket, plug my earbuds in and tune into my Spotify playlist. I spend a few lazy hours dozing and people-watching before dipping my feet into the sea. I save the visit to the chip shop until I'm almost ready to leave for home, sitting on a bench facing the water devouring my hot, salty meal. The fresh air rejuvenates me. My day hasn't been wasted after all.

Eight hours after leaving home on my mission to help Faye – again – I step off the train at Herne Hill, excited at the prospect of an evening slumped in front of the TV with a large glass of wine or two. I stop off at the Sainsbury's Local to pick up a few essentials and I have just exited the shop when my phone vibrates in my pocket. Ready with a few choice words to level at Faye, I'm not even put off when the words: *No caller ID* flash up on the screen. I know it will be her.

'Yes,' I answer acerbically. No time for games.

'Hello?' The voice is male, hesitant. Definitely not my sister. 'Am I speaking to Ren?'

I'm taken aback for a moment. 'Yes, who's this?' I ask, just as something familiar in his voice causes me to start.

'Ren, this is Leonard. I understand you've been trying to contact me.'

'Leonard!' The excitement in my voice must leave him startled. 'I'm so glad you called. I've been desperate to find out if you're okay and if the police have—'

He cuts in abruptly, his tone and words brusque: 'Listen carefully to what I'm saying,' he hisses. 'If you have any sense whatsoever, you'll stop what you're doing right now. Stop digging. You're playing a very dangerous game. Leave me alone and don't ever contact me again.'

Three short beeps and the line goes dead.

I'm left rooted to the spot, eyes wide, wandering what the hell has just happened. I stand, staring at my phone, as though it will provide me with the answers to the labyrinth questions and mysteries that just won't cease. It is the sound of voices behind me that pulls me back to the present and I shove the phone into my pocket and walk home in a daze.

***

When I wake up the following morning, I know what I have to do. The thought had been bubbling away in my head the previous day, but I had no idea if I would act on it. Until now.

There are few people in my world that I can say, hand on heart, I trust implicitly. Very few people I will put my life on the line for, and vice versa. Denny is one of them. Our time together was well grounded; borne from a friendship that saw us moving in the same circles. There was no massive initial connection, we simply came across each other at weekends when we were in London visiting from our respective universities. For a while, we even lost touch, but when he started working for a firm of solicitors not far from Kizzy's offices in the City, we reconnected. At the time, I was a year into my role as a lecturer at Upper Norwood College and he had been making moves and shaping his career as a criminal law solicitor. For a time, he had veered towards violent crime, but very early on he had made the move to specialise in fraud: from bribery to money laundering.

It hadn't taken him long to establish himself as a tenacious and knowledgeable specialist, responsible for some highly complex, and one particular high-profile, cases. The more his career burgeoned, the less time we spent together; the less we seemed to talk and laugh. Gone were the random date nights, lazy afternoons, movie nights. If Denny wasn't at work, he was preparing for it, thinking about it or studying for it. We had spent the best part of four years together and though we hadn't formally moved in together, we hardly ever spent a night apart, whether at my place or his.

There was never a point when our relationship crashed; in fact, we rarely exchanged harsh words. It wasn't just one thing, it was the sum of many small details: forgetting an important event, cancelling dates, working late hours, and conversations that revolved less around light-hearted things but more about work and pressure and climbing to the top. Neither of us really wanted it to end, but there comes a time in every problem when it's big enough to see, but small enough to solve.

I refused to be the kink in Denny's mission to set the legal world alight. I couldn't be that person. I was certain that we could have continued in the relationship, kept it afloat, even remain happy and relatively content, but Denny needed more than that. He needed the freedom to excel, his pathway unhindered. Maybe if I had the same intense ambition as he did, things may have been different, as we both battled our way to the top, but in all honestly, it felt as though his direction was more steeply inclined, more formal than mine. It probably doesn't happen very often, but the decision to break up was completely mutual and boringly cordial; a pensive time, but not melancholic. We even spent a last day together, collecting our numerous items from each other's homes before a parting evening at one of our favourite pubs, reminiscing over the good times. Just as I said, boringly cordial.

Now, I think back to the work-related stories Denny had shared with me. I think about the friends he made along the way, some at university, others early in his career in the same legal field and some who have gone into the police force.

Right now, Denny feels like my last bastion of hope. Maybe I am clutching at straws, maybe I just need to hear the voice of the person who knows me best in the world. Lots of maybes, but what I can be certain about is that something densely evil is circling around me, I sense it; I can almost touch it. Ever since the encounter with Faye and her dealer, and the start of my creative writing course, something misshapen and dark is in the air, surrounding me like a black fog and threatening to have a ruinous impact on my life. Whenever I take a step forward, another spray of sinister air is pumped out, pushing me backwards until it feels as if I am teetering on the brink of sanity.

Leonard's words yesterday were a hammer blow. I had been confident he would get in touch in his own time; but I had been expecting an empathetic conversation, one where we consoled each other for being at the nucleus of such a dreadful crime; unpicking the fibres frame by frame, matching our witness statements and expressing joint dismay at how gruesome a crime it was. We would join forces to make sure the police heard what we had to say. Maybe I would even share my exploits so far. He would be shocked but at the same time admire my purposeful approach and the risks I had taken to try and uncover the mystery. What I wasn't expecting was a point-blank shutdown and warning that my life was in danger.

Sitting here meditating, I assemble the events that have happened over the last few weeks. Jigsaw pieces that don't quite fit together. What am I missing and how has it come to this? My whole world seems to be on an axis and even in my rational and calm moments, I'm not completely focused on anything. My tutoring sessions have been substandard, there is a pile of letters and mounting emails unchecked, awaiting my attention; and even attending the writing course is pointless: the last two sessions have been a wall of white; nothing learnt and not much produced. It feels as if I'm fighting to stay in control, like flying an enormous jumbo jet solo, with no training, no guidance. There must be a saturation point. But I don't want to reach it.

One of the things I have always loved about Denny is his unflappable nature. Whilst we were together, I never once saw him react with anything but impartiality and logic. In fact, such was his common-sense approach that at times, I almost wanted to see him lose control, act irrationally, but he never did. Whenever I went into uncontrollable and sometimes unreasonable rants about my parents or Faye, he simply listened – no judgment, no aspersions. When I was certain my Deputy Head at college had graded me unfairly for a teaching observation, my angst went on for days; again Denny was there to prop me up and offer logic and reason.

Not that I can equate the causes of those meltdowns with a run-in with a drug dealer and witnessing a major crime online, but I'm unequivocal in my belief that Denny is the person I need to talk to. Just to hear his words of wisdom and advice would go a long way to alleviating my raging thoughts.

I opt for a phone call. Meeting up will seem too date-like and I don't want this to be about '*us*'. If Denny's work pattern is the same as when we were together, weekdays and weekends conflate to form one long working week. The only difference being that Sunday is his research and preparation day, with a few hours off at lunchtime and then a switch to something light-hearted in the evening. This is what I am thinking when I text him at 1pm to ask if he is free for a chat.

Hearing his voice is like balm on a wound. We engage in small talk, generally catching up on each other's lives and a brief mention of some mutual friends, including Lex and Kizzy. Then, without further pre-amble, I get down to the purpose of my call. I talk non-stop for close to thirty minutes, punctuated by the odd question from Denny. His tone is subdued throughout, simply absorbing all that I have to say. To my ears, my story sounds fantastical, but I make a concerted effort to deliver the information as factually as possible, leaving out anything emotional or speculative.

I'm most aware of his breathing when I come to the part about meeting up with Josh. I don't expect or want him to be jealous, but there is a sense of displacement to be speaking about a guy (whom I have made a connection with) to my ex-boyfriend. Denny draws in a deep breath when my story comes to an end.

'I know it sounds insane when I put it all together, but there's nothing made up, nothing left out.'

'This is unbelievably shocking, Ren,' Denny says, quietly.

'I've dealt with some strange cases in my field – cases you'd never believe unless you're involved in them. So, I know for a fact that weird things happen.' He pauses for a moment. 'There's got to be some explanation – even if it means overturning a few stones to find it.'

It is so good to hear his sensible and measured words. He asks me to go over the specific dates, names, times, locations and addresses again, and I can hear him furiously scribbling down some notes as I speak.

'The call from Leonard has really spooked me,' I add at the end. 'He made it seem as if something is going to happen to me too. But I'm sure the attacker didn't look into the camera. He wouldn't have seen me or known that I witnessed it.'

'Yes, it seems unlikely,' Denny agrees. 'But we don't know what has happened, apart from the obvious, to cause Leonard to react that way.'

I let out a silent groan. I don't relish the prospect of looking over my shoulder for the rest of my life, not knowing who I should be running from. I just want this to be over.

With all the drama I have offloaded on Denny, I refrain from bringing Faye's crisis into it; that is far too much for an ex-boyfriend to have to deal with in one sitting. Besides, the mention of her name would only throw up some memories we would both rather forget.

'Do you remember the Sherlock quote I used to say?' Denny's tone lightens, and I can tell he is smiling. I rack my brain:

'When you eliminate the impossible…' he begins.

'Whatever remains, no matter how improbable, must be the truth.' I finish the quote for him, smiling too, as I recall him saying it on many occasions, until it had become a bit of a parody.

'So you did listen when I spoke,' he says good-naturedly.

'Depends on what you had to say,' I retort.

We chat for a while longer, this time about ourselves, and then I leave him to get on with his Sunday.

'I'm really grateful to you for listening, Den,' I say sincerely. 'I don't expect you can do anything much to help, but if there's anything you can suggest—' I tail off.

'I won't promise anything, but I can definitely call in a favour or two to run the names, addresses and general things like that. Give me a few days and I'll see which trees I can shake.'

'You're a diamond!' I say, and I truly mean it.

After my conversation with Denny, I'm able to let go of some of the tension that has been crushing me. My brighter mood even allows me to regroup and get on track with my planning and paperwork.

Later, I receive a message from Josh:

Is the weekend being kind to you?

Was it really just two days ago we spent a lovely evening together, with that parting kiss which makes a vivid return when I see his name on my phone? Despite the tingly feeling that fizzes like popping candy, a torniquet tightens around my heart. I know there is a mutual attraction, but I also think Josh is going out of his way to make sure I fall for him. This is why he is already a step ahead of me, conducting his own investigation into Rusco's death, alongside the mission we are on together.

When it struck me that Josh already had Mary's address, that was the moment certain things began to fall into place. The way he is so in control of everything – unlike me unravelling at every step – he hasn't been able to leave this alone any more than I have. He just doesn't want me to know how invested he is in getting to the bottom of it. I picture him going out of his way to solve the many mysteries and then proudly proclaiming his every action to bring Rusco's killer to justice. There is a competitive streak in him, the desire to be the '*winner*' – his words. I'm not sure whether to view his behaviour as duplicitous, masterful or ingenious, but it adds to my wanting to keep my feelings for him in check, not to dive into anything until I've got to know him a bit better.

I respond to his message. *Kind, but as always too brief. You?*

Agree. But it's not too early to start planning for the upcoming one?

The question mark is suggestive.

Never too early to plan ahead. Always good to be organised. I don't help him out.

It's thirty minutes before I receive another message from Josh. This time there is a link to an event called *Rum 'n' Blues Live Music Night*. It is billed as an intimate basement experience of music, entertainment and rum tasting from a selection of unique rum blends and recipes from around the world.

Sounds like it should come with a health warning!! But sounds fun all the same. It's been a while since I've been out-out, and this is the type of social event I would love.

Our exchange continues for a while longer, but the conversation doesn't steer towards Mary/Rusco, which I'm actually pleased about. Now that I have Denny on the case, the edges of that jittery nervousness have softened, at least for the moment. Josh signs off by telling me he is looking forward to next weekend. We wish each other a pleasant week and make brief reference to our penultimate creative writing session on Thursday.

An afternoon of mellow music, and my pots and pans getting the kind of workout they haven't had in a while, my flat is alive with the smell of stewed chicken, roasted vege-tables, and macaroni cheese, as if I'm cooking for a family of four. Once I have eaten my fill and everything has been tidied away, I can't fight the desire to open my notebook and revisit the notes I made about Rusco's attack. I read through, updating some of the points and making the following additions:

- *Visit to Mary's house with Josh – what did the police find and why did they release her?*
- *The police haven't contacted me. Why?*
- *Andrew Shales -who is he?*
- *Leonard sounded scared. He warned me off. Did someone warn HIM off? Am I in danger?*

Finally, I write in capital letters:

- *DENNY IS ON THE CASE*

It is the assurance that arises from the last bullet point that ensures the rest of my day is relaxing and my sleep is blissfully dream-free and energising.

Chapter 12

Less than two weeks before the end

If there is such a thing as '*normal*', then this is how my week begins. I'm up to date with my tutoring paperwork – five sessions planned and ready to take place across the week. I've logged them onto the portal and emailed my students a reminder of the work they need to complete. I even perform the long overdue task of sorting through my box of old resources that has been sitting in the cupboard since my last day at Upper Norwood College.

I take advantage of this renewed vigour, and the next task I tackle is to go through my notes from the writing course and complete the activities I have failed to do. It may not be going quite as planned, but I still have to use this opportunity as a springboard to get my writing on track. I have decided that I want to write for an older teenage audience, something that draws on my experiences with some of the students I have met. A couple of them keep popping into my head, as if longing to be part of my novel. Nadine, the mouthy, tough nut. Bright, challenging and extremely complex. Then there's Ben, the class comedian, easy-going and amiable on the surface, but scratch deeper and there is a bagful of goodies to be explored.

Tarquin said in our first session that, by the time the course ends, we should have figured out the genre that interests us, the audience we want to write for and possibly have some story ideas or even a solid plot that we can begin to develop. I let my thoughts run riot for a bit, shaping some ideas around Nadine and Ben, expanding on some of the notes I had started. In between, I catch up with Lex and Kizzy on WhatsApp. They get a brief outline of what has been happening and they fill me in on their varied and busy weekend and start to the week. With the promise of a mini heatwave on its way, we make some pencil plans to meet up, providing Kizzy can co-ordinate diaries with Tom, or one of the grannies is available for babysitting duties.

My '*normal*' week comes to an end on Wednesday afternoon at 1:45pm when I answer my phone to Denny. He calls me while on his lunch break and I can hear from the sound of his voice that he is walking; rather quickly at that. The sound of constant traffic and intermittent voices indicate he is in a busy area. Notwithstanding, his voice is just above a whisper and I have to press the phone against my ear to hear him properly.

The greeting is hurried; such is his eagerness to get to the point.

'Ren. I've been doing a bit of, erm, digging. Something really serious is going on.' I almost sense him looking around furtively. The hesitancy of his first sentence revealing that the means of obtaining the information may have breached certain protocol.

'I know you said it all seemed far-fetched but it's not. In fact, it's a hell of a lot worse than you think.' He sounds breathless now. 'Mary Harris and Andrew Shales are dangerous. Whatever you do, do not take any more trips to Watford.' His voice is authoritative, hardened in a way I have never heard it before.

My world blows over like a house of cards and a numbing sensation begins to rise through me, right from the soles of my feet. I honestly don't know what I was expecting, but hearing these words from Denny's mouth, it is as if a volcano is about to erupt. I cannot find my voice; but there aren't even any words.

Denny continues, probably aware that I am struggling to absorb what he has just told me. 'I think you should carry on attending your lessons; just act as if everything's normal. But keep an eye and ear out for anything that seems out of place.'

'What have they done, Denny?' My voice is weak, tremorous. 'Are they responsible for Rusco's death?'

Denny is silent for a moment. All I can hear is his breathing. I know the answer before it comes. I have known the answer all along.

'Yes, they are.'

A crushing sadness overwhelms me. Poor Rusco. I recall what the neighbour had said about him not being quite right. Kept like a prisoner in the house by the sounds of it. What could he possibly have done to have been treated like that? To have his life extinguished in such a brutal, callous way?

'Ren. You still there?' Denny's concerned voice brings me back to the moment.

'Yes. Yes, I'm here,' I answer morosely. 'I'm just glad I didn't come face to face with Andrew Shales. I think he disappeared into the house before I arrived.' I look out of the window, the clear sky contrasting with the cloud of darkness in my head. 'I just can't get my head around this.'

'I know,' he soothes. 'It's a lot to take in.'

He stops suddenly and I wonder if we have been cut off. 'Denny?'

A light static fizzle, and then he is back. 'There's something else, Ren.'

My entire body sags until I am moulded into the sofa. As if I can take any more.

'I know you've been spending time with that guy you mentioned. Josh?'

'Yeah, that's right.' My words emerge as a nervous croak because I have a feeling I am not going to like the words that follow.

'You can't see him anymore, Ren.' An uncomfortable pause. 'He's involved in this too.'

And this is when the sticky tape that is holding my world together begins to peel. Like a plaster that has been saturated with oil and water, it slides downward. The ugly exposed wound mirroring my world.

'How much does he know about you?' Denny asks.

'Erm. W-we've spoken a lot, but I haven't told him loads about myself,' I stammer, thinking back over our previous conversations. 'He knows I live in Herne Hill – but he's never been to my flat. We've talked about my work, family, stuff like that, but nothing too personal.'

'Right,' Denny says, some relief evident in his voice. 'Don't let him know you're onto anything. And do your best not to have any communication with him. Okay?'

I nod, absent-mindedly, as if he can see me through the phone. I am thinking of something else. Someone else.

'Did Tarquin's name throw anything up?' I ask, nervously.

'No. Nothing at all.'

Denny tries his best to reassure me that everything will be okay, but the confusion and questions won't cease. Why haven't the police been in touch with me despite my numerous attempts to engage with them? Am I in danger? Shouldn't they be protecting me? Denny assures me that multiple investigations are taking place, with an increasing amount of evidence – some of which has only just come to light – and he is confident that the police will be in touch when the time is right.

'These things take time, unfortunately. The process is

often very lengthy,' he tells me. 'I just want you to be careful, Ren. Promise me you will?'

'I promise,' I whisper, through the sheet of sandpaper that has scratched its way down my throat.

Who the fuck are these people and what kind of crazy are they involved in? With this information forming into huge undigestible clumps, I give up trying to focus on anything else. There has got to be resolution and closure soon because I cannot hold it together for much longer. The thought of attending the online session tomorrow fills me with a pervasive dread. I know I will be in the security of my home, but the thought of sharing the same space as Mary and Josh and having to communicate with them as if everything is normal is deeply unnerving.

Disappointment and hurt. Of all the emotions fighting for prime position, these are the ones that predominate. Josh is involved. Josh has been deceiving me all along. Josh hasn't been fighting my corner, trying to win me over. Calm, sweet Josh, who has been nothing but thoughtful, respectful and caring towards me. He is complicit in this. How are they all connected? Why did Josh call the police, knowing what they would find? None of this makes sense.

As though this revelation has given me licence to be brutally honest with myself, I address those odd misgivings that crept in from time to time, that I manipulated to suit my truth, or brushed off without a second thought. When Mary turned up in the session, there wasn't so much as a raised eyebrow from Josh, before he turned his camera off. He probably knew she would be there. The way he put himself in the driving seat, taking control and I didn't even question it. My heart quickens when I think of the time I have spent alone with him. Dancing with the devil and I didn't even know it.

I close my eyes and remember how the conversation

ended at dinner. The dark, fleeting expression, the curt manner when I spoke about Mary I put that down to his irritation at my inability to stop prodding and poking when all he wanted was for us to have a carefree date, enjoying each other's company. What about the intense, mesmerising way he looked at me before he kissed me? For me, it was heart-melting, seductive. But what was going through his mind? The painful beauty and clarity of hindsight throbs away like a bad toothache.

***

Thursday morning, and I'm flitting around like a caged bird in need of release. I wake at 5am, tossing and turning, certain I will not go back to sleep – and I don't. The pulsating in my head refuses to be still so, for want of something, anything, to keep my mind occupied, at 7am I'm in my running gear, out in the park with the early morning fitness enthusiasts. My fellow joggers make it look effortless, but by the time I have completed one lap of the park, my lungs feel as if they have been lacerated and the painful stitch in my side is a stark reminder of how unfit I am. A slow walk home is all I can manage, before turning on the cold tap of my shower. The cold needle pricks work their magic. Enough discomfort to numb my mind of anything but my sore body.

An hour later, the painkillers I have swallowed have done nothing to release the pressure behind my eyes. The increased pulsating makes me feel woozy and out of sorts. I have my notebook open at the ready, my laptop open at the ready. Everything ready except for me. I have no idea how I will sit through three hours in Josh's presence without him being able to read every expression on my face and deduce every thought that runs through my mind. I think about keeping my camera off during the session, but I know I will be called out on it. Besides, it will only draw attention to me.

I take my time logging on: every minute I delay is one minute closer to the end. When I eventually join, I am thankful that it is already abuzz with conversation. No one notices my stealthy entrance. I have kept my curtains drawn – the darker my surroundings the less likely anyone can look closely at me. A quick flick through the participants' list shows that everyone expected is present. I picture Rusco, nervous and out of place. Was he aware of the fate that awaited him? Then there is Leonard. Confident, self-satisfied, a different person to the one that called me recently. Was it Josh that threatened him? Warned him off?

'So, this being our second to last session, we need to start thinking about your direction.' Tarquin's voice cuts into my thoughts.

'A round of applause to you all for commencing the journey; you've started to engage with your writer's voice and connect – or reconnect – with your imagination. Don't forget, that inner voice needs constant stimulation. So, what comes next?' Everyone looks at him blankly.

'I ask that as a rhetorical question. What is next for you? And you?' He points at his screen, directing his words to each of us individually. 'We'll use today's session to focus on harnessing our person. Who is the character you've chosen for your story? How can you continue to bring them to life?'

I think about Nadine and Ben. I write their names down, already knowing that Nadine will take centre stage: my feisty heroine. Back to my screen, and I switch to gallery view. My classmates appear in front of me. Today, everyone is in the mood to be inconspicuous. Curtains closed, no brightness or sunshine to add a bit of cheer. A sense of bleakness, an almost funereal atmosphere prevails. Or is it my imagination?

I look first at Tarquin as he continues his sermon. I have lost the thread of what he is saying. His mouth and arms move together and there is an intense seriousness about him; so passionate about his delivery. My thoughts dwell on him: his unique, off-centre character; traits which match his creative intellect. From the beginning, I focussed on all his oddities. Then after Rusco's murder, and the subsequent meeting in Wood Green, he morphed into someone with improper motives. My overactive mind allowed me to manufacture a monster when all along he is probably just an eccentric lecturer aiming to leave a memorable impression on his rapt audience. Am I creeped out by the words he wrote about me? Yes, but it doesn't mean he wishes to harm me. And, of course, he didn't spike my drink. I'm too embarrassed to consider apologising and admitting that the aftermath of Rusco's attack had pincered my brain, but at least I can cross him off the '*bad people*' list. I had even googled his award-winning book in the early hours, when sleep refused to come – something I had been meaning to do before everything went awry. Turns out he had reason to boast, it's a highly recommended read with some great reviews.

'My character is based on my younger self.' Ally's voice brings me back to the present. 'Or shall I say she draws from my younger self. I'm leaving the mundane, restrained part behind.' She giggles self-consciously. 'There's a lot from my early experiences I have always wanted to write about.'

Gillian throws in her contribution: 'The character I've been playing around with is a mish-mash of female members of my family. Not what I set out to do, but as I'm shaping her, I'm seeing bits of my sister, my aunt, my grandmother, God rest her soul…'

I tune out again as the conversation continues. This time I shift my attention to the poisoned chalice that is Mary. She is not in her usual location, but it's clear from the décor that she's in the same room. Her short-sleeved, peach blouse is unflattering and does nothing but wash the colour from her complexion. Her lips are slightly turned up at the corners, so it looks as though she is smirking. My initial impression of the sweet nana, smothered and destroyed.

Mary stares directly into the camera, a deadness behind her eyes. Every so often, her expression changes and she seems to scowl at the screen. I picture her heaving the sack out of her house and struggling to get it into the back of the blue van. What did the police find? I'm desperate for Denny to shed some light on this situation before my overthinking drives me insane. I look down at my pad unaware that I have been doodling. Inside the patterned circles I have drawn are scribbled names: *Josh* and *Mary,* double underlined and with question marks beside each name.

I have been putting it off since the session started, but now I finally turn my attention to Josh. His presence, concentrated to a little square box, seems to dominate my room. My breath catches in my throat as we make virtual eye contact and he winks, as if he has been waiting for me to look at him. Still the same Josh; hair perfectly preened and styled; a casual t-shirt fitted around his slim torso. I feel a slight tug within, as I think of what could have been. He gave the impression from the beginning that there was chemistry between us, but was it all part of a plan?

I cast my mind back through our conversations and rack my brain for anything he may have said that could have given something away. Anything that my softening heart may have ignored. The fact that he is a teacher is hugely worrying. If he is involved in this and still in charge of a group of impressionable children, that must surely be cause for concern. I grab my phone and search through my history, clicking on the link that takes me to Wayland Primary School, and follow my previous path to get to Year 6.

6JL. Josh's class. But now, it doesn't exist. The picture of Josh with the 20-strong group of happy children is no longer there! Next, I seek him out on Facebook, and after navigating my way through a list of Joshua Lees, I find him. He has quite a bit of activity on his page, and I make a mental note to have a proper look through later.

I tune back into the lesson. Everyone is busy scribbling away and I wonder what I have missed. Thankfully, Tarquin has posted the task in the chat: *Have your character engage in a conversation with someone they are at odds with.*

My thoughts meander back to Josh. I don't think he gave any details of the exact business his family is in, or did he? Something to do with retirement homes? I jump when my phone beeps and open it to see a message. From Josh.

Not in the mood for writing today?

He must have noticed my lack of participation. The last thing I want to do is communicate with him, but I have to avoid drawing attention to my growing resentment.

No, not really, I respond.

Anything I can do to reactivate the gray matter?

Thanks for the offer. I'll be okay.

Sure? You seem a bit jumpy.

How would he know that? He must be closely scrutinising me. I avoid looking at my screen, wishing a meteor would descend and paralyse the universe just for the next few hours. I decide to ignore the last comment, hoping that will end the conversation.

I turn to a new page in my notebook and attempt to write a conversation between Nadine and Ben.

Ten minutes later, I am sitting looking at a blank page, startled when someone calls my name. I look up to see Gillian and Ally staring at me. Everyone else has disappeared from my screen. It takes me a moment to realise we are in a breakout room together. 'Are you okay, Ren?'

Gillian asks, a quizzical look on her face. She must have called my name a couple of times already.

'Sorry!' I say, injecting a false cheer into my voice. 'I was miles away. It's been a busy few days and I'm struggling to concentrate today.'

'That's okay! We all have those days,' Ally responds kindly. 'I nearly fell asleep at the PTA meeting yesterday. Didn't help that we were in a room no bigger than a cupboard with no windows, and the secretary was droning on a bit.' She hiccups on a giggle.

'Any volunteers to go first?' Gillian brings us back on track. I think we are both aware that, given the opportunity, Ally will prattle on non-stop – I wouldn't mind that right now, especially as I have no idea what we are supposed to be doing.

'I will!' Ally shrills brightly, raising her hand as if we're at school. 'But before I do.' She leans forward confidentially. 'Gill, have you noticed that Jolly Josh is a bit off today? Not as on the ball and keen to share as usual.' My ears are perked, but I remain silent. I get the impression this is not the first conversation she's had with '*Gill*' about him. *Jolly Josh?* – maybe they've been discussing every member of the group and giving us all nicknames.

Gillian, (I'm not sure if she's only 'Gill' to her friends) who moments ago seemed keen to crack on, shifts position in her high-backed chair. She bundles up her long hair, placing it over one shoulder. 'Well, seeing as you mention it…' she says, 'he does seem a bit subdued, a bit distracted.'

'Yes, I noticed that too!' Ally seems pleased to be sharing a bit of gossip. 'When I logged in just before ten, I didn't have to wait to be let in, like we usually are. Josh and Mary were the only two online.' She leans in further, whispering loudly: 'It sounded as if they were arguing!' Her voice ends on an exclamation, little realising this is a very interesting revelation to me. 'Just the weirdest thing.'

My heart races, the air around me tightening as if oxygen has been sucked out with a powerful vacuum. 'What were they arguing about?' I ask.

'I only caught the end of it, but it sounded quite heated. He said something like: *Do you know what will happen if people find out*? And she called him stupid for getting others involved.'

They must have been arguing about Rusco, and their involvement in his death. Was Mary referring to Josh's relationship with me? My mind is ablaze. How could they be so indiscreet, arguing on this type of forum, knowing the barbaric secret they hold.

'Oh, Ally!' Gillian says, flapping her hand dismissively. 'They could have been acting out a conversation between characters. It could all be innocent.'

'I doubt it,' Ally says, affronted. 'I know there's something deviant about Mary. I've come across some shady characters in my time and I guarantee you, she's right up there.' My ears are so strained, they begin to throb. I am so tempted to blurt out everything I know. If nothing else, the conversation confirms that Ally is a good judge of character.

'Have you noticed…' Ally's words are halted by rustling and Tarquin's voice comes to us. 'Five minutes and we'll gather back together.' The three of us look into our cameras, eyes wide. I think we are all asking ourselves the same question: *Did he hear any of that?*

My apathy towards the lesson seems to have rubbed off on Ally and Gillian. Our 15-minute task yields nothing productive in terms of the lesson, but it is very enlightening for me. I'm not the only one being observant. Ally and Gillian may not have witnessed or experienced what I have, but they are aware of the changing behaviour of certain members in our group.

I stumble my way through the remainder of the session,

at times half tuned in to what is going on, but mostly in a world of my own, going over the conversation between Ally and Gillian. I wonder if they'll continue the chat later, (they seem to have struck up a friendship outside of the group) and if my lack of involvement will come up.

As we draw to the end of the session, Tarquin rounds off by issuing instructions for our final lesson next week. He has shared his screen, which contains a list of our names with an allotted time beside each: our one-to-one slots to discuss our next steps.

Maybe, I think to myself, I should side-step the embarrassment and use this as an opportunity to apologise to him.

Chapter 13

Less than two weeks before the end

I'm scrolling through Josh's Facebook page, mainly look-ing at pictures of him and a variety of people uploaded at random intervals. The most recent is a group of lads united in celebration, raised glasses and matching smiles. It has been liked 89 times with over a hundred comments. A quick skim read reveals it was a stag night for *Noah-The-Great*. Scrolling further back in time, there is a plethora of photos, many of them in group situations. Josh often at the centre, each one serving as a conduit into his gregarious world. The majority have been '*liked*' hundreds of times and with comments galore, giving the persona of a popular pri-mary school teacher; outgoing but well within the bound-aries of decency. He has 490 friends. A glance at his profile shows that he hasn't uploaded much by way of personal information. His birthday is 1st November and he supports West Ham. There is a keen interest in personal fitness apps and video games. All pretty standard.

The lack of privacy on his settings allows me unfettered access to his list of friends. Unsurprisingly, we have no mutual ones. I'm scrolling through robotically, not looking at anything in particular, just about ready to exit. My eyes have caught on something that my finger speedily flicked past. I slowly retrace my virtual footsteps. Rymone, Rufus,

Ronnie, RoseLynn- – backwards through the list of names beginning with '*R*'. And then there it is.

Rick-UL.

Not the exact name that has been pecking a hole in my life but it is like a straightforward clue to a name game. I click on it, and my phone screen is filled with an image. Stringy hair, piercings, the startled rabbit expression. Without question, I'm looking into the eyes of Rusco. My previous search didn't throw up the name Rick-UL. But it seems he has two Facebook accounts. How long have he and Josh been friends? I try to rationalise it. Rusco was killed in lesson three. Could they have connected after the first or second lesson? A quick scroll through Rusco's page shows that he is even less active on this Facebook account than the one I previously found. There haven't been any posts, likes or comments for over a year. They must have a connection that goes further back than the start of the writing course. The information section reveals his current town/city. Again, listed as Watford.

My heart and head pulsate ruthlessly as the events of the last few weeks pummel me like the trailer of a fast-paced action movie. A panic attack looms. I steady myself, clinging to the sofa; deep breaths in and out, slowly and deeply. I think back to my rendezvous with Kizzy and Lex in Herne Hill just last month and how simple and uncomplicated my life seemed then. I was certain that I would sail along for the next few months, comfortable with my tutoring sessions, picking up a few more along the way while taking my time to look for another full-time teaching role. I recall my excitement at having something to focus on when I signed up to the writing course. How could I have known it would be the catalyst for my world breaking apart at the seams?

I pull myself together and decide to contact Denny. I don't know how significant the pieces of information I have found out will be, but I need to share it with him all the same and ask if he thinks it's worth me contacting the police again. I summarise the conversation between Ally and Gillian and tell him about the '*friendship*' between Josh and Rusco.

Since yesterday, I have been messaging Lex and Kizzy with snippets of information and updates of the situation. Though we haven't spoken, the group chat is alive with activity, and I am struggling to keep on top of it. I know they mean well, and I'm so grateful for their support, but when my phone vibrates steadily in succession – calls from both of them – I ignore it and switch the phone off. I crawl into the cosy, safe space under my duvet and burrow there; head covered securely, finding solace in the warmth and darkness. I wish I could hibernate here until my world is clean and pure again.

***

The voices are indistinct; words that I can't quite connect with, but I hear my name being called: muffled as if I'm under water. There is a shrill, relentless alarm, signalling a warning of some sort. If red had a sound, this would be it.

Then I hear the banging. And this time my name is loud and clear. I jump out of my sleep, for a moment confused. The curtains are open but it is dark outside with only the streetlight allowing me some vision to rise and make my way to the door. I am suddenly afraid. I only ever have visitors by arrangement, and if someone is knocking on my flat door, it means they have bypassed the communal front door. Who would have let them in? Surreptitiously, I leave my bedroom. With light footsteps I can make it to the peephole without whoever is on the other side of the door being aware. Just as I reach it, I hear a familiar voice calling my name.

169

'Ren! Please open the door. I won't threaten to break it down, but we *will* call the police.'

It's Lex. And Kizzy must be with her. Relief washing over me, I hasten my footsteps, remove the safety chain and open the door.

'Fucking hell, Ren. You scared the shit out of us. We've been banging for like ten minutes!' Lex doesn't hide her relief and annoyance. 'Your neighbour upstairs let us through the front door.' They stare at me as if I have just landed from another planet.

'I'm sorry,' I croak. 'I fell asleep.'

'I called you, probably a minute after your last message, and that was about three hours ago. We've called you about ten times each since then.' Kizzy nods beside her, frowning at me.

I realise I am standing there, caught up in the moment and I haven't invited them in. I open the door wider, and they pass me, entering the flat. 'Let me just clear some space for you to sit,' I say, fussing around, picking up a stack of letters, my notebook, laptop, an empty mug; annoyed that I hadn't straightened everything out before I decided to have a nap. Heavy-headed, I literally sweep everything into a messy pile on the floor, stumbling about as if I've been spun around blindfolded. Kizzy and Lex watch me, silently, as I tidy up. I can only guess what is going through their minds.

Kizzy enlightens me when she asks: 'Are you okay, Ren? You look even worse than the last time we saw you.' Even in my fragile state, I smile. Frank words spoken by a true friend. I almost feel sorry for them having no choice but to look at the eyesore in front of them. The combination of waking from a three-hour nap, restless nights, weight loss and constant worry have ravaged me. The concern is etched on their faces, and I suddenly feel guilty for inconveniencing them when they could be doing so much more than chasing after their bothersome friend.

'I'm sorry,' I say again. What else can I say? 'Let me get you some drinks and then we can have a chat.'

I head to the kitchen, hoping there is something readily available in the fridge that I can offer them. I pull out a bottle of wine, three quarters full, and a carton of apple juice. I place them on a tray with some glasses. From the overhead cupboard I grab a packet of dry roasted peanuts and a box of Pringles, tip them into bowls then add them to the tray and head back to the front room. My footsteps are light and Kizzy and Lex are unaware of my approach, suddenly silent when they notice I am in the room. They had obviously been talking about me.

Under their close, watchful gazes, I set the tray down, pour some drinks and open the nuts and Pringles. My hands are slightly unsteady, and I hope they don't notice it. This occasion doesn't warrant chit-chat and once we are all seated with glasses in hand, Kizzy lunges straight in.

'Forget about the messages you've sent us, you need to tell us word-for-word what has happened since the last time we saw you,' she says directly.

As if in silent disapproval for all I am about to say, my head begins to throb. I gently stroke my temple, feeling the uneven, bristly skin. Lex and Kizzy listen raptly to the lengthened version of the parts that had previously been summarised into WhatsApp messages. I can almost see their brains labouring intensely to organise the jigsaw pieces. I conclude by telling them about the plan for the final lesson, and my message to Denny.

'Bloody hell. What a crap-load of madness!' Lex exclaims. 'How do we even make sense of this, especially when you add in all the bits that have happened recently?' She rises and paces the floor of my living room, repositioning herself on the window seat. 'Seeing someone killed is bad enough

171

but, when the people involved are all around you, that's just another level of nuts!'

'I wish I could get my hands on that arsehole, Josh,' Kizzy says, her curls bouncing around in harmony with her anger. 'He sounded like a decent bloke. I can't believe he's part of it.' She scratches her head in confusion, not yet finished. 'Whoever actually killed Rusco is either still on the loose or the police have arrested them. So how are Josh and Mary involved? All of you were in the session when it happened.'

'It's all a mystery, Kiz,' I respond. 'If I had to guess, I would say they organised it. Maybe they hired someone to kill him.' At the same time I express these thoughts, I'm shaking my head at the ridiculousness of it.

'But why do it in the equivalent of a room full of people?' Lex asks dubiously, then answers the question without waiting for our input. 'Unless whoever did it wasn't aware he was on Zoom with a bunch of people on camera.' It's the million-pound mystery.

Kizzy traces a continuous circle around her glass of apple juice, absentmindedly, her gaze fixed somewhere in the distance. 'So, they know you and Leonard saw what happened. Someone has obviously got to him if he's warning you off. Which means, someone might try to warn you off too, Ren.' Her gaze rests on me.

'And you've already used up a good number of your nine lives,' Lex adds, reproachfully.

'You know you have to cut ties with Josh, don't you?' Back to Kizzy. She looks at me, as though expecting some resistance.

'I've knocked that one on the head,' I say, definitively. 'As I said, we exchanged messages during the session, but I haven't responded to the last one he sent.' I suddenly remember: 'I'm supposed to be going out with him this weekend. I'll have to find a way to let him down.'

'Just tell him to piss off and leave you alone,' Lex asserts, stomping back to the table where she left her drink.

'I would, but I can't let him know that I'm onto him. I might just have to pretend I'm ill.'

'What about the final lesson next week? You're not going to attend, are you?' This from Kizzy, furrowing her brow. 'The thought of you being online with those freaks gives me the shivers.'

'It's the last lesson and I've got to try and take something away from it to justify spending all that money. At least I know Tarquin isn't a threat,' I say thankfully.

'Yeah, I guess eccentricity isn't a crime, or having poor dress sense and a bad comb-over.' Lex brings a bit of humour to our solemn conversation.

'They should refund the cost of the course to you,' Kizzy says. 'They should even compensate you for the trauma you've been through.'

'Good point,' Lex says. 'We might have to look into that once this is all over.'

I offer the peanuts around then dip my hand into the bowl, drawing out a small handful. 'To be honest, I'd settle for being able to put this all behind me and knowing everyone involved has been punished.'

We fall silent for a moment, nibbling on nuts and crisps.

'So, what about this Andrew Shales character? What exactly is his involvement?' Kizzy breaks the silence.

I shake my head slowly. 'He owns the blue van and the house I followed them to. Apart from that, no idea.'

Lex draws her arms tightly around herself and shudders. 'The whole thing is just so depressing,' she says. 'I would love to know what the police are doing.'

The thought is one that frequently plagues me. I have never been in a situation like this before, nowhere near, but I am miffed as to why the police aren't chomping at the bit to speak to me. Okay, so maybe they wouldn't fill me in at every stage of their investigation, but I would have expected more than this. At the very least, shouldn't they have followed up on my initial statement?

'I hope Denny can squeeze some more information from his contacts,' Kizzy says after we have gone round full circle, still without any conclusion that sounds credible.

'I hope so too,' I say, crossing my fingers.

'Hey. Don't even start getting all dreamy,' Lex chastises. Maybe she detects something wistful in my voice.

But I am resolute: 'No chance! After the near miss I've just had, I don't think fellas will be featuring in my life for a long while.'

Kizzy changes the subject. 'Have you still not heard anything from Faye?'

I wrinkle my nose, as if the air has suddenly become putrid. 'No. Nothing whatsoever. She hasn't seen fit to contact me after standing me up.' I use both hands to gently massage my scalp, not ready to deal with Faye's drama as well as the one I am mixed up in. 'I'm sure she's back on drugs. I don't even think there's anything I can do to help her, especially if she's not prepared to communicate with me.'

Kizzy looks disheartened. 'No one will blame you if you wash your hands of her. It's not the first time she's shat on you from a great height, is it?'

I lower my head sadly, the incident a few years ago scrabbling back to haunt me.

It was relatively early days in my relationship with Denny. I was settled in my teaching job and had just bought my flat after saving up for ages. Faye was always on the periphery somewhere, popping up from time to time, when she needed something. Lex and Kizzy had persuaded me to have a house-warming party before I got stuck into redecorating and turning the in-need-of-TLC flat into my home. I eventually agreed and thought I would invite Faye along too. She had met Denny once before, was familiar with Lex, Kizzy and a few of my other friends. I even offered to put her up for the night so she wouldn't have to traipse back to wherever she was staying at the time. (Needless to say the overnight stay ended up being three weeks.)

The party had been a great success. Loud, lively music, (probably to the disdain of my new neighbours) everyone up on their feet, inhibitions swept aside along with my sparse furniture, and enough booze to rival any London wine bar. Everyone present was worse for wear the following day.

The revelation had come some weeks later when the first of many letters addressed to an unknown *Marie Taylor* had landed on my doorstep. At first, I assumed it was a previous owner or tenant or maybe someone from the flat upstairs. It was only when the red letters began to arrive that I thought to open them and it all became clear. Marie is mum's middle name; Taylor was her maiden name. I knew Mum couldn't have used her details and my address to take out three credit cards. There was only one other person who could have been guilty. To make things worse, when I shared Faye's treachery with Denny, I was surprised when he was unable to look me in the eye. His evasiveness spoke volumes: there was something he wasn't telling me. My mind went into overdrive, thinking maybe he had been a co-conspirator in my sister's shenanigans. I literally had to drag the truth out of him. Denny had stayed over on the night of the party, and whilst I had collapsed into bed in the early hours, he had stayed up till the last person had left, tidied up a bit and then, unable to sleep he had sat in the kitchen, not wanting to disturb me or Faye – who was fast asleep on a sofa bed in the front room. When he felt arms around his neck, he instinctively assumed it was me but the sloppy kisses on his neck and the whispered: 'Come to bed with me' sent him scurrying across to the other side of the kitchen. My sister had tried to seduce my boyfriend.

I had confronted Faye over the phone about the credit cards and about making a pass at Denny. There was no apology. No outright admission of guilt. Just excuses: *I was broke. I knew you wouldn't have to pay the money back. I was drunk. I didn't mean to make a pass at Denny; he's not even my type!* I must be a real glutton for punishment to have gotten involved with her drug debt and tried to bail her out from whatever dilemma she's got herself wrapped in this time. After everything I have put up with over the years.

I put a lid on my thoughts of Faye and return to the present. 'She'll be in touch again when she needs something, or when Elis demands more money.' I shake my head.

'She needs professional help, Ren,' Kizzy says gloomily. 'Help that you're not equipped to give her.'

The evening so far has been all about me and my woes; fun and mindless chatter between us a distant memory. I ask Kizzy about her first few weeks back at work and how she is managing to juggle things. Cory seems to be settling well into his new Grandma tag-team routine. I promise her that I will come by and see him sometime and even offer to babysit so she and Tom can go on a date.

Lex is readjusting to being a Miss again, loving her single status, confident she won't be taken in by a bad egg again – as if they come with a large red X scrawled across their foreheads. She has been on a couple of dates but nothing she is interested in pursuing. On the plus side, she and Phil have found a buyer for the house they bought as a rental, so it won't be long before the remaining link between them is severed.

It's after 11pm when I say farewell to them, thankful for the restorative conversation. I see them out to Lex's car. She has offered to take a slight detour and drop Kizzy home before heading on her way. I clear away the remnants of our evening. I have a few chores to do, but even after my earlier nap, nothing is more welcoming than a hot shower and curling up in bed. Whatever tomorrow's battle is, it can be fought tomorrow.

Chapter 14

One week before the end

Most of the next day is spent batting and fielding through an excess of emails, like I've become my own personal secretary. Sharma, my contact from the tutoring agency, calls rather unexpectedly, to let me know they have three potential students if I am interested in taking on some more online tutoring. I agree for her to put my profile forward. She assures me that it should all be straightforward, and as my CRB certificate is up to date, I could be starting with some new students as early as next week.

Denny's call is the one I have been most anticipating. When he eventually rings me, in true Denny style, he is between meetings, walking and talking, footsteps clacking along as though he's in a rush.

'You okay, babe?' he asks in that familiar manner, almost as if we haven't spent the past three months as exes.

'I've had better days,' I answer honestly. 'Still a hundred and one things going on in my head. But I'm trying to tune those voices out,' I say.

'I know it's easier said than done but try not to let things get on top of you. I haven't got long but I thought it might be good if we get together. I can fill you in with what I know so far. Just a moment, Ren.' I hear him conversing with someone in the background in muffled tones, then he comes back on.

'Sorry about that.'

'No don't be,' I say. Knowing how busy he is and at the same time appreciating that he is taking time out to help me. 'You let me know when's a good time and we can arrange something,' I say.

'I'll do that,' Denny replies. 'I'll be in touch soon, okay?'

We end the call and I spend the afternoon ticking a few more things off my to-do list. I also send a message to Lex and Kizzy thanking them for being such awesome and caring friends.

All part of the service, Kizzy messages back. *The direct debit mandate will be with you shortly!*

The communication I have been least looking forward to comes in the form of a text message which pings through late in the afternoon.

Looking forward to a boozy evening tomorrow. Are you?

It's Josh. All sorts of emotions whizz through me. I know I can't ignore the message, and I stall for ages, thinking about what to say in response. Eventually, I go with a simple untruth.

Really sorry to blow you out, but I think I'm coming down with something. Been feeling off since yesterday.

You avoiding me Ren?

There's something almost menacing about his response. I try to lighten the mood.

No, not at all! If I've got the lurgies, it won't be very chari-table of me to share them with you.

My finger hovers over the send button before I add: *I was looking forward to it.* I pause again, then quickly delete the last bit.

He sends back a sad face emoji. Followed by:

I could always come round and play nursemaid?

If this had been a few days ago, I probably would have been tempted. In fact, if it had been a few days ago I wouldn't be pretending to be ill.

I think I'd be better off nursing myself. But thanks all the same, I message back.

I'm disappointed. But I'll get to you eventually!

Forewarned is forearmed. Knowing what I know now, the hairs on the back of my neck stand to attention. There definitely feels like a simmering undercurrent of threat, and I cannot wait to be at a point where I can cast him out of my life forever, without having to resort to lies.

***

The Shephard family have never been religious, so an eyebrow was always raised at Dad's fondness of the phrase: we make plans, but God has the final word. This is what comes to mind when I think of my current situation. Just days ago, I had been excited at the prospect of another date with Josh, visions of drinking, dancing, flirting into the early hours. Now, as I drag the comb arduously through my tangled mass of hair, I'm still planning an evening out, but not with the person I had originally intended. Yes, I'm looking forward to seeing Denny, but part of this is fuelled by the yearning to prise as much information from him as I can.

I dress for comfort, and to mirror the cool dampness of the last few days. My denim dress hangs shapelessly around my thinned-out frame, so that I have to cinch it in at the waist with a belt. It's long-sleeved, so it will do just fine should the temperature cool down any further. Leggings and white pumps complete my look, making it a perfect combination for an evening at the pub.

I was surprised to hear from Denny again so soon after we had spoken the day before. Knowing how full-on his schedule always was, I hadn't expected he would be able to find time to fit me in so soon. Maybe he is getting better at balancing his work and social life, I reason. He had suggested we meet at a pub in East Dulwich, not too far from me, and one we enjoyed frequenting, mainly due to its cheerful atmosphere – busy but welcoming with mellow background music. That was often where we went if we wanted a sociable evening out, but without having to yell at each other or sign and lipread across a table. For a moment, I consider taking the car, unsure whether it will be a late one. I decide against it: not only will it be a nightmare to park, but it's always nice knowing I have the option of more than one glass of wine.

We arrive at Larange within minutes of each other. Denny, punctual as ever. Me, often hit and miss.

'On time today.' Denny teases in greeting.

He kisses me on both cheeks, and I catch a whiff of something woodsy and deliciously masculine. A different scent from what I was used to him wearing, but I like it all the same. He's added a few pounds to his usual lithe physique but it's enough to suit him, more definition and a bit more character to his face. Prior to meeting Denny, if I could have drawn a picture of my ideal-looking guy, Denny would have been very close. Everything about his face fits perfectly together; squarish jaw, white, even teeth, hair always trimmed close to his head, so you could see part of his well-nourished scalp. He vacillated between glasses and contact lenses, (both looks suited him) mainly depending on the outfit and the occasion. He was well turned out, without the need for hours of pampering and preening, everything seemed effortless. I remember often feeling envious that he could throw on a pair of jeans and a shirt and look as though he'd been dressed by his own personal shopper.

'I didn't want to risk being told off by His Highness,' I retort. 'I'd never hear the end of it.'

'Still as cheeky as ever then,' he laughs, as we make our

way into the dimly-lit pub. Every fraction of every second is taking me back to a time not so long ago. Walking into the pub is like stripping back time and embedding ourselves into a space we once occupied together.

We get to the bar with ease, order without delay and before long we are seated across from each other with a bottle of wine and several packets of crisps. More old habits.

'You've lost weight,' Denny says, his disapproval evident although he tries to hide it.

'The anxiety diet is working, I guess,' I respond, trying for humour.

He looks at me gravely. 'You should have called me as soon as this happened. I know we haven't really been in touch since we split up, but we are still friends.' he says, looking deeply into my eyes as if for verification.

'I know,' I say regretfully. 'I've been swallowed up in it from the moment it happened. I think I was in such a state of shock for the first few days.' I watch as Denny fills our glasses. 'I thought once the police were involved, they would investigate it and find out what happened and then it would all be over.' I say naively, pausing to take a sip of my wine. Denny does the same. 'Well, not that I expected it to be as easy and straightforward as that,' I continue, 'but I didn't think I'd be left feeling like I'm trying to fight my way off a sinking ship.'

'It's enough to freak out the toughest of people,' Denny sympathises. 'It's no surprise you feel that way.'

I smile ruefully. 'I spend most of the time feeling jumpy and neurotic. Every day there's some new layer to add to the drama.'

Denny takes my hand and squeezes it. 'I can't imagine what it's been like. If I hadn't done some digging myself, I would have put you down as a nut job.' I know he is trying to soften the edges of the conversation.

I slap his hand playfully. 'And you have the audacity to call me cheeky!'

He laughs, then his expression changes and our eyes lock. 'I hate that you're going through such a tough time, Ren.'

My throat swells. 'Don't look at me like that, you'll only make me cry!' I swallow hard and clear my throat, not wanting my emotions to seep out. I take a deep breath. 'So what have you found out?' I ask, resting my arms on the table. 'Who did you speak to?' I take a sip of wine, this time a large one.

Denny looks around. Even in the dimly-lit pub with everyone surrounding us deeply embedded in their own huddles of chit-chat and laughter, he appears suddenly uneasy.

'Do you remember Rob Santos?' he asks.

I close my eyes and picture a hairy giant of a man, brash and intimidating on the surface but comical and affable on a one-to-one basis. He was on the fringes of our friendship group some years ago. Older than the rest of us, but he forged a great bond with Denny. At the time, Rob was doing an MA in criminology as well as a placement with The Met. He's not the kind of person you could easily forget. I nod my head in recollection.

'Well, he didn't quite follow through to becoming a detective, but he's a senior crime analyst for Hampshire Constabulary – and he is *extremely* well connected.' I note the emphasis on extremely.

'Not to mention he owes me more than a favour or two,' Denny issues a sly wink – an indication of a conversation pathway I would rather not tread. He continues: 'So I gave him a snapshot of what you told me: all the names, addresses, and so on.' He rests his elbows on the table, head close to mine.

'Mary Harris is one of three names used by the one person. She also goes by the name Belinda Havant. But her birth name is Maggie Shales.'

'Why so many aliases? Who or what is she hiding from?' My voice is increasing in volume, displeasure creeping in at the thought of this evil witch.

'She's been implicated in a number of kidnappings – three young men all with learning disabilities.' Denny takes a pause. 'Two of them have supposedly disappeared off the face of the earth.'

A deep frown creases my brow, as certain cogs begin to turn and slot into place.

'Rusco,' I mutter, almost to myself.

'What are you thinking?' Denny asks.

'Mary told everyone in the writing class that she's a carer,' I say, thoughtfully. 'I always assumed she was caring for a husband or maybe an elderly parent. She must have been referring to Rusco.'

I look off into the distance as an image of Rusco resurfaces. 'There was something about him that made me think he had learning needs. It was as if he'd wandered into the wrong place. And the way he used to look around, like there was someone nearby that frightened him.'

Denny listens intently.

'Why did the police let her go if she's dangerous? Why isn't she in custody?' I have lost track of the number of times this question has come up.

Denny's look is concealed. 'They've made arrests, but the difficulty is always the evidence. If they can't find anything specific to pin her to the crime, they have to let her out on bail, pending inquiries.'

'It doesn't make sense to me,' I tell Denny. 'They definitely found something of interest at 43 Barcourt Road. That's her house, so I would assume they have enough to charge her with something. At the very least, they could have refused her application for bail?'

'It's never that simple, Ren. If she has a decent solicitor, it wouldn't be too difficult for her to get bail until there's a trial. Besides, if she can prove she didn't actually carry out the killing – which in Rusco's case she can – it's a matter of innocent until proven guilty.'

'So who **did** kill him?' I ask irritably. 'Is that who the police have in custody?'

'There was only so much I was able to glean from Rob. He'd have to dig a bit deeper to find anything more.'

'So, what we know so far is that Mary and Andrew Shales are related, more than likely in it together. He might even be the person they've arrested.' I'm tempted to bring my pen out to scrawl some notes on a napkin. It is a good thing we hadn't ordered food; it would have cooled and congealed in front of us, so deep are we in conversation. Eventually, Denny opens the packets of crisps, tearing straight lines through the middle, making it easy for us to share.

'Where does Josh fit into all of this?' It stings to bring his name up, for multiple reasons. 'Why did he act as if we were in it together if he's involved?' That is perhaps the single, most bewildering question of all. One that I have chewed up, spat out and still not been able to mould into a credible answer. Top of my list of *what ifs*: what if he is trying to extricate himself from something that has got way out of his control. Maybe he's scared, guilty by association, but doesn't want to be in any trouble. But that just sounds as if I'm making excuses for him.

Denny shrugs, munching his way through a handful of sea salt and vinegar crisps. 'It's a weird thing to do when you know what the ramifications will be.' He pushes the crisps towards me, and I take a few.

'Rob looked into Josh's background,' Denny continues, once he has washed down a mouthful of crisps with some wine. 'Did you know that his family run a couple of assisted-living care homes in Hertfordshire? Two of the young men that disappeared are linked to one of the care homes. I'm not sure yet what the relationship is between Mary and Josh, but Rob said the police are looking into him, although I don't think he's a prime suspect.'

Through the nebulous cloud, some of Denny's discoveries are beginning to fit together. I tell him about Josh's part-time work for his family business, and the fact that his details have recently been wiped from his school's website.

'News travels fast in the right places, I guess,' Denny says. 'The slightest whiff of wrongdoing, especially where kids are involved, it won't be taken lightly.'

We sit for a moment, sipping our drinks, lost in individual thoughts.

I break the silence before Denny does. 'Are you sure nothing dodgy came up about Tarquin?' I hate to belabour the point; I have asked him already, but just to be certain.

Denny shakes his head. 'As I said before: he checks out.' As if reading my thoughts, he continues: 'Your mind was in overdrive when the attack first happened. I'm sure Tarquin understands why you were so overwrought and suspicious.'

'At least that's one thing I've been able to clear up. Even though I still think it's creepy what he wrote about me.'

Denny's eyes twinkle mischievously, and he laughs. It's a warming sound. 'He's probably making notes for his next novel. Might be something erotic with you as the main character!'

I screw up my face and pretend to stick my fingers down my throat. But it does make me giggle.

After polishing off the crisps, we order a bowl of fries, onion rings and some garlic bread. Denny fills me in on his work. Just as I thought, he has climbed another level from where he was three months ago and is still enjoying the challenges – even when a case appears hopeless. His work ethic is admirable. Hours spent away from home means he is often eating on the run, or in a range of restaurants, hence the weight gain, he tells me.

He asks about my life outside of Zoom-gate and I tell him that I am enjoying having more free time post-redundancy but will soon need to start giving some serious thought to my next permanent role.

We spend a few enjoyable hours together, settling easily back into a comfortable place, gentle ribbing, open and honest chat. When he mentions the discoloured graze on the side of my head, which I obviously haven't covered very well, I reluctantly tell him about the incident with Faye. He fights to keep his expression neutral. I'm sure he is thinking back to the scene at my flat-warming party and her blatant attempt to seduce him. Their relationship was never able to work its way beyond that: no surprise really. The only positive was that Faye was in and out of my life so infrequently, we never had to face any awkward encounters.

'Your sister still hasn't found her way then,' he says diplomatically. 'She needs to take a long hard look at her life, and if she doesn't make changes, she'll lose the one person who actually gives a damn about her.' I'm sure Lex and Kizzy would high-five him if they were here. 'I'm surprised you're still chasing after her, trying to solve her problems considering the way she's treated you,' he admonishes.

I groan loudly. 'I know I'm a pushover.' I hold my hands up in supplication. 'It's taken a while, but I realise I'm at my limit now. I agree with you: she has to take accountability for her actions.'

Denny stares at me, tilting his head to one side. 'You've got a heart of gold, Ren Shephard. A beautiful trait, but it also leaves you exposed.'

I smile sheepishly. 'Well, this heart has had one too many exposures and it needs to heal.'

We gaze at each other, a crash collision of private thoughts exploding and blistering between us. A heat that can scorch the earth if we allow it to. Eventually, I break free from the bubble. 'Let me get some more drinks.' I'm up on my feet before he accepts. I snake my way to the bar, needing a chance to be by myself and assimilate every word spoken between us in the last couple of hours, getting the sense that I am moving closer to the parapet, but still with some way to go.

I allow my mind to drift to Josh as I wait to be served. If I hadn't sought Denny's help with this, we would have been out on our date. How would that have panned out? What did he have in store for me? I shudder at the thought, glad that I didn't have to find out. If I had placed bets on anyone in our writing group being the villain alongside Mary, it would have been Tarquin. Little did I know the villain's sidekick had charmed his way into my life. *I am the worst judge of character that has ever lived*, I think to myself.

I glance back at Denny, using the opportunity to appraise him unobserved. Everything about him is stable and transparent. I can only hope I find that again, one day. Maybe driven by intuition, he looks in my direction and the smile that passes between us is wistful and filled with a deep bond of friendship.

A few rounds later, we are ready to call it a night. Reluctantly. The air outside is still, a touch humid, signalling that rain is on the way. Strangely, I feel cleansed, as if a sponge is being expanded within me, drawing in some of the toxicity, expelling it from my body. Arms linked, we stroll further down the road, separate Ubers taking us to our destinations. Denny hugs me tightly and protectively, kissing the top of my head as he used to. It is a comfortable and familiar place to be and there is a part of me that doesn't want to break away.

I float home on a cloud of nostalgia. I know these are

likely to be false feelings, instigated by the unsettled and energy-sapping time I've had of late. I remind myself that there was a perfectly logical and valid reason why Denny and I decided to split up. Nothing has changed. All the same, I'm relieved and grateful to have him in my corner. I know I will triumph over this situation, and his support will put me in his debt forever.

There is a steady stream of vehicles on the road, but it isn't overly busy for a Saturday night. Fifteen minutes later, the Uber pulls up on my road, just as my eyes are losing the battle to stay open. Not surprisingly, he has to double park due to the limited spaces. Typical Saturday night: everyone is out, but no one wants to drive. I already have my key out, ready to enter my flat and submit to the comfort of my bed. I thank the driver, and he is chivalrous enough to wait until I get beyond the communal front door before he drives off.

When I started flat hunting, I viewed another property close to this one. It was in a large Victorian house, with rooms slightly larger than what I have now. What put me off was that Flat 3 was on the third floor. I've always favoured ground floor living – that is until such time that I can afford to purchase a whole house. But living alone has made me very security conscious, and more so because I am on the ground floor. Now, as I insert the key into the lock, I sense straight away that something is wrong. There isn't the usual resistance prior to turning the key, instead there is a light wobble which indicates the door isn't as secure as when I left home earlier this evening. My heart is pounding with the dread of something terrible greeting me on the other side of the door. Should I risk going in or should I go straight back out and call the police?

Adrenaline takes over. Slowly I turn the key fully in the lock and push the door, at the same time reaching into my bag for my phone. I feel along the left wall for the dimmer switch and turn it slightly so I can just make out the outline of my furniture. I turn the dial again, shedding more light into the room. Tentatively, I step forward, into the woolly dimness. That's when I hear the tinkle of breaking glass coming from somewhere at the back of my flat, possibly the bathroom. An insurmountable fear overtakes me. I turn rapidly, slam the door behind me and run outside.

Certain that most people will either be out enjoying their Saturday night or tucked up in bed, I run the short distance up the road to number 18. If his car is there, I know he will be home. Sergio, a genial man in his mid-fifties, who works odd shifts in security and who has been kind enough to take in parcels for me on several occasions, is often home on a Saturday night. It is late, but I am desperate. His black Ford Mondeo is there. Breathless, though I have only run a few paces, I rap loudly on his door, waiting less than ten seconds before I knock again. I can see the shadow of a TV blinking through a slice in the curtain and shortly after, he opens the door, a surprised expression greeting me.

'Sergio,' I gasp. 'There's someone in my flat! Please call the police!' He stands stock still for a fraction of a second, my words catching him off guard. Then he comes to life. 'Come in, come in,' he says peering left to right before shutting the door firmly behind us. He guides me along the hallway and into his front room, where he scrambles around for his phone. In the grip of terror, it doesn't register that my own phone is in my hand.

'Police please.' Through the thudding of my heart in my ears, I hear Sergio making the call. He gives them my address and explains that there is a burglary taking place. Yes, the assailant appears to be in the flat. No, there isn't anyone in the property at the moment – at least not on the ground floor. He hangs up shortly after and motions me over to the sofa to sit down. I can see that I have disturbed his evening; I am sure he was dozing in front of the television prior to my furious knocking.

'I'm so sorry, Sergio. I didn't know where else to go.' I lower myself onto the sofa, the tiredness of minutes ago having deserted me.

'It's okay, it's okay,' he says reassuringly. 'You didn't go into the flat, did you? Did you see anyone?' His earnest, surprised tone draws attention to his fading Italian accent.

I recount my actions and tell him what I heard. 'Maybe you disturbed the person and they were escaping through the back,' he says.

We see the flashing blue lights through the window and together we exit Sergio's house. He walks just ahead of me, keeping his eye on me as I amble along behind. A male police officer steps out of the vehicle. His partner, a female officer, follows suit.

'Miss Shephard?' the male officer asks.

I nod my head.

'I'm PC Langton and this is my colleague, PC Amit. Can you tell us what happened here?'

I talk them through, from the moment I put the key into the lock to when I ran out after hearing glass shattering.

'Do you have your key, Miss Shephard?' PC Langton asks. Hands quivering, I search my pockets and handbag, trying to remember where I put it. I finally locate it in the inner pocket of my bag and hand it to the officer. 'I don't want to go in first,' I say.

He nods and takes the key from me, leading the way. 'Was the communal front door open when you arrived?' he asks.

I order my thoughts, replaying the moment I put the key into the front door. 'It was definitely locked,' I say. We move together, a tight line, walking the few paces to my flat. PC Amit looks behind at me for confirmation.

'Yes, it's this door, just here on the left,' I say. PC Langton leans slightly on the door and from my position, it doesn't appear that there's any give. It all seems secure.

'Doesn't look like a lock's been broken,' he mumbles, more to himself. 'Would you mind opening the door?' he asks, holding the key out to me.

I step forward, my fingers so inept that I struggle to perform this usually simple task.

'Was the light on when you arrived home?' This from PC Amit.

I explain that I switched it on but rushed out and didn't switch it off again. We step into the flat, gathered like a horde of sheep, looking around for anything untoward. The officers step forward and walk carefully around the room, their thick dark boots at odds with my cream carpet. They disappear along the narrow hallway leading to my bedroom, the kitchen and bathroom. Less than a minute later, they return. 'There's definitely no one here,' I am told.

To the unfamiliar eye, it looks like a relatively well-organised living area with nothing amiss, but I can see straight away that someone has been in here. I tell the officers this.

'Has anything been taken from this room?' PC Amit asks. I walk around, looking at all the things of value: my laptop, my drawing tablet and pen, speakers, my flat screen TV. Everything looks to be in its place, but it is the small detail. There is an ordered pile of letters on the floor by the sofa. That was the last thing I did before I left to meet Denny, as well as plumping up the cushions and placing my notebook on top of my laptop. But one of the sofa cushions is on the table; my notebook is wedged in the side of the sofa; the remote control is on the floor. I didn't leave the room like this. Again, I communicate this to the officers.

'Let's have a look in the other rooms. See if you notice

anything missing,' PC Langton says, his foot tapping a rhythm of impatience.

I walk into my bedroom. My jewellery is untouched. My rarely worn gold watch also snug in its velvet pouch in my top drawer. Nothing is missing, but there is an indent in the duvet, the shape of someone having recently sat down. I look under the bed as though expecting to find someone there. All that greets me is a few particles of dust.

The askance look of the officers makes me feel paranoid. Do they think I have made this up? Someone has been in my flat.

'What about the back?' I ask them. 'I definitely heard the sound of glass being smashed. Could they have broken a window or something?'

PC Langton gestures for me to lead the way. The bathroom and kitchen tell the same story. Nothing is missing.

'How do you access the garden?' I'm asked. I move the curtain that covers the door leading to my small back yard. PC Amit steps forward, scrutinising the door before taking the key from me, unbolting and unlocking it. She removes a torch from her side pocket and shines it around, stepping outside. I immediately hear the crunch beneath her feet. She bends down and shines her torch on the object. 'Looks like a broken ceramic pot,' she says.

I recall the terracotta pot that had been sitting on the low wall out there, covered in mould, waiting to be discarded.

'But what caused it to smash? Was someone trying to get away?'

'I doubt it,' PC Amit says, still carrying out her torchlight investigation. 'There are no footprints, no sign of forced entry. You've seen for yourself; the door was secure.'

Just then, I hear knocking and my name being called. I tense up, before realising it's Sonja from upstairs. 'That's my neighbour,' I tell the officers, as I head to the door.

'Oh my god!' Sonja spurts, eyes gaping, hair standing in all directions. 'I saw the police car and I thought something had happened to you.'

'I'm okay,' I say, closing my eyes briefly to ward off the swell of wooziness. 'I came home and there was someone in my flat. The police are just checking it out.'

'I've been upstairs all evening,' she says, perplexed.

The officers have wandered to the front now and are listening to what Sonja is saying. 'Are you the resident of the flat upstairs, Madam?' PC Langton asks.

'Yes, I'm right on top of Ren,' Sonja explains.

PC Langton takes out his mini notepad and pen to make some notes. 'So you didn't hear the sound of something breaking a short while ago?'

'Actually, I did hear something,' Sonja says, pensively. 'To be honest, it didn't sound close by, but I looked out of the window anyway. I didn't see anything. I thought nothing more of it.' The officer continues with his notetaking. They remain for another ten minutes or so, taking down details but convinced that my flat is secure and, because nothing is missing, the overall attitude is indifference. They probably have me down as some paranoid female, who has somehow spooked herself into believing an intruder has entered her home. I can't let them think this.

'But I'm a witness in a murder investigation.' I have to play my trump card. 'What if this has something to do with it?'

The wind changes direction. There is no disguising the shift in their demeanour, the intrigue in their expressions. PC Langton turns the page in his notepad and asks for details. While outlining Rusco's attack, I whip out the card from my purse which has the crime number and the name of the lead investigator. He takes this from me, hands it to PC Amit and without need for words, she walks to the door, radio crackling to life.

'Whether the two incidents are related or not, we still have to note this down separately,' PC Langton says. He asks a few more questions, walks around the flat again, this time checking the windows. I'm in the bathroom, splashing cold water on my face when PC Amit returns. An unreadable look passes between her and PC Langton.

'Well?' I ask, eager for information.

'Does anyone else have a key to your flat, Miss Shephard?' PC Amit asks.

'No, only me,' I say. The spare key had been with Denny but he has since given it back to me.

'It's extremely doubtful that anyone has been in here, but to err on the side of caution, I've radioed for an officer to be present outside your property, at least for tonight.'

'Does that mean you've been able to check out the attack on Ricky Usco-Lewis?' I ask hopefully.

'Does this have anything to do with the case?'

PC Amit shifts from one foot to the other. 'We aren't in a position to share any information, I'm afraid, but we would like you to be vigilant. Make sure your doors are locked securely. We will be outside until our colleague arrives.'

I want to scream in frustration. The only redeeming point is that I can feel safe tonight knowing an officer is metres away from me.

Sergio has been hovering protectively in the background during their visit. He sees them to the door and comes back in, facing me where I stand dejectedly in the living room.

'You can stay in my spare room if you want to, Ren,' he says tentatively. 'I use it as my office but there's a sofa in there.'

'Thank you, Sergio. You've been so kind already. I won't put you out. Honestly, I'll be fine, especially with an officer outside.'

'Are you sure? It won't be any bother.'

I reassure him that I will be okay, and he insists on checking again to make sure everywhere is secure. He also gives me his mobile and landline numbers and tells me not to hesitate to call him if I'm worried or scared.

He hesitates at the door. 'I'm so sorry you've been through such a bad time lately, Ren,' he says despondently.

When he leaves, I go through the process of rechecking, and it's only then I take my shoes off. I open my laptop: which is switched off, just as I left it. I know that my notebook was on top of it, not stuffed down the side of the sofa. None of the cushions were on the table and the remote control wasn't on the floor.

I leave every light on while I have a shower, put my pyjamas on and wrap myself in my nightgown. I peep through the curtain as I have done several times already. True to PC Amit's word, a single police car sits in a newly created space in front of my next-door neighbour's house. I make myself a coffee and lie down on the sofa. I can only hope that the weight of tiredness bears down upon me at some point.

Chapter 15

The days leading up to the end

I have heard people talk about feeling violated when someone enters your home, your sanctuary, with malicious intent. I'm left feeling as though someone has opened me up, stripped out a vital part and roughly sewn me back up again. PCs Langton and Amit were convinced that no one had been in my flat but they wouldn't have been ordered to station a car outside if someone in the force hadn't thought there could be a link to Rusco's killing. This is the conclusion I come to. I wish I could have been privy to their conversation on the way back to the station.

My personal protection lasts for 24 hours, and within 48 hours of the incident, I have called out a locksmith to change the front and back locks and add security locks to the windows too. I purchase and arrange the installation of a video doorbell, so I can see any activity outside the property. As far as the internal goes, I strip my bed, remove and wash the throw on my sofa and the cushion covers, scrub and polish everywhere possible to erase the feeling of being defiled. I have even shampooed the carpets and jet washed the small patio area at the back. By the time I am satisfied with my manic decontamination spree, I feel as if I have sanitised my soul.

But an inner war still rages. How do I extricate myself

from this mess and get back to a place where my world feels normal and stable? If the intruder was a figment of my imagination, it boils down to one thing: Rusco's murder is affecting my sanity. I wish I could press the reset button and never have embarked on this course. Now with the whole incident potentially putting my life in danger, I am on tenterhooks to the point that I can't even trust my own judgement.

I undertake a slow hike through the early part of the week. Every step, every action, every decision is like climbing a mountain with no foothold or handgrip; no gravity to harness me. I'm torn between attending the final Zoom lesson or cutting this volatile chapter from my life once and for all; drawing the line under everything before the mountain collapses with me still on it. But there is also a part of me that, strangely, equates getting to the end of the course with bringing closure to this horrendous ordeal. Not to mention the achievement of seeing the course through to the end. Whatever happens, I still intend to prioritise my writing when the course is over.

My greatest contest this week is having to communicate with Josh, fielding off his numerous attempts for us to meet up again. Fobbing him off with the excuse of being under the weather reaches its shelf life, so, I come up with another excuse that I hope will put an end to his efforts:

I still have feelings for my ex-boyfriend. I don't think it's fair for us to keep seeing each other. Unvarnished, straight up, no apology. I can't be sure if this is another lie, or if there is some truth to my words.

His response: *That's a shame.*

I speak to Denny about the intruder and even he sounds sceptical, but he still offers to stay with me for a few days which I decline. It wouldn't be fair to draw him into this. He has done enough already. I just have to deal with it myself.

Thursday morning begins with a thunderstorm. It has been brewing for days, bringing a much-needed downpour to the arid few weeks we have had. The type of thunderstorm that communicates anger, violence, the universe being at odds, and all not being well. The best place to be on a day like this is indoors; preferably wrapped up in a duvet in front of the TV. Thankfully, the '*being indoors*' part works for me, but wrapping up in front of the TV will have to come later. First, I have an important event to attend: my final creative writing session.

It has taken two cups of coffee and a 30-minute meditation session before I feel as ready as I can be to retreat into the virtual world once again. My laptop sits in front of me, my notebook open to a new page with my pen lying on top. I am sitting cross-legged, listening to the rain beating its fury against the window, but the steady snapping sound is somehow soothing.

A temporary distraction comes in the form of Mum and Dad. We haven't had any communication since I fired off my angry rant about their poor parenting skills and neglectful attitude towards Faye.

Hi Sereny,

We're still in the middle of a heatwave and your mum is still contorting herself into 101 different positions. Your sister has been in touch. She sounds better.

Not much to glean from that. Maybe this is Dad's indirect way of addressing my fury at their behaviour. I don't feel the urge to respond just yet, but at least they've had some communication with Faye.

I'm logged in and waiting at 9:56am. *Nothing to lose, nothing to fear…* I repeat to myself.

One by one, faces emerge on the screen; positive and eager, perhaps relishing the final day of the course and thinking about the possibilities that exist beyond. At 10am, we are all present, the indistinct background noise from mics not switched off, awaiting Tarquin's greeting and overview.

Mary, at first, appears slightly pixelated and grainy, giving the impression of someone not meant for this world. Her expression is blank; staring straight ahead into the abyss. I focus on her, wondering about this face of immorality. What is going on in her head? In her world? She leans downwards towards her left, distracted by something out of camera shot. Her blank expression turns into a wide smile as she returns to an upright position. In her arms she is holding a glossy black cat which nuzzles into her neck, seeking attention and a gentle stroke which she loyally obliges. A sight like this would ordinarily arouse an 'Ahhh, how cute', but watching Mary, the only thought that comes to mind is: evil witch. I shiver slightly and divert my attention away from her.

My eyes travel across the screen, briefly taking in each of my fellow classmates. I'm trying hard to keep my attention away from him, but like an itch that needs to be scratched, I stop at the little box allocated to Josh. One of the quirks of technology is that it can be difficult to judge real emotions, but Josh wears his for the world to see. He looks troubled. Resting his chin on his hand, he drums his fingers rhythmically and restlessly on his upper lip. At times he looks directly at me, his eyes flashing with heat. A glare of defiance, challenging me to communicate with him. The charming warmth of a week ago, buried underneath this other Josh.

'Well done, Seedlings, you've made it to the end!' Tarquin's sense of joy is uncontainable. 'For every one of you, the journey is just beginning, and you should be exceptionally proud of yourselves.' His enthusiasm is contagious. Ally, Gillian and Michelle Mac smile and nod like excited children. It's a pity I haven't been able to inject the same level of dedication to the course as my counterparts. For me it has been a hybrid: making tentative steps to engage with my creative side, juxtaposed with the worst experience of my life.

'Your journal should be bursting with variety and flavour!' Tarquin continues, clasping his hands together. 'Ideas, characters, descriptions, scribbles, sketches. Of course, you won't be making use of all your workings, but I hope that the seed of an idea has sprouted from something you've written during the last seven weeks.'

I graze through the pages of my notebook: A few spider grams; some scribbled thoughts, character notes and descriptions of Nadine and Ben, some short paragraphs of plot ideas. There are some other isolated pieces of work on my laptop; but altogether this is disproportionate to the amount of work I should have completed so far. My shoulders slump for a moment. I can't help thinking that if the world hadn't gone into deep freeze; months of lockdowns and isolations resulting in a boom in distance learning, things would be very different. I would be sitting at a table across from real-life fellow aspiring writers, conversing face-to-face, looking over each other's shoulders, sharing biscuits and ideas in the same physical space. There would be no mystery murder keeping me on edge and disrupting my life.

Tarquin's voice infiltrates my thoughts. 'So, for most of the session you'll work independently to continue moving ahead in your individual directions. What aspect of your creation would you like to explore? Is it a character? If so, flesh them out. Is it a plot? If so, harness it and step into it.' He pauses to take a sip from a mug beside him.

'You are all sailing your own boats, masters of your own seas; I'm expecting the voyages to be very different. It will be interesting to know what is next for each of you.' He takes a moment to lean back and smile patronisingly at his 'Seedlings'. Is he expecting a round of applause?

When everyone remains silent, he continues: 'So that leads me onto my next point. You should all be aware of the one-to-one tutorial times that I shared with you last week. So, from 10:30, I'll begin the ten-minute feed-forward slots as allocated, whilst the individual work continues.'

I have about an hour to complete some work before my scheduled slot, and I need to use the time sagely. No more daydreaming, attempting to crime-solve. I need to get my head into gear. I minimise the Zoom app on my laptop and open the Word document I created for this course.

I still have my sights set on a teenage audience. I want to explore relationships, vulnerabilities; I want to tap into their world. And from an altruistic perspective, I want them to read more. For my novel to work, I need to re-engage with my teenage self. They can't read a work of fiction that sounds as if it's been written by their mum. My years of experience working with teenagers will come in handy. I revisit my notes on Nadine and Ben and wonder what exactly I am going to do with them, or the sketchy ideas I have. How do I fit them together?

The rain continues to beat an unyielding rhythm, as I seek out the last page of notes I made of some possible storylines. But something I can't quite place my finger on is amiss. Frowning, I flip backwards and forwards, suddenly realising that there are some frayed strips in the spiral binding. A page has been carelessly ripped out, leaving small fragments of paper jutting out in between my pages of written notes. I'm lost for a moment. I took Tarquin's early advice not to get rid of anything we write: one-off activities, scribbled drafts, even careless doodling – all part of the creative process, he had said. I look at the pages preceding and following the missing sheet, and then like an unexpected punch, it hits me. The bullet-pointed notes I made about Rusco's case! I turn the pages again, hoping I have somehow missed it. My hands slacken. It is no longer there. Someone has removed that page. I sit for a long time, staring into space.

When the police came round to investigate the intruder in my flat, I had sworn to them that my notebook had been moved. This is the confirmation that I need. It was not my imagination. Someone had been in my flat. They had bypassed my laptop, my jewellery, various electronic gadgets, a few expensive handbags, yet they ripped a single, specific page out of my notebook.

The vibrating ping alerts me that an hour has passed by already, a reminder of my one-to-one slot with Tarquin. This latest revelation has thrown me, and an invisible layer of film wraps itself around me, restricting my breathing. I manage an acute, agonised inhale, then I maximise my Zoom app. Re-entering and waiting to be connected, I switch my camera back on. I'm there for less than a minute before Tarquin's thin face appears, dominating the right side of my screen. Seconds pass while he simply looks at me, a watery smile playing around the corners of his mouth. From this close position, I notice there is a slight dishevelment to his appearance; the buttons and holes of his shirt mismatched at the top. His eyes have taken on a beady look, as if he is searching for something through the screen. Is that a trace of left-over breakfast on his lower lip?

I break the silence.

'Hello again, Tarquin.' My voice sounds awkward, as if it belongs to someone else.

'Ren! What will you do next?' I'm not sure if I expected him to mention our encounter of a few weeks ago, but I'm surprised there is no small talk, no preamble, instead he skips to what feels like the end of the conversation.

'Well, err,' I stutter, caught off-guard. 'I definitely want to continue writing.' What a stupid, obvious response. My temple gives in to the slow onset of a headache. 'I want to write for teenagers.'

'Okay.'

He's not helping me, with his overly consuming stare and clipped response.

I go on to tell him about the characters I've been playing around with and some of my ideas.

'Have you thought about—', his image fizzles and distorts, giving him the appearance of a gremlin. His voice is stuttery and robotic; I'm catching every third or fourth word.

'I think you're losing connection, Tarquin.' My voice is elevated. 'I can't hear you properly and your screen has gone funny.'

He appears, reformed, for a few seconds. 'Sorry. My connection has been in and out this last hour; might be to do with the weather. I'm just going to reposition myself closer to the hub. Can you give me a minute, please?'

His camera goes off and he switches to mute while I sit and wait. Moments later, he is back; somewhere in the same room by the look of the wallpaper behind him.

'That should be better,' he says, and I nod to indicate that I can hear him clearly again. We continue the conversation where we had left off, but I'm grappling for coherence; my sentences are disjointed and unintelligent. Something in his background is biting for my attention and I can't focus on it and talk to Tarquin at the same time.

An open shelving unit stands solidly behind him displaying the usual paraphernalia: a framed painting that looks like a couple of magpies on a roof, a couple of mini trophies, something that looks like a snow globe and a pair of small circular speakers. I take this all in quickly with cursory glances. It all looks very busy and cluttered. But it is the certificate just behind his left shoulder that demands my attention. When he speaks, moving his head and hands, I catch glimpses but I'm unable to view it in its entirety.

'I can direct you to some of the courses that might be suitable for you,' Tarquin informs me. 'I'll just make a note of the points we've discussed so I can send you some links later.' He inclines to his left, assumedly to write on a pad on the surface in front of him, and at this point I'm able to lean forward and read the words on the certificate behind him.

Open Learn
Professional Studies
Statement of Participation
Awarded to:
Andrew Shales

A flame ignites and then a whole fire erupts at my core. A legion of emotions pass through me in a heady, agonising rush. I battle to assume a poker face and extinguish the blazing heat. My breaths are raspy; only my fingers digging painfully and deeply into my palms stop me from screaming.

What do I do? What do I do?

Tarquin, oblivious to my emotions, is busy mumbling to himself whilst jotting down some notes. Without diverting my eyes from the screen, I drag my phone along the table towards me, unlock it with my fingerprint and swipe left to my camera app. Hurriedly, I direct my camera at the screen, zoom in and take a picture – just as Tarquin looks up.

The fractional downward movement of his eyebrows makes me gasp. Did he see me?

I come to my senses quickly. 'Sorry, I was just sending a message to my friend,' I say, my voice wobbling, false and hollow to my ears, trapped in the type of questionable lie my students used to tell me when they had been caught accessing a social media site during a lesson.

I hold my breath, expecting to be confronted by an irate,

affronted Tarquin, but he simply continues to observe me, blinking rapidly, before adjusting himself to his previous position. The remainder of the conversation is like being encapsulated in a soundproof bubble. His lips are moving, I'm responding, but I have no clue what's being said by either of us. It cannot come to an end soon enough.

As soon as I hang up, and before we are called back together for our final encounter as a group, I leave a garbled voice message for Denny, as well as sending him a picture of the certificate. I guzzle down a pint of cold water to quell the raging fire.

Tarquin St John is Andrew Shales?

I can't think of any other explanation. Have the police connected the dots already? What is his relationship to Mary? Are they husband and wife? The questions, like discharging missiles, come quickly and resound loudly against a brick wall. Any thought of Tarquin being misunderstood – just a quirky, harmless character – has been intercepted. I am now unequivocally certain that he is a very dangerous man.

***

The Insight Academy creative writing course ends with a Kahoot quiz and lots of well-wishes from one to another, whilst I hover in the background caught in a net with my hands tied behind my back. There is nothing in Tarquin's demeanour that tells me he's aware of what I saw. Josh sends me a message minutes before the end:

I hope this isn't it for us, Ren?

Always an interrogative; his attempt to initiate a dialogue. I ignore him.

I have been checking my phone every few seconds, hoping for a response from Denny. Nothing. I had hoped (wishful thinking I know) that the end of this course would come with some sort of closure to this mystery. But, like a game of Whac-a-Mole, every time my mallet hits upon an explanation, something else pops up. I'm pacing the floor of my living room, annoyed that the soothing sound of the rain has now ceased. When my phone beeps, I am almost disappointed to see a message from Kizzy in our WhatsApp chat. I don't bother reading it, but I open the chat and send a clipped summary of what has happened. I can't even remember if I told them about the intruder in my flat. In less than ten minutes, Kizzy calls me. Something in my rapid, muddled monologue troubles her.

'Ren, I'm not keeping up with what you're saying,' she interrupts. 'Look, why don't we meet? I had an appointment first thing this morning in Blackfriars, but I'm not going back to the office. I can take a bit of a detour and meet you for lunch somewhere?'

My stomach rumbles in response, protesting at its need for a proper meal. Stepping out of the confines of my flat would probably be a good idea; at least I won't be counting the seconds until Denny gets in touch. I agree to meet Kizzy in Clapham. I can jump in the car and be there in twenty minutes. Her journey from Blackfriars will take double that time.

Before heading out, I dig out the telephone and reference number I was given when I reported the crime. Surely the police are onto this already. But without any way to confirm or refute it, I feel duty bound to report today's discovery. This time, I'm not met by the gruelling task of trying to get through to the right person. I navigate my way smoothly through two helpful staff members and then I am speaking to someone who has the crime details open on a screen in front of them.

'So that's how I made the connection between Tarquin St John and Andrew Shales.'

PC Grayson has been kind enough to listen to my recount without interruption or sending out any negative vibes. I can hear the tap of his keyboard interlaced with my words, so I gather he is taking me seriously.

'Okay, Miss Shephard,' he says, still typing away. 'Thank you for reporting this to us.'

'So what happens now?' I ask urgently. I don't want to give him a chance to utter a quick goodbye and then hang-up on me.

'The information you've given me has been fed into the system. Both cases are still open... and active,' he says guardedly. When he realises I'm waiting for more, he clears his throat. 'Unfortunately, I can't disclose the nature of the investigations, but every piece of information is being treated with utmost importance.'

I have no choice but to accept his words. They are pretty much what I have come to expect. Maybe they are already aware of the connection and the investigation is moving forward. I take a breath, about to ask if there's any way I can be kept in the loop, but the continuous drill informs me that my conversation with PC Grayson has ended.

The streets are soggy and washed out after the earlier deluge, which equates to more traffic on the road and a prolonged journey. With parking restrictions forming a circle of exclusion around the majority of Clapham, I swing my car into Asda's car park. I will have to be mindful not to exceed the maximum two-hour parking limit. I make a mental note to pop into the supermarket afterwards to pick up a few items.

I rush into Costa, twenty minutes later than we planned to meet. Kizzy is already there, her attire contrasting with mine: scruffy house jeans, and my old mac thrown over a creased, stained t-shirt, whilst Kizzy looks like the professional city worker she is – pencil skirt, kitten-heeled shoes and a striped lilac shirt, an ensemble which suits her. Her handbag has been chosen to match; expensive and big enough to fit Cory, and a few of his nappies too.

When she hugs me, she comments on how frail I am. Encased in her solid and loyal embrace, the barriers that have been strained to capacity suddenly burst, and I can't hold back any longer. The tremors ripple through me as loud, unruly sobs bubble their way to the surface. 'I feel as if I'm going mad, Kiz,' I cry, my face tucked into her shoulder. 'I just can't believe what's happening. I know I'm not crazy, but I feel as if I am.'

Kizzy makes soothing sounds, hugging me tighter. 'It's okay, hun. It's okay.' She strokes my hair gently, not caring that my outburst is attracting curious looks from people around us.

'It will be alright. Just let it out for now.' She rubs my back lightly until my sobs have subsided, holding out a tissue for me to wipe my streaming eyes and nose.

'It's like the worst hellish nightmare you can imagine,' I say, once I find my voice. My throat feels raw, and I can barely see out of my sore, watery eyes. 'I know it sounds really horrible to say this, but Rusco seems to have paled into insignificance now. It's everything else that is happening. It feels like I'm drowning in responsibility and – and – I have to get to the bottom of it before I can start to live again.'

'You're not responsible for this, Ren. You are not the one who—'

'I know I'm not to blame; I know that.' I jump in because I don't think she really understands. 'But I feel so close to this, as if there is something I have to do to solve it. Maybe something I've missed.'

Kizzy clasps my face in her hands. 'Ren, will you listen to yourself!' she says in exasperation. 'This is not your battle.

Yes, you witnessed the most awful crime possible, I don't doubt that for a minute, but it is not your responsibility to solve it.' I've never heard Kizzy speak so decisively, authoritatively, before.

I sniff loudly and shake out of her grip. 'I know. But look at everything that's happened since I saw Rusco killed.' The spotlight shines on a trailer of stills in my mind: Rusco, a knife to his throat. Mary, heaving the sack. The police, cordoning off Barcourt Road. The scene of crime officer, delicately removing the body bag. Then I see Josh, glaring at me. And, finally, Tarquin/Andrew, putting something into my drink? It now seems likely my original outburst was well-founded.

'Listen to me, Ren.' Kizzy moves her chair closer to mine, so our knees are touching. 'I can't say I know what you're going through because I don't. But you've reached breaking point now.' She nods, confident that her statement cannot be disputed.

'You've contacted the police; you've got Denny finding out what he can. You've got to step away now and think about your wellbeing and your safety.'

I nod, solemnly. It's time to prioritise. I have to wipe the slate clean, maybe take a holiday somewhere and try to heal from this trauma. I know it won't be easy not to think about it, but I can't sink any further into this cesspit. Kizzy orders some coffees and two rounds of cheese and tomato paninis. I eat and drink mechanically, glad for the refuelling but not tasting the meal as it goes down. Kizzy's harsh but sensible words help to ameliorate my current state of mind, just a bit. However, I'm conscious that her time is precious, and she should be at home working or resuming her mummy duties.

'I'll just pop to the loo,' I say, aware that on top of my swollen eyes, I am also dishevelled and in need of a shower. I splash cold water on my face, blow my nose then return to our table. Kizzy follows suit while I sit and wait for her, gazing mindlessly out of the window. I hear an unfamiliar chime and notice that Kizzy's phone, which is beside me on the table, has lit up. I glance at it, seeing Lex's name flash up. I'm not being nosy but with the message right in front of me, I am able to read it before it disappears from the screen.

What's the verdict? Something's definitely up. I think she's losing it.

I have no doubt that the message is about me. Is this what they think? That I'm crazy? This is obviously one in a stream of messages they've exchanged. I feel despondent; let down. My closest friends, conversing about me behind my back, questioning whether I'm sane.

There is nothing more for me here. I pick the phone up and tuck it into Kizzy's bag on the chair beside me, zip it up and place her coat securely on top. Then I get up from my seat and head back to my car. I don't even bother to stop in Asda to do any shopping.

When I arrive home, I double lock myself into my flat, fastidiously checking (in a way I have only started doing since last week) that the doors and windows are all secure. Denny must have rung me while I was driving home, because when I take my phone out, there is a voice message from him.

'Ren. Sorry I missed you earlier. I can't believe what you sent me. I'm really shocked! I haven't been able to speak to Rob, but I've left a message for him.' There is the clack-clack of foot-steps, and I can hear a car revving loudly in the background. *'Do you want to meet soon?'* He pauses. *'I think we should. I'm on a course in Sheffield today but I'll be back tomorrow afternoon so if you're free in the evening, or Saturday, let me know. Oh, and if you call and I don't answer, I'll call you back as soon as I can. It's a bit full-on at the minute… Okay… Look after yourself, Ren. Speak soon… It's Denny by the way!'*

The last sentence is tongue-in-cheek, a little in-joke we used to share. I manage a weak smile and replay the message, in need of something positive, just a droplet of comfort to cling to.

I must get it together. I have online lessons tomorrow that I need to prepare for. Thankfully, Sharma, from the agency, hasn't got back to me with details of my new students. I don't think I could muster the enthusiasm to engage with them right now. Notwithstanding, I put together an introductory PowerPoint presentation in readiness, then I prepare tomorrow's lesson, including several links so I can send them off to do some independent work.

Later that evening, I receive an email from Tarquin/Andrew. Keeping to his word, he has included some links to courses available for writing for a teenage market. He has also included a message:

Dear Ren,

Thank you for your participation in the creative journey introductory course. I am sorry about the negative experience you encountered along the way and I hope you are able to get back on track with your writing.

I couldn't help but notice that you appeared distracted during our one-to-one session. I hope you are okay.

You will be interested to know that the police investigation into the crime you witnessed has gained traction and I for one have been working with the police to ensure the matter is concluded imminently and justly.

Attached are the links to the courses we discussed.

I wish you the very best of luck on your continued creative journey.

All the best,

Tarquin St John.

What a sophisticated liar! I can only wonder if this man believes the nonsense that comes out of his mouth. This is obviously some sort of ploy to lure me away from his evil stench. I stare at the email, sure that the police will be interested in reading it, which means another phone call to the crime team to get the email address I need to forward it to.

I decide not to cut off my nose to spite my face, so I click on one of the links Tarquin has recommended. It takes me to an Insight Academy course: Writing for teenagers. A year long, distant learning study programme with five modules. Just as he recommended, all the courses I glance at relate to my interests, so I '*star*' the email, promising that I will go through each of the courses in detail when the time is right, but with no intention of signing up to another course with Insight Academy.

Now I focus my attention on the missed messages and calls from Kizzy and Lex, all sent after I left the coffee shop in Clapham. Six unread messages and three missed calls. I don't want to hear anything they have to say, and neither do I want them turning up on my doorstep. Without reading any of the stream, I type a quick message:

Hi both. Just need some time out please. Catch up soon.

I hope this is enough to act as a deterrent and keep the wolves away from my door.

I'm not sure when I fall asleep, but I wake in darkness. For long moments, I try to gather my bearings. I'm on the sofa, fully clothed, curtains drawn. Something woke me, but it is a moment before I am aware of a gentle tapping on my window, at the same time my doorbell app alerts me to motion outside. In my sensitive state, I'm tempted to crawl under the table and hide, but this is not me.

Opening my phone, I access the black and white image of a large figure in dark clothes. He has retreated to the front gate, and I squint at my phone, trying to clear the sleep from my vision. I let out the breath that I hadn't realised I was holding. It's Sergio. I rush to the window, part the curtain slightly and tap the glass so he can see me. I mouth to him that *I'm coming*.

I grab my bunch of keys, slip on my trainers and exit the flat, pulling the door shut behind me. Then I head to the front door.

'I just wanted to check on you, Ren,' Sergio says, his attentiveness causing me to well up.

'Thank you, so much, Sergio,' I say, earnestly, swallowing the lump in my throat. 'Do you want to come in?'

'No. I just wanted to make sure you're alright after the other night.'

'I'm fine, honestly. I've changed all the locks, and installed a video doorbell, so I feel much safer,' I say, only partly true, but I am hardly going to unburden myself to Sergio – lovely as he is.

'That's good,' Sergio says, giving me a thumbs up. 'If you need anything, just let me know. Okay?'

I'm so touched by his kindness, and slightly guilty because I had been hoping he would decline my offer to come in. He is a sweet chap and he's proved to be a great neighbour, but I don't feel like company. At some point, I will buy him a bottle of something nice to thank him for his neighbourly concern.

He is leaning forward, peering at me curiously. He points to the side of my head.

'Your head, Ren. You're bleeding.' I touch my temple. My hand comes away sticky with fresh blood. At the same time, I feel the burning sensation of a reopened wound.

'It's okay,' I say. 'I had an accident some time ago and it's taking a while to heal. I've just been lying on my side, so I've probably scratched it on the edge of my sofa.'

He nods. 'Okay. Go look after your head. Take care and remember what I said.'

'Thanks again, Sergio. You've been amazing.'

'Just being a good neighbour,' he says shyly. 'Bye, Ren.'

I close the door and pull the chain across before scampering back into my flat, going through my usual security routine. My sleep hasn't done much to shake the bulky load of tiredness that makes my eyelids feel as if they are being weighted down. I check the side of my head in the mirror. It's bleeding but not badly. It tingles a bit, and I can see where I have scraped at the healing scab. I press some dressing against it, taping it down at the edges. I strip down to my underwear, not even bothering to shower, throw on my night-dress and climb into bed, eager to put another day of ambiguity behind me.

Chapter 16

The day it ends

On Friday morning, I wake feeling refreshed after a good night's sleep. My head is still slightly tender, but thankfully the bleeding has stopped. I spend most of the morning and early afternoon delivering my online lessons, which are well received by my keen students. It provides a much-needed distraction, and I'm not even fussed that both lessons overrun.

Sharma sends me an outline of four students I can add to my worklist, with dates and times when they are available, alongside a summary of each of their tutoring requirements. This is good news for me: more students equate to more money, and a chance to spend a bit more time in the wilderness before I knuckle down to looking for something full-time. Tapping into the thought I had yesterday, I toy with the idea of going away for a break somewhere. I can continue my lessons from any of the destinations I would choose to visit. Even though I must think about my purse-strings, after the recent ordeal I've had, I think a holiday is justified.

My spirit deflates when my phone alerts me to a message from Josh.

Hey Ren,

Shame I won't get to see your pretty face light up my screen anymore. But we will get together soon.

A flagrant disregard of my previous message. Which part of *I don't want to see you* does he not understand? There is a cocky assuredness about him, almost as if it is only a matter of time before he reels me into his clutches.

I ignore the message.

When my phone pings again, a short while after, I clench my teeth, expecting another message from Josh, and pondering briefly if I'm going to have to change my number. I pick up the phone in annoyance, but I'm pleased and relieved that the message is from Denny:

Hiya,

All okay? On way back from Sheffield. I've spoken to Rob. Been some developments. You free to meet this eve?

I read the message over again: Please let this be the news that brings an end to this saga and the justice that Rusco deserves.

Hi Den,

Okay thanks. No plans this eve, so yeah, be good to meet up. I can come to your end this time, save you another journey after your trek back from Sheffield.

He responds within minutes:

Veya – 7pm?

Sounds lovely! I respond.

Great. Will book.

A cache of fond memories dance around as I recall some great times spent at Veya – all involving Denny. The best being my 25th birthday where Denny laid on a surprise dinner with all my favourite people and some of our mutual friends. Our relationship had still been in its embryonic stage, the year of celebrating our firsts as a couple: first birthdays, first Christmas, first holiday – all leading up to our first anniversary. Since then, it had become one of our go-to places when we wanted the guarantee of fantastic food without the risk of exploring somewhere new. It's a fusion restaurant with an ever-expanding menu, blending the most basic dishes in a way that galvanises them straight to food heaven.

The thought of delicious food is enough to allow the purpose of our meeting to take a back seat. In fact, the hours I have spent today, without the unrelenting thoughts of Rusco-gate assailing me, have reinforced the need to cast this depressing episode to the yonder regions of my brain. I will make it clear to Denny that although I'm grateful for everything he has done to help me, today will be the end of any more sleuthing and poring over Rusco's murder. The police are the ones responsible for bringing the criminals to justice. Kizzy is right. As long as I am safe and well, that should be the extent of my concern. I should be grateful that I never have to see Josh, Mary or Tarquin/Andrew again.

I contemplate how I have allowed my involvement in all this to shunt my relationship with Kizzy and Lex. The strength of our friendship will see to it that we are okay; it can't be easy for them watching me fall apart. Any conversation they've had in my absence would have been with my best interests at heart. I don't have the right to be mad at them. Since I entered this dark world, not only have I missed a significant event in my friend's healing journey, but every conversation has centred around me. I make the decision that after I've met with Denny this evening, my priority will be to put things right with them. They mean the world to me, and I can't imagine being at odds with them for any length of time.

For the first time in a while, I'm making positive, pragmatic decisions and looking ahead with clarity and hope. Small steps to reconnect with the Ren Shephard that existed before this nightmare began.

I take my time getting ready. My hair would benefit from the magical fingers of my hairdresser, but I make do with a deep condition. I blow dry it, and then set to work with my curling tongs, giving it some light curls that add body and bounce. Not one for face paint, I moisturise my skin, add a layer of mascara and my favourite Rimmel lipstick with the nude shimmer. I opt for smart slim-fit jeans, a frill-neck top, and my check boucle blazer. I assess myself in my full-length bedroom mirror, feeling pleased with the overall result.

***

Veya is in a great location close to Oxford Street station, which makes it a straightforward journey for both Denny and me. The weather is dry and mild, so not surprisingly everyone is out and about making the most of their Friday evening. I take a leisurely stroll along Oxford Street, dodging between groups of tourists, commuters, people heading out for the evening. By the time I enter the eatery, it is 7:05pm and I'm sure Denny will be there already.

A cheery waiter takes my name and leads me to a window table in the large restaurant, decorated to reflect the spirit of the Far East. I decline his offer to order a drink just yet, but he informs me that he'll bring a jug of water and a couple of glasses. The table is ready for us, and I use the time to peruse the menu. I'm already drooling at the sound of a Singapore Sandwich, Vietnamese Pizza, Pad Thai Taco, thinking that we may need to go for the taster menu, so we get to sample as many goodies as possible.

The music in the background is louder than it needs to be, but the tune is melodic and easy on the ear. With the air conditioning blowing nearby, it feels a bit too cool to take off my jacket. Maybe after a glass of wine. It's been a while since I've sat down to people-watch, and I lose myself in the activities occurring beyond the glass. A large group of women in a rainbow of short skirts and high heels, move together as one, like an ocean wave, giggling uproariously. The prospect of a fun-filled night ahead. Then there is the Asian couple, (the Union Jack bandana around the man's neck a giveaway to their tourist status) who have stopped to consult their map, either lost or planning where to go next.

The mishmash of people makes it easy to sit back and watch the world go by, making up stories about who they are, what brought them to this part of London and how their night will end. I'm so caught up in a world of make-believe that when I look at the clock on the wall, I'm surprised to see it's 7:25pm. Around me, diners are tucking into a host of scrumptious smelling meals, causing me to rub my hungry stomach. I check my phone, certain that Denny would have messaged or called to let me know that he is running late, but there is no word from him.

When the waiter saunters over a few minutes later, I order a bottle of wine. I'm sure by the time it's sitting in front of me, Denny will be here. It doesn't take him long to return, tray in hand and an inviting bottle of pale Rosé. I take the liberty of pouring a glass for each of us. I also send Denny a message.

I'm at Veya. Hope you're okay? I can usually set my watch by you.

I return to people-watching, sipping my glass of wine, which hits the spot perfectly. Five minutes later, I put in a call to Denny. When it goes to voicemail, I'm in two minds whether to leave a message, I'm sure he wouldn't have forgotten about meeting me. That's not like him. I decide to leave one, just in case.

Now the restaurant is almost full and I begin to feel anxious. I know he booked the table. The reservation had been made in my name. Could he have done this whilst still on the train from Sheffield? I quickly check through the news channels, hoping there hasn't been any breaking news of a major train incident or anything similar. Nothing comes up.

An hour goes by, and I'm still sitting at our table, alone. I'm thankful for the waiter's patience, but it's clear from the swelling crowd that I have overstayed my welcome. I've had a glass and a half of wine, and with my stomach starting to ache from hunger, it's not a wise idea to consume any more. I send another message to Denny; a mixture of worry and disappointment filling the empty space opposite me:

Not sure where you are but I'm heading home. Please call me.

I beckon the waiter over, apologise for Denny's no-show and pay for my bottle of half-drunk wine. I rise too quickly and I'm accosted by a wave of dizziness. I take a couple of mouthfuls of water poured from the jug on the table. I'm sure I receive a few sympathetic glances from some of the diners as I take the *'I've been stood up'* path, right through the middle of the restaurant and back onto Oxford Street. The thought of heading home doesn't come with its usual temptation. Perhaps I'm holding out hope that I will get a frantic call from Denny with a valid reason why he's been held up. The moment I head down into the bowels of the underground there will be no chance of any communication until I exit the tube at Brixton Station.

I take a slow walk heading towards Piccadilly Circus. I can always jump on the underground from there. The air is mild and slightly cloying with all the bodies manoeuvring their way in different directions. It's been a long time since I walked along these streets. I stop and look in a few shop windows, not paying much attention to anything, simply whiling away some time and getting lost in the busy bustle of the West End. When I reach Piccadilly Circus I extract my phone, even though I've had it in my bag clutched against my side in the hope I would feel it vibrate against me. No messages. No missed calls. There seems no point hanging around. Something has obviously come up and I just hope he's okay. Deflated, I disappear down into the station. Now I'm eager to get home.

The unnatural heat of the underground, like having warm air pumped beneath your clothes, leaves me in a sticky, damp sweat, so by the time I exit Brixton underground station just after 9pm, I'm desperate for the coolness of the outside air. The uninterrupted flow of activity that keeps Brixton operating like a mechanical Lego city adds to a feeling of safety. I've never known anywhere that is filled with such an eclectic combination of folks. From the homeless duo, woven into Brixton's tapestry, to the wealthy suited types who now occupy many of the expensive Victorian properties. The mix is also reflected in the eateries that cater for all budgets.

My flat is a ten-minute walk from the station. I could jump on a bus for two stops, but looking at the slow-moving traffic, it's not worth waiting. I pass the snaking queue of Saturday evening revellers, eagerly waiting to indulge in some finger-licking chicken, then on past the famous Windrush Square and the many bodies that loiter around. Music blares from more than one source as they participate in their own little outdoor raves. I can't help but smile at this sense of freedom and unconstrained enjoyment. Past this point, the roads are well lit, but then it becomes more residential. I turn onto Saltoun Road, leaving the trail of activity behind me.

The transition from vibrant sounds to fading tones makes my sense of sound more acute. That's why I'm sure that as well as my own footsteps, someone else's are present not too far behind me. I turn swiftly but all I see are parked cars and tall streetlamps, glowing down on me. I cross the road and head towards Kellet Road, thankful that this part of my journey will put me back in touch with activity and bodies. I can already hear the boisterous drinkers spilling out onto the street in front of The Green Man; some remaining to loiter outside, others staggering away. I pass them by, wondering what level of clean-up operation will be inflicted upon the poor staff come throwing out time.

The final part of my journey takes me beyond the pub, along a connecting residential street, past the now-closed phone repair kiosk, and then onto Braisley Road. Five minutes, at my steady pace, and I'll be home. The first thing I plan to do when I get in is find out where Denny is. If another phone call is left unanswered, I'll do a ring round, see if anyone has heard from him. The numbers of his closest friends are still stored in my phone.

My feet snap loudly on the pavement, the Saturday evening volume being turned down with each step I take. There is a sudden shift in atmosphere as the street takes on a shadowy darkness. When I look up, I realise that the streetlight nearest to me isn't exuding any light, causing a rim of gloom to settle around me. The hairs on the back of my neck feel sensitive; that feeling that indicates danger is nearby. I turn again, but apart from the vague outlines of people in the distance, the road is clear. Without slowing my pace, I reach into my bag and extract my phone. I yank it out too quickly forcing my bunch of keys to eject and clatter noisily to the ground.

'Shit,' I mutter, stooping to pick them up. Rising, I sway and wobble. Light-headed. The car beside me acts as my stabiliser. I shouldn't have had that second glass of wine. I tuck my keys back into my bag. This is the instant when I know there is a presence behind me. That sixth sense. No need for proof. My heart concertinas in my chest. There isn't enough air in my lungs to inhale. I know before I turn around who it's going to be.

'No need to panic, babe,' Josh's breath is hot against my neck, his voice menacing to my ears. 'And if you want to see Denny again, you definitely aren't going to make a noise.' He grips my arm so that even through my jacket, I feel it, pincer-like and steadfast.

'Josh!' I finally find my breath. 'W-what are you doing here?' I ask stupidly, wincing from the pain in my arm.

Josh takes charge, walking us quickly in the opposite direction to my route, further away from any activity or light. I catch a glimpse. A cold panoptic dread hovers and settles. His eyes are an inferno, the rage so intense it frightens me to the bone. I recall the words he'd said in jest: *Wait till you see my ogre impression.* But there is nothing remotely amusing about the ogre that has latched himself to me.

'Where's Denny? Please don't hurt him,' I implore.

'Shut up and keep walking.' A patronising singsong tone but filled with venom.

'What is this about, Josh? I don't understand what's going on!' Not totally true, but I hope I can talk him out of whatever he is planning to do.

'Don't play stupid, Ren. You know what it's about. You should have left well alone when you had the chance. Not rushing around playing detective as if you knew what you were doing.' He spits out every word, his voice becoming irate and frenzied.

The shutters have come down on my brain. How many movies have I watched where the victim, in their panicked state, knows exactly what to say and what action to take to free themselves from a dangerous situation? There must be several things I can do and say, but none of them come together in a co-ordinated way. If anyone were to see us they would assume we are a couple, walking as if we have merged into one. That is until they look closely and see my expression of abject terror and the intense anger of my predator.

But this isn't just about me, it's about Denny too. I can't allow Denny to come to any harm. This is my battle. Hurt me, but don't hurt him.

'Where are you taking me?' I ask, tempering down my rising hysteria.

Josh doesn't respond. He continues to speed walk, the grip on my arm unceasing. How does he even know this area? Has he been watching me for some time, aware of my every movement? Was he in my flat?

In the distance, I see the silhouette of a small group of people heading in our direction. I tense. Josh senses it. He leans into me. 'Don't even fucking try it,' he whispers balefully, emphasis placed on each word. As the group draw nearer and their voices become more distinct, Josh pushes me against a nearby wall, pinning my arms behind my back. He leans in and his mouth closes around my trembling lips. He presses close to me, every contour of his body fused with mine so that I'm overcome by an insurmountable surge of nausea. I feel my whole body implode. I know I'm losing the last vestiges of control. My eyes are squeezed tightly shut as though I can smokescreen this moment out of my life. My chance of help slips through my fingers as the voices of the small group, oblivious to the distress I am in, reach a crescendo and then start to fade, like the ending of a song.

He doesn't release his grip immediately. His hands wander around my waist, tugging at my top, releasing it from the waistband of my jeans. 'No, Josh, don't,' I try to say but his mouth is still encamped around mine. Whatever he is planning to do to me, it can't be this. Surely, he won't.

His hands, like slime, rub my naked back and just when my cluttered mind dives into action, discerning an opportunity to pull my leg back and knee him in the crotch, I feel the sharp pierce of a needle in my side. Josh releases me. My hand rushes to cover the sting.

'What have you done?!' I cry, hysterically. 'What have you...' My brain and my speech have lost connection. Warm liquid hums sluggishly through my veins. Despite this being a sure sign that I'm wholly exposed, totally defenceless, it cannot alleviate the blissful release, the weightlessness that comes with this drug that has been administered to disable me. As if every bone has been seamlessly and simultaneously extricated from my body, I flop to the ground like a ragdoll.

Chapter 17

The night it ends

A tunnel within a tunnel. If such a thing exists, then this is where I am. In conflict, trying to disentangle myself from the deep chambers of a dark evilness, but even if I succeed, the evil will still surround me. I'm contorted into an unnatural position. My limbs gelatinous. Useless. The alternating smooth and jerky movements, symptomatic of being in a vehicle. My jaw feels slack. The tunnel is interminable. Every time there is a fragment of light, it is quickly swallowed up by the gigantic darkness. If only I can hold onto the light when it comes, maybe I can find my way out. If only I can inhale one full breath, maybe I can scream. If one limb can function, maybe I can kick or throw a punch. If only. If only…. The effort to harmonise my movements with my thoughts is painful and distressing. So, despite my intense desire to triumph, to save Denny; to save myself, I give into it. I let the murky gloom claim me once again.

***

I exit the tunnel gradually, my eyelids fluttering open. This time it is not a complete blanket. I draw my hands up towards my face, testing for movement and coordination. I can wriggle my fingers. I can make fists. My face feels bloated and clammy. My head throbs. I press my palms against my cheeks, heat transferring between them.

I'm in a room, lying on a bed, on my back. A burning acid rises from my gut, travelling at speed towards my throat. I must raise my head. If I vomit, I will choke. But I know I will do myself an injustice if I rise too quickly. My eyes are adjusting to my surroundings. I try to move my legs to place my feet on the floor, but the effort is too great: my legs are tied together. I raise my body, slowly, consciously feeling around me. A thick rope has been hurriedly wrapped around my ankles; my shoes removed. Twisting and pulling, I undo the awkwardly formed knot.

The scene from earlier replays blurrily. Walking home. Josh following me. His anger and venom. The needle prick and then oblivion. We travelled somewhere in a vehicle. Where? For how long? I don't know.

I lie down again, this time on my side. I will only be useful if I can commandeer some energy to get me through whatever challenge awaits me on the other side of the door. Deep breaths – in for five, out for five, wiggle my toes and move my feet around, get the circulation back. I close my eyes; completely removing one of my senses to focus on another. There are outside noises: the gentle rustle of branches, a door being slammed, a baby crying in the distance. But there are no nearby sounds. Maybe that is a good thing.

It takes a few minutes to restore some steadiness into my weakened body and mind. Precious minutes I can't afford, but neither can I afford to break. I resume the breathing exercises; images of Denny flashing before me. Is he nearby? Is he okay?

My phone! Where is it? If it's in the room, I can call the police. I pat the bed, feeling around the shadows. My hand connects with something solid on the floor. My shoes.

I continue, relying on my sense of touch, but there is no handbag and no phone. The panic threatens to swell again. I can't lie here waiting for my fate to be sealed. I need to act. I use my arms to pull myself up, so I am now in a sitting position, lowering my legs until my feet are firmly on the floor. I root around, managing to slide my feet into my shoes. Taking a deep, shaky breath, I pull myself up, gently unfurling into a standing position. I am okay. Hollow and shaky, but I am okay.

I take measured steps to the window, the wall helping me along. The heavy curtains form a shroud around the window. I bring my hands together to open a small gap in the centre where the two curtains meet. I'm looking down onto a dark, quiet street. A familiar street. My eyes perform a zig-zag movement, taking in the blue Ford van; the spot opposite the house where I parked my car a few weeks ago. Barcourt Road. *Please don't let my fate be the same as Rusco's.*

I let go of the curtain. It obliterates the little bit of light. I tiptoe to the other side of the room, silently praying to a god I have never called upon before that the door will not be locked. I clasp my hand around what feels like a brass knob, inhale a breath of courage. The slow twisting of the knob sounds like a whistle is being blown in the silence of the room. I pull. Nothing. I try again. Still nothing. My heart sinks, as I lean my head on the door in defeat. But I can't give up. I feel along the frame and that is when I realise my mistake. I turn the knob again, and this time I push. The door opens with a sweeping sound.

One small victory.

Peeping out, I listen for sound or movement, and to try to get a sense of my bearings. To my right, I can see a flight of stairs and there is a light on somewhere down below. I tiptoe along, hoping the floorboards are secure and won't creak under my weight. The only sound is my growling stomach, and I clutch my hand to it, desperate to hold the rumbling in. I want to storm down the steps and force open the front door which is straight ahead at the end of a narrow corridor. But the light is coming from the one visible room down below, and now I hear the muffled voices. To reach the front door, I will need to pass this room. But if I head towards the exit, I may not find Denny. My journey downstairs is painstakingly laboured. Halfway down, the voices become clearer:

'She knows too much already. If we don't sort this out, we're all going down like a lead balloon.' Tarquin. Andrew.

'You should have sorted this out right from the beginning.' Mary's tone is harsh, recriminatory. A pause as if directing the next part at someone else. 'And as for you, putting on that stupid show; police crawling all over the place.' Maybe it's in response to her voice that a black cat appears from somewhere unknown '*meowing*' in surprise at the stranger creeping down the stairs. I stop. The cat stares at me. If I take another step, will it alert its owner of my presence? Will it pounce?

The conversation continues.

'How many times do I have to tell you? It was to throw her off the scent. Ricky wasn't killed here. No one even knows Richard Usco-Lewis is a name we made up for him. I knew the police wouldn't find anything. How was I to know you've been burying your dead cats in the garden!' Josh. In Mary's presence, his voice has lost some of its confidence. The weakest link of the three.

'This is turning into a right shit show,' Mary again. 'No one should have witnessed the killing. Bloody amateur! Ricky was supposed to disappear without a trace, and we carry on receiving payments for the retard, exactly the same as the others. A dull bang, as though she's taking her anger out on a hard surface. I picture her glaring at them with venom in her eyes. 'A useless brother and a half-wit for a nephew,' she hisses.

My eardrums tingle and burn. The conversation I had with Josh: his absent parents. The domineering aunt and the dismissive uncle that brought him up. Mary and Tarquin!

'There's no point standing around arguing about it,' Tarquin/Andrew says. 'The police haven't connected the dots yet. We just have to get rid of the loose ends.'

My heart is in my mouth, feet stuck, refusing to move as they help me to slot some of the missing pieces into place. These evil bastards are making a career out of killing vulnerable people and claiming their money through the '*homes*' Josh's parents own. Are his parents complicit too?

The cat hisses, arches its back then saunters off. I refocus on my downward journey. Two creaky steps, concealed by the heated conversation. I finally reach the bottom. My eyes are drawn to the floor, and I stare at what looks like blood splatters against the bottom step. To the right of the hand-rail there is a red trail leading towards the rear of the house. Denny?

I switch off from the conversation still taking place a few feet away. The red trail leads to concentrated pools of blood, followed by a smear as if someone has been dragged along, then it stops at a door. The door that leads to the basement. I push. Wood scrapes against wood as it opens.

Squinting, I adjust my eyes to the darkness beneath. The musty smell of long-forgotten furniture, that has dampened and dried many times over, rises to meet me; causing my nose to twitch. A furtive glance behind me: no one. I can still hear the muffled, exasperated voices. I know it won't be long before they come looking for me where they'd left me.

I lean forward, pushing the door further open, relying on the dim light from the hallway. Now I can make out the distorted heap, blending in with the darkness below.

Denny! There is no doubt in my mind. Is he alive? I must help him. But which battle do I tackle first?

Thoughts scrambled and with a rising panic setting in, I know my best option is to get out and call for help. *I have to move. Now!*

The front door. About fifteen metres away, just beyond the room where this demonic, murderous family is still condemning each other, little realising they all deserve to rot in hell.

With one final glance below and whispered words: '*Hang in there,*' I take a step towards my only escape route. And then I hear it: a sharp, uneven inhalation of breath. Instinctively, I turn around. The expression on his face: Hatred. Irritation. The hint of an apology?

His move is swift: there is nothing I can do to deflect it or protect myself. Tarquin yanks me towards him. Acute pain, as something heavy and cumbersome is smashed against my head. A shove sends me somersaulting backwards. The kind of somersault that is only ever performed by a stunt person in an action movie. But this is no stunt person. It's me, Ren Shephard, with a broken head – a head still in recovery from its previous attack; a head that hasn't been able to expose what I have just found out – falling and flailing into the abyss, saying goodbye forever to the life I haven't yet fully lived.

Chapter 18

After the end

The two women stand either side of their unmoving friend. Their red-rimmed eyes indicative of the tears they have shed. The curtain had been drawn around the bed to give them privacy, a chance to say a few quiet, comforting words.

'We love you, Ren. Always have and always will,' Kizzy says, dismally. She takes her friend's still warm, but lifeless hand and gently rubs it between her own. On the other side, Lex does the same.

'You're the best, sweetheart,' she says, trying but failing to remain strong. The shock and disbelief of the situation causing her voice to wobble.

There is movement behind the curtain, softly spoken voices, making them aware that their time is up. They look at each other, the anxiety mirrored in both their expressions. Lex reaches out and Kizzy takes hold of her hand, so the three of them form a crooked circle. A ring of friendship which is at odds with the monitor and equipment surrounding them.

The curtain is pushed back and the doctor, accompanied by a member of her team, enters. Lex and Kizzy look eagerly at the doctor. She nods. No words needed. 'Can we just let her parents know? They're in the waiting room,' Lex says, tenderly lowering Ren's hand back onto the bed.

There is no need to go looking for them. Al and Angie sweep into the room, the door swinging open dramatically; a whistle of air causing the curtain to ripple. Healthy-looking and tanned, they are in stark contrast to their daughter's pale, thinned-out frame. But their faces have taken on a weariness, combining a sleepless night with reacclimatising to a now unfamiliar time zone. Lex and Kizzy step back, allowing Al and Angie to take up their previously occupied positions.

Angie is sobbing quietly, her threadbare tissue in need of replacing. She leans over her daughter and kisses her gently on the forehead. 'I didn't expect the next time I saw you to be like this,' she says sorrowfully. 'Dad and I are here.'

Shoulders slumped, Al responds by laying his hand clunkily on top of Ren's. 'You've always been my special girl,' he mutters. 'I should have known you needed me,' he adds, guiltily. He closes his eyes briefly, a host of thoughts and unspoken words rampaging around in his head.

Lex stands soldier-still at the far end of the small room. She'd expected her and Kizzy to be asked to leave, but nothing has been said, so they remain. But it's difficult to concentrate on the sentences now being spoken by the doctor, instead they come at her as random medical words and phrases. *MRI, brain injury, damage to the temporal and frontal areas.* She tunes out and focuses on the low acoustic music from somewhere nearby, allowing her to drift into another realm while the doctor's voice fades further into the background.

***

No tunnel. No dark dungeon. This time there is a light, and I'm drifting towards it. The peace and weightlessness are beyond description. Somewhere far away, music plays. A song with no

234

words, strange yet soothing, but I can't reach deep enough to fully enjoy it. It feels as if the world is smiling at me, even the intermittent beeping in the background blends in seamlessly with the music. I hear words being spoken, the voice reassuring yet mechanical. A professional voice, someone who wants to help, not harm.

I am loved! The surety comes at me with a force that sends spasms and surges through my body. Delightful ripples that give me the green light to let go. I don't need to fight anymore. The war is over. I can choose to walk, run, sail or fly into the light. The view beyond is idyllic, unblemished. I sense it. That uninterrupted view of green that I so love. I'm being pulled towards it. And just as I make the decision to fly, my world seems to spin on its axis so that I'm facing against the brightness, peering into a dim, opaque world. I try to turn back towards the light, but invisible arms wrap themselves around me, stilling my movements.

'But I want to fly.' Do I say the words aloud?

Now there is a strange sensation wading through me as if I'm being recalibrated. Something irretrievable from the enclave of my memory is battling to pierce through the slush.

'But I want to fly,' I say again. 'I want to be with Denny.'

The moment his name leaves my lips, I feel the dampness on my cheeks. I feel my arms being caressed ever so gently and affectionately. Someone is leaning over me.

'Denny?' I breath.

'Ren. It's me, can you hear me?'

I'm smiling and spinning; the light keeps coming at me, creating a kaleidoscopic effect. If I can just open my eyes, I will see him. I will touch his face and know he's okay. But the peace and calm and weightlessness, the beauty that I am just an arm's length away from, is fading and I don't want it to, because anything else will bring pain, heartbreak, and more uncertainty.

'That's it, Ren. Stay calm. You're doing great.'

It's not Denny. The voice is unfamiliar, female. If I can reach her, she will take me to him. I'm fighting, like I've never fought before. I can't reach the final page only to crumble at this point. I must be victorious; I must know how it ends. Something is pressing down heavily on my chest, restraining me. If I can just break through this final constraint, I will be okay. We will be together.

But my brain is like smashed glass, roughly and hastily repaired. Jagged and useless.

'She's coming round,' a familiar voice.

It's a numb kind of pain; one I can tolerate. I am almost there. So very close. I allow my breathing to harmonise with the sound of beeping. And with a power that comes from some place I never knew existed; I open my eyes.

She's a blurry vision. The woman in the white coat, peering down at me, a compassionate expression on her face.

'Do you know where you are, Ren?'

I'm so confused, but I have no way to articulate this. One eye is struggling to focus, but through the other, I can see people: Lex, Kizzy. Mum? Dad?

'Sereny, darling! You've given us quite a scare,' Mum gushes, her voice filled with an uncharacteristic emotion.

The woman in the white coat and someone beside her are fussing around me, checking a monitor, adjusting the needle in my arm, making notes on a chart.

I blink hard. Once, twice. Something isn't right. Something is hugely amiss here. The calm, floaty feeling of moments ago is replaced by an expanding weight form-ing across my chest. The timeline of events is unclear, but I remember exactly what I've been through and why I'm here.

'Did the police find Denny? Did they find Rusco's body?' My voice is a dry, urgent whisper. The tickle in my throat a precursor to a fit of coughing if I don't moisten it. As if reading my thoughts, the doctor reaches across to a nearby cabinet, and I hear liquid being poured into a glass. She tilts it towards my parched lips and despite the chore of swallowing, my throat instantly feels better. But it doesn't replace the crushing doom, the sense that the exchange of unreadable glances between the people in the room hides something big.

'Is Denny dead?' I choke on the words. If the answer is yes, I might be better off not knowing.

Lex steps forward. I notice the look of confusion that causes her brows to flicker. 'You were attacked when you went to meet Faye,' she says. 'Someone pushed you from behind and you hit your head against a wall. Do you remember?'

I try to raise my hand to my temple, but the effort is too great. The bruise, the scab that keeps opening. Elis, his greyhound physique and puffed out bomber jacket, those intimidating eyes. 'But that was ages ago,' I croak. 'That was before Rusco was killed.'

'This is all down to your no-good sister.' Mum's voice invades the room, heated, piqued. Gone is the emotion of moments ago. 'She's already confessed that she set the whole thing up. Her thug friend was supposed to nick your purse and your jewellery, not damage your brain.'

'I don't think she needs to hear all this just yet,' Dad interjects.

I start to cry. I don't understand what they're saying. Their voices: so strangulated, robotic, as if they're being churned up in an industrial cement mixer. My brain is taking forever to declutter this information and turn it into something that makes sense. Why are they talking about Elis and Faye? Am I dead? Is this why I'm so confused. My head and my body should be in pieces after being smashed in the head and cruelly shoved down the cellar steps by Tarquin. But I only have a slight headache. I raise my head slightly. I'm still wearing the carefully chosen outfit for my date with

Denny, but my boucle jacket lies crumpled at the bottom of the bed. There are dirt marks and a jagged rip at the front of my top. Strands of hair tickle my nose and cheeks. I vaguely remember blow drying and patiently styling it before going out. I must look like a colossal mess. My trembling fingers are dirty, hands scratched and sore. From my tumble down to the cellar? Did that happen today?

'Yes, she does need to hear it!' Mum's voice again. A different emotion, maybe in response to my crying. 'She's been running around playing detective for weeks, getting herself into all sorts of scraps because her brain isn't working properly. You heard what Lex and Kizzy told us!'

'Please Mrs Shephard. This isn't what Ren needs.'

I blink away the tears and look around me. Where did Mum and Dad spring from? Why are they here? They've never been the people I would call on in a crisis. It won't be long before they let me know how much my misfortune has cost them. A fresh pool of tears form, and I allow them to obliterate the image of my parents. I look around for the faces that will bring me reassurance: Lex and Kizzy, my sanctum, my confidantes. But they aren't here anymore.

'We had to sedate you, Ren.' Slow and measured words from the woman who now sits on a chair beside the bed. I glance at her name badge: Dr Eline Missour, Consultant Psychiatrist. 'You were in quite a distressed state when you were brought in on Saturday. Your neighbour found you asleep in the back of your car.' She stops, as though her words are explanation enough. It must be my quizzical expression that urges her to continue.

'Ren, I know this isn't making complete sense right now, but I'm here to work things out with you.' She pauses again. 'You sustained a head injury when you were attacked some weeks ago. Even though you appeared to recover from it, any injury to the head needs to be taken seriously.' She looks at me with kindness and sympathy. 'I'm aware that you refused to have a CT scan at the time because you felt okay. It may be that the psychological and emotional reaction to the attack has triggered some psychiatric issues, which have led to you misinterpreting and altering some of what is happening in your environment. Or there may be some trauma to your brain that needs to be investigated.'

I become aware that I'm shaking my head vigorously. The head they think is damaged, dysfunctional. Shaking these harmful and untrue words away. The mechanics of my brain are fully engaged. 'What about Tarquin and Mary? What about Josh?' I shout. 'I saw what that man did to Rusco. I saw what he did! And now I know exactly why he did it!'

I jerk forward into a sitting position, taking the doctor by surprise. 'I can prove it. I can prove everything. The police know what happened. They haven't been very helpful, but they took my statement; I have a crime number. They know what I witnessed. Insight Academy have it on record too – and… and Leonard. He was a witness. There must be cameras to show when Josh took me. It was in Brixton. I saw a group of people walking past, but they didn't realise he was kidnapping me.' I'm gabbling, my words overlapping, my brain racing, eager to make this woman see sense. My face is sweating, and I use the sleeve of my top to wipe my forehead. 'My phone. I have messages, photographs, emails…' I slump. 'But Josh took it. He took my phone. I have to—'

A coughing fit interrupts me, forcing me to stop, at the same time I realise that my missing phone will likely reduce the credibility of my argument. I take a breath, side-stepping the urge to throw up.

'Denny. He's been helping me. He knows everything about Tarquin and Mary, and Josh. If Denny isn't…' I can't bring myself to continue. Instead, I am overcome by a crushing tiredness. The conversation, my parents, the drug that Josh injected into me, have sapped my energy. I flop back onto the bed. The doctor's watchful, appraising gaze pins me down. She stands and pours me another glass of water. Whilst I swallow it greedily, she reaches into the cabinet beside me and pulls out my handbag which she places on the bed beside me.

Inside, nestled in the zip compartment beneath a packet of tissues is my mobile phone, intact, informing me that today is Monday, 6pm. My heart leaps, knowing there will be so much on here to corroborate what I have been saying. I sense the doctor looking at me, but I take no notice of her. The battery image flashes red – 7% of life left. First to my pictures: a quick scroll shows that I haven't taken many pictures in the last few weeks, so I can easily locate the snaps I need: The certificate on Tarquin's wall, blurry, but wasn't this what proved the connection between him and Andrew Shales? A grainy image of Mary H walking towards 43 Barcourt Rd. The registration number of the Ford van. I don't see the pictures I took of Tarquin's notebook when I met him in Wood Green, but I can check for that later.

Next, my call log and messages. Names of the people I have communicated with recently flash up: Lex. Kizzy. Josh. Dad. Faye. Interwoven with nameless numbers – some of which are calls to the various police departments.

'See!' I say, excitedly, to the doctor, proffering my phone to her. I know the battery won't last long enough to go through each stream of messages, but it's all here, in black and white. She takes the phone from me and places it on the cabinet. We are both distracted by a gentle knocking at the door. 'Please excuse me for just a moment, Ren,' she says, lightly squeezing my shoulder. I close my eyes and rub my damp face. Have I said enough to convince her? Reaching for my handbag, I check in the hope that my charger is there, but as expected it isn't. I can picture it plugged into the wall in my front room. No use to me now.

I make an instant decision. I'm not prepared to wait for the doctor to return and find me in this bed. I'm not sick. I'm not an invalid. I shouldn't be here! For the second time in as many days, I swing my legs off an unfamiliar bed and test if there is any strength left in them. If need be, I will find Lex and Kizzy and ask them to take me home. They know what I've been going through. They'll help me to face whatever sorrow awaits when I learn of Denny's fate. I grab my jacket and with the little energy I have, I brush it down, fighting the urge to cry when particles of dust and dirt descend to the floor, reminding me of the cellar and Denny. I struggle into it and shove my feet into my shoes. I hear a muted voice as I slide my phone off the cabinet and into my bag.

'Yes, she'll be admitted under Section 2… We've arranged a CT scan, so we'll be able to see if her brain has sustained any damage.' An indistinguishable response. Then the doctor again: 'It could be that what she's experiencing is a psychological response to a very frightening and traumatic incident, which she hasn't yet dealt with.'

No. No. No. This can't be happening. They can't do this to me! They can't keep me here against my will. I need to leave. I need to make sure Tarquin, Mary and Josh don't get away with this. I steady myself; measured breaths: must appear calm so I can explain this to the doctor. The door opens slowly.

'Doctor, you have to listen to—' And that's when I see him. A frown of concern, which he tries to mask with a tiny smile. Pale, clean shirt and faded jeans, hair formed into a neat afro. How could it have grown that much in the week since I last saw him? There's not a scratch or injury in sight. No sign of the weight gain I noticed last week. If anything, it's the opposite.

'Hi, Ren.' Denny's tone is subdued, tentative. 'It's been a while.'

Lightning Source UK Ltd.
Milton Keynes UK
UKHW011842120622
404319UK00001B/43